DOCTOR
LOVEBEADS

A NOVEL

GARY REILLY

Running Meter Press

DENVER

Published by
Running Meter Press
2509 Xanthia St.
Denver, CO 80238
Publisher@RunningMeterPress.com
720 328 5488

Cover art by John Sherffius
Composition by D. Kari Luraas

ISBN: 978-0-9847860-5-3

Library of Congress Control Number: 2013948345

First Edition 2013

Printed in the United States of America

Other Titles in The Asphalt Warrior Series

The Asphalt Warrior
Ticket to Hollywood
The Heart of Darkness Club
Home for the Holidays

CHAPTER 1

I was sitting in my taxi at the cabstand outside the Brown Palace Hotel pondering the nature of my latest miscalculation. I was fourth in line, with two cabs parked behind me, and frankly I needed to go to the restroom. But I was leery of leaving my cab for fear that a crowd of fares would come out of the hotel and I would not be present to take any of them to Denver International Airport.

It had been a slow day. It was nearing five in the afternoon, and while I had earned back my seventy-dollar lease payment and the ten dollars worth of gas I had bought at dawn, I still hadn't shown any profits for the day. Ergo, I was afraid to leave my cab for fear of missing out on a decent ride that would put enough money into my pocket to make the day worthwhile. It looked like it was shaping up to be one of those shifts when I would be lucky to take home twenty bucks profit.

Let's cut to the chase. The fear I was experiencing was a form of mental illness known only to cab drivers. Nobody was coming out of the Brown and heading for the airport. I had been sitting at the stand for fifty minutes and the sidewalk was dead. I had sipped two cups of 7-11 joe prior to pulling in, and now I had to activate an emergency Number 1, but I kept thinking that an avalanche of human flesh would spill from the doors while I was down in the classy johns in the Brown Palace. If you've never been inside the men's room at the Brown, you really ought to visit it the next time you're in Denver. Each urinal is bordered by privacy walls made of exquisitely attractive polished brown marble. When you close your eyes you feel like you're in New York City.

Anyway, I put up with my own nonsense for fifty-one minutes, then I climbed out of my cab and entered the Brown and went down to Times Square. I was gone two minutes. When I got back out to the sidewalk there was not a taxicab in sight, except mine—Rocky Mountain Taxicab #123 was alone at the curb. I read the tragic tale the way Natty Bumppo could read the secrets of the woods in up-state New York. An avalanche of human flesh had spilled out of the hotel while I was gone.

Just to confirm my irrefutable conclusion, I walked over to the doorman, William, a black man who had been guarding the palace gates longer than I had been hacking the mean streets of Denver.

"Where did all the taxis go?" I said, falling into the technical jargon employed by born losers.

"DIA," he replied. "It was like a circus out here for two minutes."

I nodded at William. I knew that the odds of another avalanche occurring within the next half-hour were slim to nonexistent, like everything else in my life. I had blown an entire hour in front of a hotel and had not made a dime. Everybody who had ever driven a cab in his life was laughing at me right at that moment because the way you make money in a taxi is by taking calls off the radio, i.e., jumping bells and not loafing in front of hotels or in the cab line out at the airport. You prowl the streets, you keep your ears attuned to the radio and your right hand gripping the microphone ready to pounce on any call. When you sign on for the day, you don't sign on to eat Twinkies and sip joe and read paperbacks. You sign on to hump the asphalt, jump the bells, get the fares in and out of your backseat as fast as possible. That's how a pro puts money into his pocket.

By the way, that isn't me talking. That's a friend of mine named

Big Al, the cabbie who taught me how to hack fourteen years ago. It's the standard speech that he makes at the end of a training day, after putting a student through the wringer. He even has it printed on a sheet of paper that he gives to all the newbies before turning them loose. The sheet costs only a dollar but you have to buy it—that's what he told me anyway.

Here's the funny thing though. It never would have occurred to me to eat Twinkies and sip joe in front of a hotel if Big Al hadn't mentioned it in the first place. I guess there are some things you should never say to people, and I'm one of them.

When I first started driving a taxi I had every intention of working hard. It was like when I got drafted into the army, I had every intention of being a good soldier. But at the end of my first week of basic training I happened to be sitting in the day-room watching television. I saw *Caught in the Draft* starring Bob Hope and my army career went to hell.

I wandered back toward my cab. "Wandered" is the operative word here. I felt like wandering right past it and continuing until I found an easier way than cab driving to earn money. This, of course, is a scientific impossibility. There is no easier way to earn money than driving a taxi, which is what makes it so difficult to bear when you actually do not earn money. Not earning money is virtually impossible in a taxi, and yet somehow I had managed to do it. I felt like someone who had disproved Einstein's Theory of Relativity. A lot of nuclear scientists are going to be loitering in breadlines when that day comes.

"Got any spare change?"

I froze.

Was I talking out loud again?

I recognized the cadence of that sentence. I'll admit it. I once panhandled on the mean streets of Philadelphia. I tried it only one time though, and the pedestrian said no. It made me feel like a fool. I felt like someone who was only pretending to be a panhandler. I assumed the guy said no because he could see right through me and knew I wasn't a hobo. He was right. Truth be known, I was walking to an agency that paid guys like me to pass out handbills, but I tried panhandling because it seemed like a good way to get free money. I'll try anything to get free money. I buy lottery scratch tickets, but let's move on.

"Spare change, mister?"

I finally emerged from my self-pity and looked around. Three hippies were standing on the sidewalk looking at me with entreaty in their eyes. I know entreaty when I see it. I used to employ it when applying for employment.

My heart soared like an eagle, which is hard to pull off when you're bummed out. Wow, I thought to myself, when was the last time I used the term "bummed out"? Probably in college. There were still a few remnants of hippies around back in my college days. I somehow managed to get in on the tail-end of hippiedom. After the army I grew my hair long and went to college on the GI Bill. This was at Kansas Agricultural University (KAU) in Wichita, Kansas, the town where I "grew up." I had failed as a soldier, so I thought I would try my hand at failing as a college student. I succeeded. I tried to fit in with what was then defined as "The Youth Culture." I did this by attempting to talk cool. When all my college buddies were cramming for their finals, I was studying the writings of cultural icons such as Ken Kesey, Timothy Leary, and Frank Zappa, trying to learn the lingo, the diction, the idiom of our nation's troubled youth. I figured the only way to become "in with the in crowd" was to trick them into thinking I was groovy. I'm pretty sure I tricked a couple of them, but they were freshmen.

Even though the three hippies had long hair, I could tell they consisted of two girls and a boy, whereas back in the sixties not too many people from my parents' generation could ascertain the difference when the kids had long hair. I was never entirely certain why it was necessary to know the sex of a total stranger unless you were dating him or her—or "it" as me ol' Dad used to say. But I had no trouble differentiating among the three panhandlers who were gazing at me with entreaty. Maybe the inability to recognize girls was an element of what had been known as "The Generation Gap" during the sixties. Or maybe my parents were just being sarcastic.

The two girls were wearing ankle-length dresses, sort of like Mama Cass used to wear. The boy had a headband and bell-bottoms, but rather than go into a detailed description of the rest of their outfits, I'll just let you use your imaginations. My Maw once told me that radio is superior to television because it allowed people to use their imaginations. "What imaginations?" I said sarcastically. She subsequently sent me to my room where I sat on my bed and tried to imagine the plot of that night's *Gilligan's Island*.

I dug into a pocket of my jeans and felt around for some quarters. I specifically give quarters to panhandlers because I myself don't like getting nickels and dimes from fares, so why should I treat mooches any differently from myself? I pulled out three quarters. Three hippies, three quarters, I said to myself, then dropped them into the outstretched palm of one of the girls, who looked seventeen or eighteen. Obviously she wasn't a real hippie. A real hippie would have been in her late forties. This made me wistful. I always get wistful when I meet people who aren't real.

"Thanks, man," the boy said.

All three of the kids smiled at me. I noted that they had perfect teeth. I pegged them as middle-class. They were obviously trying to redefine themselves. I didn't blame them. I had spent the last twenty years trying to redefine myself. I wanted to be redefined as "rich," but so far no dice.

"You're welcome," I said, then I glanced around at William who was frowning in our direction. I looked at the hippies. "Listen kids," I said, "let me give you some advice. This isn't a good place to hang around asking people for money. You might get hassled by The Man."

"What man?" a girl said.

Nope. They weren't real hippies. But rather than give them a sidewalk seminar in the lingo, the diction, and the idiom of The Youth Culture, I simply nodded in the direction of William. "That man."

"But people give *him* money," the other girl said.

Yipes.

"He receives tips for carrying people's suitcases," I said.

"What's a tip?" the boy said.

Yipes 2: The Sequel. But I shouldn't have been surprised. There isn't an American male under the age of twenty-five who knows what a tip is. I don't know what the hell our schools are teaching our children, aside from Latin.

"It's sort of like money for work," I said. "But the thing is, you're working that man's corner, and the man might call the cops. You know how grownups are."

They nodded. I had finally gotten through to them. Maybe that's the key to getting through to teenagers: call the cops.

I decided the best thing to do would be to get the kids out of there. I hated the idea of William calling the cops just to get rid of a few kids who didn't have the street smarts to stay away from hotels. And I hated the idea that I could have helped to avert a disaster but chose instead to walk away from it. Sure, their fate was none of my business, but what's that got to do with my life? I've never had any business doing anything anyway.

"I'll tell you what," I said. "Why don't you hop into my cab and I'll give you a free ride down to Larimer Street. You'll have better luck picking up spare change there." This was pure speculation on my part. Tourists wander around Larimer Street, and I have learned that where there's people there's money. Criminals seem to grasp this theorem, too.

I opened the rear door and let the kids climb in. As I opened the driver's door I glanced at William and gave him a quick thumbs-up. He gave me one in return. I liked to think he understood that I was deliberately removing the hippies from his area of operations. I was probably wrong. But sometimes I like to pretend I'm a smooth character in a movie who has the ability to communicate complex ideas to people through the use of subtle hand gestures, knowing nods, significant winks, and meaningful smiles. I realize this might make me sound like an idiot, but I learned it from Alan Ladd, or at least the characters he plays. Or played. I always have trouble utilizing the present tense when it comes to dead people. Ladd appeared in film noir movies as well as *Shane*. He was a smooth operator, so I always act like him whenever I'm forced by circumstances to impress strangers. I don't know what makes me think my audience ever has a clue as to what's going on inside my head. My idiotic fantasy behavior frequently gets me into trouble, often on first dates.

I pulled away from the curb and drove around the corner toward Broadway, crossed over to Lincoln, turned left, drove up to 18th, and made another left. If that's too complicated to picture in your mind, blame the government agency that changed the two-way streets of downtown Denver into one-way streets. What a snake pit. You can't go anywhere in this city without going somewhere else first. Lewis Carroll would have loved Denver.

CHAPTER 2

The top of the D&F Tower loomed in the distance. I planned to drop the kids off near that landmark and let them get on with their lives, which hopefully included wising up and going home and eventually entering college where all young people belong when they're not in my taxi.

"Nice ponytail," one of the girls in the backseat said.

"Thanks," I said.

"Are you a hippie?" the other girl said.

I gritted my teeth. This was a delicate moment. I had been wearing my hair long ever since the army let me go home, and I only began sporting a ponytail relatively recently. But I wasn't a hippie even though I could have been mistaken for one in a police lineup.

I decided to be honest since a tip did not hang in the balance.

"No," I said, "I'm just a Baby Boomer."

"My dad is a Baby Boomer, too," the other girl said.

"Does he have a ponytail?" I said.

"No … he sells life insurance."

I love non sequiturs. I decided to push the envelope. "Does your dad listen to the Beatles?" I said.

"Who are the Beatles?" the girl said.

That was the day my world ended.

I recovered quickly. "They were a rock 'n' roll group back in the nineteen-sixties," I said tentatively. "Didn't you ever hear of the Beatles?"

I glanced around at the trio. They were shaking their heads no. "But that's *impossible!*" I said loudly before I could stop myself. And then it happened. I saw it in their eyes. The three hippies began to retreat from me psychologically. I realized what was happening. They were pegging me as a grownup. I'll never forget the day I asked my Maw who Julius LaRosa was. She cut me out of her will.

"You can drop us off here," the boy said in a tone of voice so polite that I knew he didn't care for my company anymore. I hate politeness. It's a dead giveaway.

I pulled over to the curb and parked. I felt bad. In my attempt to bridge the Generation Gap I had only widened it. Ergo, in order to try and salvage what was left of my ego or my dignity or whatever the hell I was trying to salvage, I turned in my seat and watched as the girl nearest the curb opened the rear door. Then I said with entreaty, "Have you ever heard of a music group called Wings?"

The girl stopped pushing the door open and looked at me with her eyebrows raised. "You mean the band that Paul McCartney was in?"

"Yes," I said. "The band that Paul McCartney was in."

"Yeah," she said, giving me the sort of smile that sales clerks give to strangers. "My mom still listens to Wings."

"Well," I said, "Paul McCartney was in a popular band called the Beatles before he …" I swallowed hard, "… joined Wings."

"That's nice," the girl said politely. "Thanks for the ride, man." The three of them hustled themselves out of the cab, shut the door, and got on with their lives.

I stared at the kids as they moved down the sidewalk in what I thought of as a tightly knit group. I put the cab into gear and pulled out onto the street and drove past them. I glanced in my rear-view mirror. The girl to whom I had given the quarters seemed to be handing coins to the others, splitting the dough, divvying up the profits, which is to say, redistributing the wealth.

That made me feel sort of good, in the way that the end of the Civil War probably made Americans feel sort of good. But I felt empty, too. How could anybody alive today not have heard of the Beatles? This made me start thinking that all knowledge is useless, in the sense that almost everything we know has no practical application. The fact that those kids didn't know who the Beatles were didn't seem to have any effect on their ability to walk or talk. It made me wonder how many things a person could not know and still not die.

These were not good thoughts to have in a taxicab at five in the afternoon. I've always said that a taxi is a terrible place to have an epiphany—but was this an epiphany? It seemed more like the realization of the total insignificance of everything I ever believed in. Well, maybe it *was* an epiphany, but I didn't have time to dwell on it because a call came over the radio for a fare waiting outside a Walgreen's Drugstore. It was only two blocks away, so I jumped it.

It's always risky to jump a bell for a customer who has called from a store—a grocery store, a drugstore, or a 7-11—because the call is usually made from a phone booth, and "The Phone Booth People" as I call them have a tendency to evaporate before you get there. I don't know where they disappear to, although I suspect they hail passing cabs. It's not the customer's fault really. A cab comes by, they innocently wave to it, and the cabbie stops and picks them up. I've picked up plenty of people who have miraculously appeared out of nowhere, often standing beside phone booths, but let's move on.

The Walgreen fare wanted to go to east Aurora, which slightly blew my mind, as the hippies used to say, because it turned into a twenty-five-dollar ride. He told me he had originally intended to take a bus but decided he didn't want to wait around. Impatience can be as lucrative as snow when you drive a cab, although it can be detrimental when you whack out novels, but let's not get into that.

As soon as I dropped him off I jumped a nearby bell and picked up a woman who wanted to go to Cherry Creek Shopping Center, which again blew my mind. In the space of less than an hour I had earned my profits for the day, which is fifty bucks. Forget the Beatles. Fifty bucks is the minimum amount of money I need to make my life meaningful.

Here it was only six o'clock and I could afford to head home. I was quitting work one hour early. I drove back to the Rocky Mountain Taxicab Company (RMTC) whistling a medley of tunes by Wings. I was the beneficiary of a story as old as cab driving, and God only knows how old that story is, although I suspect the first hacks were Egyptian slaves, but let's leave pharaohs out of this. The title of the story is "The Vail Trip," which means that a cabbie might be having a lousy day, experiencing flat tires, disappearing Phone Booth People, etc., only to end up catching a fare that nets him a hundred bucks. You just never know. That's part of the fun of being a cab driver. People who play poker know what I'm talking about. Every time you're dealt a new poker hand you feel a small thrill as you pick up your cards to see what fate has in store for you. Three-of-a-kind? Straight? Royal flush? Nah. A pair. But still, you can't wait to ante up again and look at your next cards. Cab driving isn't as nonsensical as poker, though, because at least with cab driving you go home with money in your pocket.

After I turned in my taxi, I got into my two-tone (red doors/black body) 1964 Chevy and whistled my way back to my crow's nest, which is what I call the place where I live. It's the top-floor apartment of a three-story building on Capitol Hill. I parked my heap in the dirt lot behind the building and climbed the fire escape.

After I got inside I dropped my cab accoutrement on the kitchen table and breathed a sigh of relief. Thursday was over with. I was back on my normal schedule now, which consisted of Monday, Wednesday, and Friday. I have to drive on Tuesday and Thursday when the rent comes due. That means I work one normal-person week per month. Five days, sixty hours. However I already had shaved one hour off the week bringing it down to fifty-nine hours, which made me feel like I had just climbed out of a time machine where I had finessed reality by going back in time one hour.

But then, as I was heading into the living room to turn on the TV prior to cooking a hamburger, it occurred to me that I would have had to travel ahead one hour in order to finesse reality. I paused before turning on the TV. I frowned, which is something I've seen other people do and which is supposed to help you think. Even though I live somewhat of a nonconformist lifestyle, I imitate other people when it comes to thinking because imitation was how I learned to talk. It has always amazed me that infants can learn to talk without sitting in a classroom with an English teacher standing over them with a bullwhip—it kind of makes you wonder if school is a fraud. I mean, they wouldn't even let you *into* school if you couldn't talk, and yet as soon as you get into school they stick you in a class called "English." Teaching people how to do what they already know how to do strikes me as redundant, if not a scam. It seems like the billions of tax dollars we spend on public education could be better spent teaching kids how to tip.

I never did get the TV turned on. One thought led to another, and an hour later I still hadn't figured out whether my time machine should have traveled forward or backward in time, but by then it was moot. The hour was gone forever. I was back in the present, just in time to watch *Gilligan's Island.* I shook myself out of my reverie and switched on the TV, then walked into the kitchen and started frying up a hamburger. While it was sizzling, I reached into my shirt pocket and pulled out the fifty dollars I had earned for the day, plus the eighty bucks that would be going to pay my cab lease and gas on Friday morning.

"TGIF," I said aloud even though it was only Thursday. But I was alone in my apartment as far as I knew. I deliberately avoid making whimsical incorrect statements in public. You would be surprised at how many people get irritated if you say "TGIF" on the wrong day. By "people" I mean "English professors." To most English professors it would be inconceivable to say, "Thank God it's Friday" on a Thursday. I don't know if that's because they are strict adherents to the rules of language or if they are mentally ill. And I don't want to know.

I went into the living room and pulled my copy of *Finnegans Wake* off the bookshelf. That's where I hide my money in my apartment. I used to keep my money in my copy of *Lolita*, but the book kept getting stolen, usually during parties. I decided that the only way to keep from going broke was to stop putting my money into *Lolita* or else stop having friends. Both plans worked.

I got settled in front of the TV with my burger and watched *Gilligan's Island*. It was the episode where a surfer accidentally travels all the way from California to the island. I have never been fond of Gilligan episodes where outsiders come to the island, partly because the outsiders always go back home, and this seems to contradict the fundamental thesis of the show, which I define as "the strandedness." It leaves me feeling uneasy. It's as if I am being asked to believe something that defies logic, in the way that quantum mechanics makes a shambles of Newtonian physics. Whenever a low-budget TV show causes me to ponder physics, I grow uneasy.

I much prefer it when the castaways have to deal with an island-specific plight on their own, such as an active volcano or cannibals. I don't mind cannibals visiting the island now and then, since they come from tribes indigenous to the South Pacific—assuming of course that there really were cannibals inhabiting the islands of the earth's southern hemisphere between the years 1963–65. I can't imagine why Sherwood Schwartz would make up something that could be disproven by anthropological evidence. Unless he was strapped for a plot.

But here's the thing. As I watched the big dumb blonde surfer boy wandering around the island being baffled by his plight, I started thinking about hippies. The island itself was not unlike a hippie commune. Even Gilligan had once been a bohemian named Maynard G. Krebbs.

As an aside, if you ever want to win a bar bet by an obscure trivia question, ask your friends what the Skipper's real name is, and I don't mean "Alan Hale," I mean the fictional character on the show. If you don't know his name, do some research. I would tell you myself but I don't want to spread it around—I rake in more than fifty dollars a month posing that question, just enough to cover my bar tab. Most suckers say "Alan Hale" and that's when I clean up.

Anyway, the castaways had—accidentally, as the opening song makes crystal clear—gone to this tropic isle and built a functioning society. This had been the goal of all hippie communes in the 1960s. I had never visited a hippie commune but I had read quite a bit about them in contemporary history books and R. Crumb comics, and it struck me that the communes of the 1960s might have succeeded if only they had included a millionaire and his wife.

The absence of free love and drugs may have contributed to the success of the Gilligan communards, although the presence of Gilligan himself arguably diminished their odds of survival. But think how boring the show would have been without Bob Denver. I'm not naive enough to think that Hollywood TV scriptwriters are fountainheads of deep philosophical profundity, but I personally think Gilligan was symbolic of something. Let's just leave it at that. Nothing destroys the beauty of a poem faster than parsing it line by line, so you can imagine what it does to sitcoms.

CHAPTER 3

After I finished watching *Gilligan's Island*, I turned off the TV and looked at my personal computer. It was set up on a desk in a corner of my living room. My steamer trunk used to occupy that spot, but I had moved the trunk into my bedroom. I had originally put the PC in the bedroom, but every time I sat down to write a novel I found myself lying down on my bed in order to "get inspired," and would fall asleep. I had learned from a how-to book about the technique of lying down for inspiration. Did I mention that I'm an unpublished novelist? I've been unpublished since—well—since I was born, but what I mean is, I began writing novels when I was in college.

My decision to become a novelist coincided with my realization that after I graduated I would have to get a job, and writing novels seemed like a much easier way to get money than working. This is also why I became a cab driver. I was right about the cab driving, but I sort of missed the boat on the novel part.

The reason I bring this up is because I only recently had acquired the personal computer. By "recently" I mean the previous Christmas. And now here it was June and I still hadn't gotten around to actually writing a novel with it. My evil brother—correction—my older brother Gavin gave the PC to me as a Christmas present. He told me that somebody he knew had achieved success as a novelist only after acquiring a word processor.

Gavin said that writing novels with a PC was supposed to be

easier than writing with a typewriter and bond paper, or with a pen and foolscap, or with a chisel and a granite obelisk imported from Greece. I shook my head with pity as he related this canard to me. Non-writers are always filled with advice for writers, but I decided to go ahead and humor my poor brother and accept his gift with the promise that I would stop using my reliable Smith Corona to produce novels.

However, it seemed like every time I searched for inspiration I woke up three hours later. By then of course it was too late to write. Not that I had anything else to do, but I felt that by inadvertently letting three hours go by, I had technically fulfilled my obligation to my brother and therefore I was legally free to do whatever else I chose. More often than not I chose to watch TV, which I felt was morally justified by the fact that I had at least made an effort to do some writing—if collapsing onto a mattress can be defined as "effort." In my world, it is.

That lasted all the way through January before I decided I was getting entirely too much rest. So I moved the steamer trunk into the bedroom and transferred the PC into the living room. This switcheroo required quite a bit of beer to accomplish, so it was another week before I was able to sit down in front of the computer without any inspiration whatsoever and attempt to write my first novel using "light" rather than "ink."

The brand name of my PC is "RamBlaster 4000." I like that name because it sounds like the title of a kid's adventure show on TV. I like anything that reminds me of TV. In one of the many how-to books I've read over the years, I was told that a novelist ought to write what he cares about, and since the only thing I care about is TV, I tried to come up with a plot about a television. Then one night while channel surfing, I happened across a movie called *The Twonky*

(1953) starring Hans Conried. It was a story about a talking TV. Leonard Maltin gives it one-and-a-half stars. The upshot? There went my TV novel. But this is one of the oldest stories in the book of novels. As soon as a writer thinks up a story line, someone else has already beaten him to it.

But it gave me an idea. Hollywood is always doing remakes of movies, so why couldn't I do a remake of a novel? There must be at least five movie versions of *The Hunchback of Notre Dame,* so why couldn't I write a "remake" of, for instance, *Catch 22* or *Valley of the Dolls*? This seemed like a much easier way to make money than thinking up an original idea. I have to be honest. I got so excited about this plan that I had to run to the bathroom, but let's move on.

After I got out of the bathroom I immediately sat down at my RamBlaster and wrote a letter to a few publishers, whose lawyers immediately wrote back and explained why I couldn't produce "remakes" of their novels. The letters were sort of like rejection slips only worse because a novelist is lucky if an editor scribbles "Sorry" on a return letter, much less "We'll see you in court."

Anyway, on Thursday night I decided to go ahead and try to get started on a novel. It had been six months since I had unwrapped the PC, and by now I was used to both its existence and its presence. I guess I'm a fairly normal person when it comes to new things. I hate new things. Every once in a while someone will hand me a new novel and I'll react to it the way Dracula reacts to garlic. "Get it away from me!" I reply, although not verbally but rather through body language.

This consists of closing my eyes and abruptly turning my head to one side, while simultaneously raising my hands palms-outward in front of my face. The message I am sending states, "I don't want anything new going into my brain!" This was how I reacted when an army buddy tried to give me *Catch 22.* I tried not to read it, but he was bigger than me and always stayed awake during judo class. Admittedly, getting *Catch 22* put into my brain was a good thing, but I still don't like new things going in there. I have enough old things I want to get rid of first.

The downside of avoiding new things is that it took me ten years to open a book on how to write novels. Prior to that I had never cracked a how-to book. The way I figured it, I was a college graduate and I had read *Catch 22,* so why would I need a book to tell me how to write a novel? I'll admit it. I was displaying the arrogance of youth. The day I turned thirty was the day I trudged down to a local bookstore and asked if they had any instructional manuals that could teach me how to write novels. Christ but I was embarrassed. I felt like an alcoholic going to his first AA meeting: "Hi, my name is Murph and I can't string two sentences together." When I walked out of the bookstore my how-to book was hidden between two AA manuals.

But the book didn't help me much. Or should I say—"books." You heard me right. Plural. During the past fifteen years I have read forty-five books on how to write novels. I also happen to be forty-five years old. And guess what—I've written forty-five unpublished novels. That doesn't include my screenplays.

After I got the RamBlaster warmed up, I stared at the screen for a while trying to think up a novel. This runs counter to the advice given in all the how-to books. They tell you to plan your novel first. But the way I always figured it, if I thought up a novel while actually seated in front of the screen, this would save me the time it would take to move from my easy chair—where I do all my planning—to the chair in front of the PC. By shaving a few seconds off the time, I would get my novels written all that much sooner, thus receiving a book contract faster. It was just like in grade school where I always sat at the desk closest to the door so that when the bell rang I could dash out of school ahead of everyone else. "Planning is everything," according to Sluggo.

Well, the bells weren't ringing that night. And suddenly I knew why. It was Thursday. No cab driver in his right mind ever tried to write a novel on a Thursday. Thursday was when an asphalt warrior psyched himself up for the challenge of Friday, the busiest day of the week. I had been known to earn sixty dollars on a Friday, which I normally try not to do because the acquisition of wealth makes people complacent, and ultimately lazy. This is what the how-to books say anyway. They are very adamant about not writing for money. I realized that by trying to write a novel on a Thursday I was risking making myself lazy, so I switched off the RamBlaster and turned on the TV. Close call. I don't know why I take risks like that.

The next morning I drove to work and parked in the dirt lot outside the on-call room. The parking lot was filled to maximum capacity. Everybody was driving, the old pros as well as the newbies. When I walked into the on-call room to pick up my cab, the joint was packed. The newbies were bright-eyed with ambition, and the old pros were bright-eyed with experience. Friday is money day in the world of cab driving. On Friday everybody in America seems to be going somewhere, and while I have no idea why anybody goes anywhere, I'm glad they do. In fact, I wish everybody I know would go somewhere.

Rollo was in the cage as usual. He's the day-man who hands out trip-sheets and keys. Rollo and I don't see eye-to-eye on everything, and given the opportunity he will stick it to me, whatever it is, which is why I am extremely polite during my brief interactions with Rollo. I am generally opposed to giving people opportunities to do anything, but especially Rollo. But on Friday mornings he is too busy making change and handing out keys and trip-sheets to give me more than a cursory frown of disapproval. This isn't specific to me though—Rollo disapproves of everybody, which is his only saving grace.

I paid my seventy-dollar cab lease, then walked out of the on-call room and hunted down Rocky Mountain Taxicab #123, which had been driven by a newbie during the night shift. I found it on the far side of the lot, a distance of at least one hundred feet. I knew then that 123 had been driven by what we cabbies call a "cherry newbie," meaning the newest of the new drivers. Probably his first night shift. I checked the body of the cab for dents, didn't find any, then climbed into the driver's seat and checked the gas gauge. One-quarter tank left, meaning the cherry did better than most newbies but not as well as he would do someday, assuming he stuck with driving.

If there is ever more than half a tank of gas left, I know the newbie will never come back to work. The record after fourteen years of checking is three-quarters of a tank of gas, which was left by a cherry who was so baffled by his first night shift that he brought his taxi back to the company after having netted six dollars for a twelve-hour shift. All right. I'll admit it. It was me. I keep hoping that a more incompetent newbie will someday beat my record, but so far no dice. And why, you might ask, did I stick with taxi driving? The answer is simple: what else was I going to do for a living?

As I cruised out of the parking lot in 123, the radio was jumping with calls. I turned the radio off and headed for a 7-11 store to gas up and buy a Twinkie and some joe. After gassing up I drove to the Brown Palace Hotel to check out the length of the cab line. I like to spend half an hour eating my Twinkie and sipping at my coffee and reading a few pages of a paperback before leaping into the asphalt fray. This is why I always leave my radio off in the morning. The radio is worse than a slot machine—worse because you know you're going to win money if you take calls off the radio. Slot machines are different.

Every once in a while I do listen to the radio, and I end up earning one hundred dollars for the day, which throws my *modus operandi* out of kilter. I start getting ambitious, which is not a good thing for a cab driver. The minute a cabbie starts getting ambitious, the gods make a note of it and schedule a few flat tires to remind him that if he wants to earn The Big Money he has to wear a suit. I once wore a suit. I don't want to talk about it.

I was second in line at the Brown Palace and daydreaming about the fifty dollars I would earn if a businessman climbed into my cab for a ride to the airport, when suddenly I saw them again. The hippies. They were at the far end of the block panhandling pedestrians who were coming out of the palace gates. I didn't know if it was my ego or my innate fear of cops, but the sight sent a rush up my spine. What was the matter with those kids? If I had wracked my brain, I suppose I could have come up with an image worse than hippies in jail, but right at that moment it seemed like the worst-case scenario imaginable.

I looked at William, but he was too busy dealing with new arrivals and ordering his assistants around and collecting tips to take notice of the hippies. But I knew that when things quieted down, the odds were good that the kids might end up getting busted for vagrancy or any of the other charges that poor people have to juggle along with starvation. In theory, the kids were correct to panhandle outside a classy hotel because classy hotels are where people with money go—witness my own presence outside the Brown. But in my experience, theory and reality rarely have anything to do with each other, similar to the relationship between Algebra and reality. I felt like climbing out of my cab and going up to the kids and shooing them away. But at the same time I felt like letting them take the fall. They needed to learn a lesson. They hadn't listened to me and now they were going to suffer for it. This sometimes happens to people who *do* listen to me, but that's neither here nor there.

Then the cab ahead of me pulled away from the curb with a load of passengers, and I was forced to cruise up to the first spot in line, which altered the matrix. I was no longer free to abandon my taxi in an attempt to save the world. Fifty bucks hung in the balance. I kept glancing from the front door of the hotel to the hippies panhandling down the block. It reminded me of Thursday. On Thursday I had to go to the restroom but I was afraid to leave my cab, and now here I was again, wracked with indecision.

Then I recalled that on Thursday I had made a decision that turned out to be wrong. So I decided to stay in my cab and let the hippies fall where they may. They weren't my responsibility anyway. I don't know what makes me feel compelled to help people who are in trouble. I write it off as boredom.

A woman came out of the Brown Palace and climbed into the backseat of my taxi. "Cherry Creek Shopping Center," she said.

Normally this would have infuriated me, since I always expect to go to the airport from a hotel. But a trip to Cherry Creek would keep me in town, which meant I could come back to the Brown and see if the hippies had been busted. I had finally decided to try and help them but only after my DIA dream was shattered. This is how most of my decisions are arrived at: total collapse, followed by surrender.

"Yes, ma'am," I said.

I dropped my flag, turned on the meter, and guided my hack over to Broadway.

CHAPTER 4

Whenever I get a rich person in my taxi I always drive a bit faster than normal—and when the got-rocks is female, I take the concept of velocity to the legal limit. I drive rich males fast because I hope they will give me a big tip. Most of the rich men I chauffeur are businessmen, and I know that to a businessman time is money. I know this because I was once forced to attend a time-management seminar when I had a real job at a place called Dyna-Plex, which is located in the Denver Tech Center south of the city.

I had an office job there. I wore a suit and a tie to work every day. I wore shoes and socks too—the whole nine yards. I was a corporate writer. Every month I wrote a brochure for the company. I averaged 1,000 words a month, which meant I was paid almost two dollars per word per annum. I had my English degree to thank for this. I had the GI Bill to thank for my English degree. And I had World War II to thank for the GI Bill. Just think—if Japan hadn't bombed Pearl Harbor, I never would have streaked Wichita.

It's a long story.

During the time-management seminar, the teacher explained that every hour that a businessman does not earn a predetermined amount of money, he is in fact losing money. For example, if a businessman thinks his time is worth fifty dollars an hour, and he goes to a barber and spends forty dollars for a haircut, he is already out ninety bucks—the forty bucks he spent on the haircut plus the fifty bucks he didn't earn because he was sitting in a barber chair. This freaked me out. After that, whenever I tied my shoes I felt like money was flying out of my billfold.

Of course, I did realize that the time-management concept was just an illusion, but illusions are all I have to cling to so I take them seriously. For instance, the reason I drive faster when I have rich women in my cab is because they make me nervous. For some reason that I don't understand, I always get the funny feeling that at any moment a rich woman will demand that I justify my existence, and I have enough problems making correct change.

I dropped the woman off in front of Saks Fifth Avenue. She handed me a ten-dollar bill on a eight-dollar-and-forty-cent ride and told me to keep the change. My plan at that point was to deadhead back to the Brown and help the hippies, but then a matronly woman came out of Saks carrying three shopping bags.

"Oh driver!" she said in a high-pitched voice. "Can you give me a ride?"

Ordinarily, if a customer wants a cab at Cherry Creek he or she can go to the main entrance of the mall where a cabstand is located. There were no cabs at the stand right then so I said, "Sure," and hopped out and opened my rear door and helped her with the packages. At least, I'm pretty sure there were no cabs at the stand.

"Where to?" I said, as I made a quick U-turn and got the hell out of there before a Yellow driver spotted me.

She wanted to go to an address on 8th Avenue, east of Monaco Parkway. This annoyed me to a certain extent. I wanted to get back to the Brown, and now I was going even farther east than I intended. It was Lewis Carrol time again.

"How long have you been driving?" the woman said.

"An hour," I replied.

"Is this your first day?"

"Excuse me, ma'am, I misunderstood you," I said. "I've been driving for fourteen years."

"Do you enjoy driving a taxi?" she said.

The hair on the back of my neck prickled. I started to get nervous.

"Yes, ma'am," I said. "Taxi driving is enjoyable and easy to master."

"My brother Horace drove a taxi in St. Louis when he was a young man," she said.

I began to relax. The rich lady was just shooting the breeze. During my years as a taxi driver I had learned that anybody who ever drove a taxi, or had a relative who drove a taxi, would always work it into a conversation as if confessing a shameful secret to a priest.

"How long ago was that?" I said.

"Right after the war," she said.

I nodded even though I didn't know which war she was referring to. But I decided to go with World War II. The Big One is always a safe bet.

After we arrived at her house, she tipped me four dollars on an eight-dollar fare. That's another thing about people who are connected with "The Industry." They're hip to the tip.

As I drove away from the house I kept the radio off. I was afraid I would end up jumping a bell that would take me farther east, and I wanted to get back to the Brown Palace. I had earned twenty-two dollars for an hour's work. I have to gross at least eleven dollars an hour to keep my profits down to fifty bucks per day, so I already had earned two hours worth of loot. This is one of those "delusions" that I am partial to, because for all I knew I wouldn't earn another dime for the rest of the day. Unlike Las Vegas, cab driving doesn't make any promises. In Vegas, you know you'll die broke, but cab driving is a roll of the dice.

I drove up to 13th Avenue and aimed the hood ornament west, although 123 didn't really have a hood ornament. Whatever happened to hood ornaments? By the time I got to Colorado Boulevard I figured William already had called the cops and the hippies had been hauled away in a paddy wagon. By the time I got to Lincoln Street I figured the boy was making big rocks out of little rocks in Cañon City, and the girls ... well ... I didn't know where the State of Colorado sent its bad girls but I figured it wasn't pretty—we're talking "caged heat" here.

I drove up Lincoln and turned left on 18th and cruised down to the Brown Palace. There were three cabs at the stand but I didn't pull in and park. Instead I slowly rolled past the front door. William was standing there doing nothing. Cab drivers and doormen have a lot in common, except doormen have to stand.

I didn't see the hippies anywhere.

I cruised back around to Lincoln and up to 18th, making the circuit. I had a choice: I could park at the Brown and forget about the hippies, or I could cruise around for a bit to see if they had drifted farther down the street. The one thing I didn't want to do was ask William if he had called The Man. For some reason, I didn't want to know the truth. The truth is always a letdown or a calamity, like everything else in my life.

I decided to make a slow circuit of the area and see if I could spot them. Maybe they had headed toward the D&F Tower. What the hell, I had twenty-two dollars in the kitty, which was like having an extra hour tucked into my shirt pocket. Having that extra hour put me into a kind of dreamlike state. It took me back to the days when I used to set my watch ahead ten minutes in order to give me the illusion that I was perpetually ten minutes ahead of everyone else in the whole wide world. That lasted until I had to actually know what time it was, meaning when I got a job driving a cab. Cab driving is the nexus where wristwatches intersect with reality.

An hour later I hadn't spotted the hippies. Eleven of my twenty-two dollars had evaporated in terms of economic delusion, so I had to get in line at the cabstand in front of the Hilton in order to grab a fare and stay financially even. An hour later I was still at the Hilton and the line wasn't moving. I was down to zero and starting to sweat. I really should have stayed awake during that time-management seminar.

By noon I had barely grossed fifty dollars out of the one hundred and thirty minimum that I needed in order to cover my rent for the next month and still live what I like to think of as a normal life. My definition of "normal" means I could take all of next week off. But the way things were shaping up it looked like I might have to work next Monday, or one of the other days that make up a week, not counting weekends. I never work on weekends. By "never" I mean once in a while, but only in emergencies, like when I need money so badly that I start getting sentimental about Dyna-Plex.

I won't deny it. When I was a white-collar worker I was earning a bundle. I owned two pairs of shoes and I got my hair styled at a salon in the Tech Center, which cost me forty dollars per session. This was *a priori* the time-management seminar. I was rolling in dough. And guess what? I was miserable. How could that be? Up to then I thought money was the key to happiness. How could my core belief be so wrong? Was I a hippie at heart? An army sergeant once accused me of being a *college boy* because I couldn't figure out how to work a potato-peeling machine. But nobody ever called me a hippie. It was only after I started driving a cab that I realized that mere money is not the key to happiness. *Lots* of money is the key to happiness. Preferably millions.

But after giving it a great deal of thought, I concluded that I would never earn millions of dollars driving a taxi—nor betting at the dog track, which is a long, though relevant, story that I won't go into here. No, there was only one way for me to earn millions of dollars and that was by writing best-selling novels. That was a coincidence because I had been doing that since college.

Let me clarify:

Trying to write bestselling novels—that's what I had been doing since college.

The fact that all along I had been doing the very thing I ought to have been doing seemed like a form of kismet, if not outright irony. It even nudged me toward a belief in determinism, which I quickly squelched because if I started to believe that my fate was carved in a block of cosmic granite I might quit cab driving and end up lying in bed all day waiting for the Blue Fairy to bring me hamburgers. Free will, on the other hand, was even worse because if I had a free will I would lie in my bed all day and do nothing. This led me to conclude that the fundamental flaw in every philosophical argument related to the stomach.

But it didn't matter. I hadn't yet earned millions writing bestselling novels. Nor had I earned seventy bucks driving a cab and it was a *Friday!* I started to hate hippies. What was I doing rushing around like an idiot worrying about three kids I didn't even know? Was I neurotic?

I have been known to ask myself that question on certain occasions, usually when I'm wearing swimming trunks and lying on a beach towel spread out on my living room floor during no-work week, or "spring break" as I call it. With the gentle crashing of waves on Gilligan's beach, I sometimes remove my sunglasses and frown at the ceiling and wonder if my seemingly uncontrollable habit of getting involved in the personal lives of taxi fares amounts to little more than an ego trip of gargantuan proportions. I don't know how many times I've vowed to myself that I would never again get involved in the lives of my fares, and I don't know how many times I've broken that vow, but I assume they add up to the same number because I have never not broken that vow.

But it's hard not to break vows. For one thing, there is no enforcement mechanism involved in a vow. Vows aren't like laws. Hell, you can break a vow in front of a cop in broad daylight and he can't lay a goddamn finger on you.

I decided it was time to forget about the hippies. I decided to concentrate on earning money. I even went so far as to turn on my two-way radio, which shows you how desperate I was. Money does that to me. Or perhaps I should say the lack of money does that to me. Money itself has never done anything except make me lazy. If I ever earn a million dollars off a best-selling novel, don't hold your breath waiting for best-seller number two.

CHAPTER 5

Ten minutes later I picked up a fare at the Hilton Hotel and took him to an auto-rental agency six blocks away, which almost started to annoy me. It reminded me of the time I picked up a female flight attendant in an apartment building near the Tech Center down south. I figured she was going to DIA, but she told me to take her to a bus stop a half-mile from her place. She said she always took the bus to DIA, which was thirty miles north. Moments like that take the wind out of the sails of a cabbie, unless he's a true asphalt warrior.

An asphalt warrior has to remind himself that in cab driving, as in life, all things even out. Well … that's not true in life but it's true in cab driving. For every lousy short trip you get, there is always a long trip waiting for you down the road. The proof of this "theorem" is a cabbie's IRS return. If he is as professional as I am, he will earn the same amount of money every year no matter how many good or bad trips he gets. If he is more professional than I am, he will earn more money, but it will be the same more money. You can't win in the taxi game, and you can't lose. You will always earn the same annual income and pay the same taxes. If you are like me and have no desire to work hard, or harder, you will be satisfied with your life. For some reason the image of a man lying sideways on a wooden pallet in an opium den comes to mind. But not all cab drivers stay as satisfied as I do with the situation, and they eventually quit the taxi game and move on to more lucrative enterprises, such as selling real estate or working at 7-11 stores. The move is usually preceded by a wedding. It gets complicated.

The upshot of the deal is that I didn't get annoyed at driving the businessman to the auto-rental agency. I simply recited the prayer of the asphalt warrior, which goes like this: "It doesn't matter, it doesn't matter, etc …" Then I switched on the radio so I could listen for bells.

There are variations to the prayer of the asphalt warrior, including body-language prayers, such as the quick roll of the eyeballs, or the shoulder-shrug. The prayer is just a way to let off steam before getting back to the job at hand. You have to let off steam. A taxicab is a terrible place to violate the laws of physics. A roll of the eyeballs, a quick shrug, a mumbled, "It doesn't matter," and you're ready to seize the steering wheel.

It worked.

After that I jumped a bell at 11th and Broadway, which turned out to be a call from a phone booth. This took an extra-special added prayer because, as I said, people who call from phone booths frequently disappear before the cabbie arrives. Consequently, just before saying, "It doesn't matter," I gritted my teeth and shrugged my shoulders twice. When I arrived at the intersection, my eyeballs nearly popped out of my head because it was a female flight attendant with a suitcase who, as it turned out, was going to DIA.

We made small talk on the way to the airport. I wanted desperately to know what the hell she was doing standing with a suitcase at the corner of 11th and Broadway. If you've ever been to Denver, you would want to know that, too. But I decided not to ask. It was obvious that kismet was rolling out the red carpet again. Only a madman asks questions when life starts treating him like royalty. When we got to DIA, she gave me sixty dollars and told me to keep it. I vowed that I would keep it until the rent came due.

Since me and kismet were getting along so well that afternoon, I took a quick run down to the staging area to see how many cabs were waiting for trips out of the airport. I had a fantasy that, since it was Friday, the line would be moving fast and there might be only two or three cabs waiting. I missed the mark by seventy cabs.

The staging area is to kismet what kryptonite is to Superman— but then I had known that ever since DIA opened for business. It takes three to five hours to get a fare out of DIA, but that doesn't guarantee you'll get a fifty-dollar trip to downtown Denver. You might get a twenty-dollar trip to downtown Aurora. Imagine waiting five hours to earn twenty dollars. Believe it or not, this has never happened to me out of DIA. When I first realized how the economic dynamics of the cab-staging area at DIA were adding up, I made the only rational decision of my entire life, which was to stay out of the staging area.

But I do make runs past the staging area to see if the line is short. It's just a kind of fun thing—like dreaming about finding the Dutchman's lost gold mine, or buying a scratch ticket.

I deadheaded back toward Denver. But then, just as I was coming up on the I-225 interchange, a bell came over the radio for an Aurora fare. It was another phone booth, this was located at a 7-11 at Colfax and I-225. It was a tough decision—a phone booth *plus* a 7-11. Double threat. I gritted my teeth, gave my head a little sideways shake, inhaled deeply, and mumbled, "It doesn't matter." Then I jumped the bell and drove to the 7-11.

Two men were standing by the phone booth. They were wearing caps, black leather jackets, blue jeans, and boots. Both were carrying small but heavy-looking satchels. I pegged them as hit men, or else truck drivers. I was right. They were truck drivers. They wanted to go to the truck stop at I-70 and Quebec, which is near the old Stapleton International Airport site.

As we were cruising west on Interstate 70, they told me they were going to the truck stop to pick up a semi-tractor-trailer and drive it to California. My heart sank. Why wasn't I driving to California? What could be more wonderful than driving to California in a semi-tractor-trailer? I hadn't been out to sunny California since ... well ... since the time I went there to find a girl I was suspected of murdering, but let's not get into that—it was just one of those nutty mix-ups that could happen to anyone.

The truck stop near Stapleton is located north of I-70, and is like a gas station for giants. On that day there were semi-tractor-trailers scattered all over the place, some of them were parked at pumps where they were gassing up on diesel fuel, if "gassing" up is the proper usage of English fuel language. The roofs sheltering the diesel pumps seemed miles high, and the pump islands seemed miles long. It made me feel like I was driving a Tonka Toy. I felt small and unimportant.

After I dropped off the two men I parked near the snack bar, which is actually a monstrous sort of 7-11 with a cafeteria. The place even has shower rooms fer the luvva Christ—I tell ya, truck drivers live in a parallel universe.

I used the men's room, which was normal size as far as I could tell, then I went into the store and bought a Twinkie and a cup of joe. Too embarrassed to buy a regular-sized cup of coffee, I bought a large paper cup, which was a mistake. But I didn't want the truck drivers lined up at the cash register to think I was a candy-ass and laugh at me. I wanted them to think I was a hardy gear-jammer who had just come into Denver after highballing across the eastern plains on the superslab and needed a monster boost of caffeine before tackling the Rockies in my nineteen-wheeler.

I say mistake because the cup was too big and thus too hot. I burned my fingers hurrying out to my taxi, then I spilled half the cup trying to get my door open. A couple of truckers laughed at me. I felt like I was in Dodge City being badgered by town loafers. I expected them to throw lug-nuts at my feet and yell "Dance, pilgrim!"

I wished my imagination would take off like that when I was sitting in front of a keyboard. I never had thoughts like that when I was alone in my apartment. Then it occurred to me that I ought to bring a portable typewriter with me whenever I drove my taxi. Considering the fact that working a taxi consists of sitting and doing virtually nothing for twelve hours a day, I might have been able to squeeze in a couple hundred words of prose fiction.

As I drove out of the land of the giants and back onto Interstate 70, it also occurred to me that if I had been bringing my typewriter with me during every taxi shift for the past fourteen years, I probably could have written a lot more failed novels.

I started calculating how many words I might have produced. Figuring a minimum of one hundred words per hour, which may have been highballing it, I could have written twelve hundred words a day, or thirty-six hundred words a week for fifty-two weeks. I had to pull off the highway and park my cab and take out a pencil and a sheet of paper to multiply thirty-six hundred by fifty-two, but who doesn't?

The answer was 187,200 words per year. I then multiplied that by 14, which took awhile. Let's jump ahead to the correct answer rather than wading through the less-correct answers: 2,620,800.

Two-and-a-half-million words plus!

I sat there staring at the answer for a long time. The sun moved a few degrees west before I woke up from what I later surmised was a state of shock. It subsequently took me a while longer to get up the nerve to take the next step in this series of calculations. For those of

you non-writers who might be scratching your heads with bafflement, writers spend an awful lot of time making calculations involving anything from word counts, to page counts, to the amount of
money publishers will advance them on unwritten novels. As non-
writers, you probably assume arithmetic has nothing to do with pro-
ducing a novel, and you're right.

The next step was to divide the figure by 100,000, meaning a
novel one-hundred thousand words long, which I use as a kind of average. The answer came to 26, meaning I could have written twenty-
six novels during the past fourteen years while driving my cab. I put
my pencil and sheet of paper away, started the engine, and began
driving toward Denver along the back roads. I didn't dare take the
Interstate. I kept drifting in and out of a kind of trance, which was
not unlike the state of shock I mentioned earlier. I don't remember
arriving at the Fairmont Hotel, but that's where I found myself when
things finally returned to "normal."

The source of the shock of course was the full comprehension of
all the time I had wasted during the past fourteen years. Prior to this,
the idea of wasting time had never bothered me. Heck, I had taken
pride in my ability to waste time ever since high school. Then there
was the army, college, and Dyna-Plex, and each of those "epochs"
of my life were opportunities to invent more creative ways to waste
time. It had never once occurred to me that I could have actually accomplished something during those years.

I then wondered if the Dyna-Plex bosses had enrolled me in
the time-management course for reasons that I had not been fully
cognizant of at the time. I was the only person in our office who
was required to take the course, although there were students from
other companies in the class. It was held in another building in the
Tech Center, offered by a private firm that specialized in both time-

management as well as financial-planning seminars. It seemed to me that the other students were just a pack of losers, but I nodded off before I was able to give them a thorough evaluation.

Anyway, I sat there in front of the Fairmont Hotel trying to come to grips with the fact that I could have written a lot more novels than I already had if only I had taken a portable typewriter with me since Day One of my cab-driving career.

Suddenly I wanted those years back.

I felt like Gig Young in that episode of the *Twilight Zone* where Gig visits the hometown of his youth and realizes he has gone back in time to the 1930s, so he walks to his parents' home and scares the hell out of his mother, and later he gets on a merry-go-round and hurts his leg and blah blah blah and so on, but anyway, to sum it up briefly, I began to feel melancholy about the swift passage of time.

I made a feeble attempt to put things into perspective. I was fourth in line at the Fairmont, it was already past four o'clock in the afternoon, and I had grossed more than one hundred dollars for the day, so I was doing all right. I figured that if I worked until seven o'clock I might make sixty-dollars profit or even more, but I had no intention of doing that. Fifty bucks, that was my goal, the only goal I ever shoot for. When you start thinking about numbers like 60 and 70, you're just kidding yourself. I am anyway. It means I'm starting to get ambitious, and anybody with ambition has no business driving a taxi.

I started the engine and pulled away from the cabstand. I decided I didn't want to sit outside hotels and brood about the swift passage of time. I would save that until I got home and had access to beer. There was a strong possibility that I would even light up a cigar before the night was through. When I succumb to despair, I go whole hog.

I switched on the Rocky radio as I drove and began listening to the endless litany of Friday bells. The ideal situation would be to cop a trip to DIA, which would put me way over the top financially but leave me blameless in the ambition department. I don't actually dislike it if I make more than fifty dollars a day, as long as I can prove in a court of law that I wasn't liable. "Luck," "Chance," and "Kismet" are the concepts that absolve me of blame when things start going right.

The odds of getting a DIA run off the radio were slim of course, so I didn't give it serious thought. I decided to put in a couple hours making Capitol Hill runs before heading back to the motor. I swung my cab over to 15th Street and headed toward the gold dome of the state capitol building. It was there that I saw the hippies again.

CHAPTER 6

I f you've never been to Denver, let me tell you about the capitol building. It's a big fancy gray granite affair with a dome on top covered with gold leaf. The dome sort of looks like the dome on top of the congressional building in Washington D.C. The building sits on top of a gently sloping hill that overlooks Lincoln Street and comprises the western edge of what is known as "Capitol Hill." I don't know who named Capitol Hill, but it may have been the same genius that named the orange.

The hill is covered with a blanket of grass and bums. During the 1960s, the bums were known as hippies, but that *nom de plume* was just a flash in the pan. Panhandlers, street people, hippies, punks, beatniks, bummers, gold miners, buffalo hunters, Lewis and Clark, they're all the same—people with no place to sleep at night who converge on what was doubtless envisioned as a garden of paradise back in the olden days when landscape artists had been hired to make Denver look important. There are a lot of Greek columns and water fountains in that part of town. The City and County Building is located a few hundred yards west, facing the capitol building. That's where I have to go every year to renew my taxi-driving license. For some reason, a Denver taxi license is called a "Herdic" license. End of history lesson.

The hippies were standing near the eastbound bus stop at Colfax and Broadway. This didn't surprise me. That particular stop is where the #15 bus loads before going up the hill and rolling straight east to

Aurora. The 15 is kind of legendary in Denver. It takes nerves of steel to ride the 15. The 15 is a cross between the Mardi Gras, the bowery, and a John Waters film. I don't know how the ride shapes up by the time you get to Aurora, since I've never ridden the 15 all the way to Aurora. It may very well be that no fare has ever made it all the way to Aurora, but I do know one thing: the bus passes the site of the old Fitzsimmons Army Hospital. That's where President Eisenhower recovered from his heart attack in the 1950s, although I don't think the 15 had anything to do with it.

I was relieved in a pointless sort of way. I really hadn't believed those kids had been busted and sent to the clink. It's just that sometimes my brain starts acting like a television and I get easily distracted by the show going on, when I should be watching the road. The sad part is, I watch the TV voluntarily. Whenever the script starts getting truly ludicrous, I sort of sit back to see how far my brain will take the premise. The more outrageous it gets, the less willing I am to switch the program over to what I call "The Maturity Channel," which is similar to PBS.

The kids appeared to be panhandling. I felt bad for them. A bus stop is not the ideal place to panhandle, since the sort of people who take busses are not that far removed culturally from the sort of people who panhandle. From my point of view, the kids were engaged in an amateurish approach to mooching. I know a few things about mooching. I've been on both sides of that fence, and I have learned that form and style have as much to do with success as the amount of money a moochee has to "spare"—as in "Got any spare change?"

Professional mooches understand this of course. I myself never really rose to the level of "professional" because I did most of my mooching in college, usually at The Campus Lounge. When it came to cadging free beers, I thought of myself as an Olympic amateur—good, but not good enough to compete with John Elway.

I glanced at the kids as I rolled past. Two girls and a boy dressed like hippies. They stood out from the crowd. All the other people at the bus stop were just sort of "normal" poorly dressed.

I decided to circle the block. Even though I was no longer worried about the kids getting shipped off to the state prison at Cañon City—which is pronounced "Canyon City" for those of you who don't speak tilde—I still felt a few ragged vestiges of desire to help them out. Okay. I'll admit it. I wanted to make up for shrieking, "That's *impossible!*" when they told me they had never heard of the Beatles.

I circled around the capitol building and pulled back onto Colfax, and saw the kids trudging up the hill. I drove past them and pulled into a no-parking zone and watched the kids in my rear-view mirror. One of the girls was holding what must have been spare change in her open palm, and the other kids were leaning over to look at it. The pathos was unbearable.

I waited until they were adjacent to my taxi, then I tapped my horn. They stopped and looked at me. I leaned across the seat and spoke to them through the shotgun window. "How's it going?" I said. I thought about adding the word "dudes" at the end of the sentence, but I wasn't certain about the proper etiquette for speaking to contemporary ragamuffins.

They squinted at me as if I was some sort of creep. Then the expression on one of the girl's faces changed, which is to say, she smiled.

"It's the Beatle man!" she said, and she leaned into the window.

"How are you guys making out?" I said.

"Okay," she said. "We're trying to get enough money together to take a bus out to Red Rocks."

I was momentarily nonplused. Red Rocks is—among other things—way out of town in the foothills.

"Why Red Rocks?" I said.

"The concert," she said.

"What concert?" I said.

Instead of replying, she reached into a purse made out of macramé and withdrew a long rectangle of paper. She handed it to me.

I quickly scanned it. It was an advertisement printed in a psychedelic font announcing a rock 'n' roll retrospective at Red Rocks Amphitheater featuring a nostalgia band called Plastic Infinity. I was familiar with them. They were a '60s cover group like Sha Na Na, whose gimmick was to be nostalgic for the 1950s. It made me wonder if the people of the 1740s were nostalgic for the 1720s.

I then realized that the sheet of paper was in fact a ticket for admittance to the concert. Price: twenty dollars.

I tried to withhold judgment on that, then I gave up. "The tickets ate up all your bread, huh?" I said. Right at that moment I couldn't have cared less if she took offense at what was subtle sarcasm. She could have bought a couple of Beatle albums for that much money and heard the real thing instead of a cover group.

Plastic Infinity.

Give me a break.

"The tickets didn't cost anything," she said with a smile, as I handed the ticket back to her. "They were free."

This statement somewhat ameliorated my admittedly irrelevant umbrage. But just as I am quick to take umbrage at things that are none of my business, so too do I admire anything that's free.

"Groovy," I said. "Where did you get them?"

"A guy was handing them out down by the bus stop," she said. I nodded. Then frowned. Why would anybody hand out twenty-dollar admittance tickets at a bus stop? The answer came quickly: Plastic Infinity was giving away tickets because it couldn't sell them. I almost started thinking about the world of publishing, but instead I said, "Is there a bus that goes out to Red Rocks?"

She shrugged. "I don't know. I guess we'll have to ask a bus driver."

In a strange way I sort of enjoyed her reply. It was as if I was talking to an actual hippie, a person completely out of touch with The Establishment.

"What time does the concert start?" I said.

"Six," she replied.

This gave the kids barely an hour and a half to mooch bus fare, query a bus driver, find the right bus, and ride it to Red Rocks. In my estimation, it would take someone who was out of touch with The Establishment approximately forever to accomplish these things. Let's cut to the chase.

I already had my fifty dollars minimum for the day, it was only four-thirty in the afternoon, the sun was still up, and I had nothing to do for the rest of my life. I knew the kids would never make it to Red Rocks in time for the concert. And I still felt guilty about yelling at them for not knowing who the Beatles were. Any of the above excuses was reason enough to give them a free ride to Red Rocks, but I liked the Beatle one best.

"Listen," I said to the girl, "why don't I run you out to Red Rocks for free? I'm finished working for the day but I have to keep my cab until seven o'clock. I can get you there early so you can find a good seat. It would take you a really long time to get there on the bus."

"Oh wow, man," she said.

If she wasn't an actual hippie, she certainly had the patois nailed. She stood away from the window and spoke to her friends for a moment, then leaned back in and said, "Thanks a lot, man, we really appreciate this."

She pulled open the rear door. She and the other girl climbed in and shut the door.

I looked at the boy, who was standing on the sidewalk waving at them.

"Isn't he coming?" I said.

"No," the girl said. "He doesn't have a ticket to the concert."

I frowned, then said, "What do you mean? I thought you said some guy was handing them out for free."

"He was, but we got the last two tickets. Billy was just helping us get some money for the bus. He isn't going to the concert."

I nodded, then reached up to drop my flag and turn on the meter. I stopped myself in time. It could have freaked out the hippies if I had turned on the meter. They might have thought I was a capitalist pig who had lied about the hidden cost of the free lunch. I smiled to myself. I hadn't thought of the phrase "capitalist pig" in a long time. I felt like Gig Young again.

I pulled out onto Colfax and went through the complicated side street business of getting my vehicle aimed west. Eventually we were rolling along Colfax but I was thinking about cutting down to 6th Avenue. There are a number of ways to get to Red Rocks from central downtown. There are fast ways and slow ways and cheap ways and expensive ways. I always drive somewhere in between. That's on normal days. But since I was giving a free ride to two hippies, this was not a normal day. I opted for fast.

Sixth Avenue turns into a highway beyond the city limits, so I decided to cut down to 6th and get this altruism over with as quickly as possible. Red Rocks is not really all that far from Denver. As I say, it's in the foothills near a little town called Morrison. I went to high school with a kid named Morrison. I don't know why I bring that up.

When I came to Kalamath Street I turned left and headed south toward 6th. Up to then I had been busy making cabbie calculations and not paying any attention to the girls in the backseat. Normally I don't have to make calculations because normally I go to the same places over and over again, DIA, Cherry Creek, etc., but Red Rocks was unusual, and unusual situations force me to think. That might be true of everybody.

"Mind if we smoke?" one of the girls said.

I was just getting ready to swing west onto 6th Avenue, looking in the rear-view mirror, checking traffic, playing the road game, so I said, "I don't mind," which I did, but only because I hate to see young people light up cigarettes. I couldn't care less if an adult wants to set his couch on fire and inhale the smoke, but not many kids own couches. I always have the urge to lecture young people about smoking, but I consciously try to avoid situations in which I pretend to be a grownup. That's what started me smoking at the age of seventeen—I wanted to be a grownup. The army cured me of that desire. But it still took another ten years before I finally managed to become a kid again and quit smoking. I didn't really *quit* smoking though—I gave up. Giving up is the solution to everything.

And then, just as I wheeled my taxi onto 6th Avenue, I realized that the girls in the backseat were not smoking tobacco.

CHAPTER 7

I glanced in my rear-view mirror and saw one of the girls surreptitiously hand the other girl the cigarette, or "joint" as I believe hand-rolled pot reefers are sometimes referred to. Yes, two teenage girls were smoking marijuana in my taxicab and were doing so apparently with my permission.

I don't want to go into boring detail explaining why I happen to possess the rare ability to recognize the distinct odor of burning marijuana, but it partly has to do with attending midnight movies. I glanced around to make absolutely certain that I was seeing what I thought I was smelling. As I looked into the backseat I saw the second girl hand the first girl the "joint." They were keeping it below window-level, which indicated to me that they were familiar with the concept of "police."

I looked ahead at 6th Avenue and tried to think of something to say. I wouldn't have let the girls light up the joint in my cab if I had known that's what they had in mind in the first place. I would have told them that they would have to wait until the ride was over. But the joint was already half-smoked, so I decided to say nothing. I did not want to startle or frighten them. From what I've been told by experienced "tokers," pot can make people paranoid, and the last thing I needed in my taxi was two freaked-out females. One freaked-out male was enough.

This was an awkward situation for me. It wasn't so much the legal ramifications. Hell, you wouldn't believe some of the laws that have been broken in my backseat, usually after 2:00 A.M. on Saturday nights. But those situations always involved adults. These two kids looked underage. What if a cop in a passing cruiser spotted the girls handing a cigarette back and forth and pulled me over to investigate?

I started to feel like an idiot. That calmed me down. Whenever I feel like an idiot, I'm in my own element.

"Are you guys natives of Denver?" I said conversationally. I had decided to treat this as a normal ride with two normal people, and work my way around to finding out more about them, which cab drivers usually do for reasons that involve tips.

"Yes," one of them said.

"No," the other said.

They burst out laughing. I glanced in the mirror. The girls were looking at each other, doing that eyeball-to-eyeball secret communication thing that, again, experienced tokers have told me reefer smokers sometimes engage in—although in my experience girls look at each other that way all the time, especially when giggling. My sisters used to look at each other that way when my Maw yelled at me.

Then the girl who had said no looked at me in the mirror. "I'm from Vermont."

I nodded. I didn't have any response to that statement. I have never been to Vermont, although I've heard rumors—but who hasn't?

"Did you move here recently?" I said. I was just making small talk, the tiniest, most minuscule talk I could muster. Red Rocks is just on the outskirts of town, not that far away, and I was hanging on by my fingernails.

The girl giggled softly, then said, "I don't remember."

This got the two of them laughing uproariously, and I have to admit that under different circumstances I might have enjoyed the conversation—like for instance if my taxicab was a college apartment where a kegger was being held and we were surrounded by a dozen engineering majors, physics majors, and a sprinkling of English majors having a noisy get-together at KAU in Wichita, which was where I wished I was right then. This ride was starting to take forever.

Suddenly I rolled down my window.

I had been told that marijuana sometimes makes time seem to slow down, and I realized that I had been inhaling fumes for the past ten minutes. I didn't really believe I was getting high. As an experienced taxi driver I knew that unpleasant situations could make a road seem to stretch to infinity. Did I ever tell you about the time I found a stray cat and decided to drive it to the Dumb Friends League?

"Would you like a hit?" one of the girls said, leaning forward in the seat. Thank God she didn't hold the joint out to me. The last time someone offered me something that you're not supposed to accept as a cab driver, it involved an eighteen-year-old girl whom I supposedly "murdered" but that's a long story and I don't want to get into it save to say that she offered me a hit from a bottle of vodka while I was driving. She held the bottle in front of my nose. But this situation was different, from a legal, moral, and chemical standpoint, which was a new record for me.

"No thanks," I said.

She sat back in the seat without pressing the issue. She and her friend continued to toke the "doobie," as I believe it is called. By this time we were coming up on the 285 interchange, so I went through the road game of checking the traffic and making the exit off 6th Avenue. Then I aimed the hood ornament south toward Morrison.

I started thinking again about the time the "murdered" girl offered me a snort and how I later decided I ought to have taken the bottle away from her but didn't. Now here I was in a similar situation. How many times in a person's life does he tell himself, "Man oh man, if that ever happens to me again I'll do things differently." Yet here I was, not doing things differently. Something told me that I ought to tell the girls to put out the joint, and explain that I had misunderstood them when they asked if they could smoke. But isn't this how it always is? One minute you're drifting along living your drab life, and the next minute you're a passenger on the *Hindenburg*. This happens to me frequently, so you might assume I would be used to it. But my problem is that I'm not used to everything. Just waking up at dawn is like starting over at square one.

But I knew I had to do it. For once in my life I had to act like a grownup. Twice, if you counted the army.

I looked in the rear-view mirror, preparing myself to be mature. Then I saw one of the girls take a last puff off of what I am told is referred to as a "roach." She snuffed out the ember and rolled the paper into a ball. She cracked the window on her side and tossed the "remains" of the "doobie" out the "window." This came as a relief. I didn't have to act like a grownup after all.

"How late does the concert last?" I said, reverting to small talk.

The girls giggled for a bit, then one of them said, "We don't know."

"Does it say on the ticket?" I said.

One of them pulled out a ticket and studied it, then said, "No."

"How are you guys going to get back to Denver?" I said.

"We'll probably hitch a ride," the other girl said.

This made me feel bad. As much as I enjoy reading Jack Kerouac's novels, the idea of stoned teenage girls hitchhiking home from a rock concert didn't sit well with me. All of a sudden I started to get a funny feeling. What was I doing giving a free ride to two girls in the first place? It was possible that they might not have even made it to the concert if I hadn't intervened. I tried to calculate whether or not I had broken my supreme vow, the one that I break constantly, the one that states that I will never again get involved in the personal lives of my fares. But had I actually gotten involved in their personal lives? After all, I was just giving them a cab ride. I do that to people all the time. Is interacting with the human race three days a week tantamount to a violation of private space? I had learned to ask questions like that in Philosophy 101.

I was just beginning to feel wracked with guilt when one of the girls said, "What's your name, mister cab driver?"

"Murph," I said.

"Murph," she said with a giggle. "That sounds like a puppy dog ... murph murph."

The other girl giggled.

I sort of giggled, too. Then I glanced back and said, "What are your names?"

"My name is Sunshine. My friend's name is Moonbeam."

"Is that your real actual names?" I said.

More giggles.

"My real actual name is Janet," one of them said.

"My real actual name is Vicky," the other said. Then she said, "Is Murph your real actual name?"

I started to say yes, but then realized it wasn't. "My real actual name is Brendan."

"That's a strange name," Vicky said.

"I come from a strange family."

More giggles.

By now we were nearing the entrance to Red Rocks. A lot of people had shown up for the concert. Cars were parked along the road, as well as vans with psychedelic paint jobs, daisies, peace signs, the whole ball of wax. People dressed like Janet and Vicky were strolling along the dirt shoulder of the road toward the entrance. All of a sudden I didn't feel so bad. The scene reminded me of the opening sequence of *Woodstock*. Lots of happy hippies all in this together. It sort of made me want to stay for the concert. I had never attended a rock concert before. If I remembered correctly, the Woodstock concert was taking place while I was on KP.

Red Rocks is an interesting place. It's a part of the Denver City Park system. The amphitheater was built in the early 1940s. Every Easter a Catholic Mass is held there. It's called the "Sunrise Service." Another interesting fact about Red Rocks is that in 1964 the Beatles played the amphitheater during their first American tour. The tickets cost $6.60 apiece and the concert lasted thirty minutes. Mull that one over.

I drove as close as I could get, then parked the cab at the side of the road and turned around and looked at the girls. "Will you guys be able to get home okay?"

"Sure, man," Janet said. "We hitchhike all the time."

Then I did something weird. I reached into my shirt pocket and pulled out a twenty-dollar bill and handed it to Janet. "Listen," I said. "If you have any trouble catching a ride, just call a cab. Here's twenty dollars. This will get you back to town."

"Oh we can't take your money, man," Janet said.

"Sure you can," I said. "It's just paper. It doesn't mean anything." Now I was really getting weird. But I was trying to talk hippie-talk. "If you ever meet someone who needs help, pass it on. The twenty will come back to me someday" like a bad penny.

Janet shrugged and accepted the money. "Thanks, man."

"Yeah, thanks, man," Vicky said, and the two girls climbed out of the backseat.

I watched them trundle toward the gate. Then I made an illegal U-turn and headed back toward Denver. I made the illegal U to take my mind off the guilt, indecision, remorse, self-reproach, and overall sense of ruefulness that helps me get to sleep at night. Counting sheep is for amateurs.

It worked. As I threaded my way back down the road, I started looking around for cops, which is something you usually see at large gatherings of people. I expected John Law to step out from between two parked cars and flag me down and ticket me. There are some things that cops will not let a cab driver get away with, and breaking the law is one of them.

Pretty soon I was back on 6th Avenue headed for Denver, glancing in my rear-view mirror every now and then for the sight of a flashing red light. I figured that any foot patrolman who saw me hang a u-ey might radio ahead to a rolling patrol. Whenever I flaunt the law, my imagination takes off like a Redstone rocket. If I could just figure out a way to break the law while writing novels, I might get a few acceptance slips.

It was six-thirty when I pulled into the parking lot at the motor. I had thirty minutes left on my shift and I was twenty dollars down for the day. This was the worst Friday I had driven in a long time. Friday is money day for cab drivers, and as I say, I often earn as much as sixty or seventy dollars on Friday without even trying. But I want to emphasize here that I do not do it on purpose. I am never to blame. It just happens. It's the nature of a Friday. People go places on Friday. I don't question it, and I don't fight it. But every once in a while I get a Friday like this one, where things fall apart. Ergo, like Kenny Rogers I never count my money until the game is done, which happens every April 15th. And guess what? It always averages out to fifty dollars per Friday per year. You never win and you never lose when you set your sights as low as I do.

CHAPTER 8

B y the time I got back, the night-shift drivers were arriving to pick up their cabs. The night driver for #123 was an old pro named Edwards, who had been hacking six years longer than me. I always feel good when an old pro drives 123 because I know I'm leaving my cab in good hands. I never have to worry about dents or dings or general body damage that can occur when a newbie drives 123. I always feel edgy when a newbie takes my cab out at night because I'm not certain I'll ever see it again in one piece, and I had gotten used to 123.

For most of my fourteen years I had driven Rocky Mountain Taxicab #127, which accidentally burned to a crisp one day. This event took place around the same time that I became the prime suspect in the kidnaping, robbery, and murder of a homeless man. It had nothing to do with the murder of that eighteen-year-old girl, which wasn't a murder but a ridiculous misunderstanding. And I assure you that I had nothing to do with the murder of the homeless man, which turned out not to be a murder at all but a suicide, which it actually wasn't. It gets complicated. Mostly I try not to think about it.

Before going into the on-call room to turn in my key and trip-sheet, I got to work cleaning up the interior of my cab. I believe in The Golden Rule of Cab Driving, which states that you should always hand your cab over to the next driver in the same condition that you yourself would want it. This means making sure he doesn't have to police up Twinkie wrappers or pop cans or any other forms of solid or liquid left on the seats or floor by either yourself or one of your fares. I also emptied out the ashtrays. I do this after I've had smokers in my cab, especially if they've been smoking pot. I suppose I have a somewhat naive faith in circumstantial evidence. I pulled out both of the door-handle ashtrays and carried them across the parking lot to a trash barrel and shook them out. I wiped them down with a piece of newspaper that was lying in the barrel. I carried the ashtrays back and replaced them, then continued to police up the cab.

That's when I found the love beads.

They were lying on the backseat where Janet had been sitting. They were sort of jammed halfway beneath the space where the back meets the cushion, the same space where fares tend to lose the occasional billfold. If you've ever removed the rear seat-cushion of a taxi-cab, you know what I'm talking about. It can be a treasure trove. It's similar to couch cushions but more lucrative. I have found cameras that have slipped down behind the rear cushions of cabs. I always turn in the cameras and billfolds to the lost-and-found, but practically everything else I find is fair game. It's like the salvage rule of the sea. Remind me never to tell you about my collection of combs.

I crawled into the rear of the cab and knelt on the cushion to separate the space, then I gently pulled out the string of beads. I didn't want to break them. I knew that they belonged to either Janet or Vicky. Each bead was made of hand-carved wood, about the size of a marble. They were painted in different colors. Some of the beads had intricate designs on them, nothing recognizable, just random patterns. It was a long necklace, the kind you would have to loop twice before you could wear it. The string had little wooden clips on each end that must have come apart. Whoever lost it probably hadn't even noticed it due to the giggling or something. Probably the something.

As I raised the necklace to examine it, it rattled. I lowered the necklace to the palm of my left hand and listened to the interesting noise the beads made. I lifted and lowered it again. I liked the rattley sound. Is "rattley" a word? It is now.

I knelt in the back of 123 raising and lowering the beads and wondering if I could invent a toy that made the same noise. I envisioned little kids all over America raising and lowering beads and being mesmerized, like kids in the 1930s listening blindly to radio programs. Maybe I could get rich off a toy like this. Then I heard a strange knocking sound, as if someone was locked inside the trunk of my taxi.

Startled, I looked up to see Edwards standing behind 123 rapping on the lid of the trunk.

"Hey Murph, whatcha doing?" he said, coming around to the door.

Embarrassed, I lowered the beads into my palm and crawled out of the cab.

"Policing up," I said, stuffing the beads into a pocket of my jeans and shutting the door. "Did you just get here?"

"Yeah," he said, pointing his thumb at his car parked nearby. "You're coming in kinda early, ain'tcha?"

"Aaah, I had a terrible day," I said. "I decided to quit while I was behind."

"Streets dead?" he said with a worried look. I knew what he meant. It was Friday. Whoever heard of a dead Friday?

"Nah," I said, giving him a doleful smirk. "I was just out of synch with the bells. I couldn't catch up with the eagle."

He nodded. Then he grinned. "Did you leave me any gas?"

"I doubt it."

We both chuckled the universal "insider's" chuckle that always annoys "outsiders."

I grabbed my briefcase and trip-sheet and key, and together Edwards and I went into the on-call room where I was required to hand my key to Rollo, who then handed the key to Edwards. I couldn't have just handed the key to Edwards, which would have been logical. The Rocky Mountain Taxicab Company is regulated by the Public Utilities Commission, a government agency. Nuff said.

"What in the hell is that thing hanging out of your pants!" Rollo shrieked.

I glanced down at my jeans and saw part of the necklace that hadn't quite gotten stuffed into my pocket. I didn't have much experience with necklaces so I had done an incompetent job of hiding it from public view. If you think it's easy to stuff a long necklace into your jeans pocket, try it sometime. The bastard takes on a life of its own.

But since I was no longer officially on duty, I didn't reply to Rollo's query. The government doesn't regulate small talk—not yet anyway. I scooped up the dangling beads and shoved them into my pocket, then I nodded at Edwards and said, "See you on the asphalt." I walked out of the on-call room.

My first instinct upon leaving the building was to drive back to Red Rocks and track down the hippies and return the beads. This was a knee-jerk reaction to having in my possession something that belonged to someone else. Call it honor, call it duty, call it obsessive/compulsive behavior. I call it Catholic guilt.

But I realized that a necklace made of wooden beads did not fall into the same category as a 35mm Nikon. It was more like a comb. I still felt bad though because the necklace was kind of cool. But I doubted that Janet's world would come crashing down on her head when she realized she didn't have her love beads.

I thought about tossing them into a trash barrel as I walked to my Chevy. I doubted I would ever run into the hippies again. But then I thought maybe I *would* run into them. That's what always happens when you throw away something that's been gathering dust in your garage for twelve years—people show up the next day and demand their lawnmower back. Maybe I would see the girls panhandling on the streets and I could return the necklace.

I hopped into my heap and kissed RMTC goodbye for the millionth time and headed home. I arrived at my apartment at precisely seven o'clock, which is normally the time that I "clock out" as they say in places where the employees do real work.

I once worked as an assistant maintenance man in a plastics factory where the employees had to clock out at exactly five o'clock. If the line of employees at the clock was too long and you ended up clocking out one minute after five, the foreman would call you in and give you a warning. It didn't matter to him that the crowd of employees scrambling to jam their cards into the clock was too long. It didn't matter that it was impossible for two physical objects to occupy the same space at the same time—the two objects being workers and the time being five o'clock. The foreman of the factory didn't give a tinker's damn about Newtonian or Einsteinian physics. All he cared about was the extra minute of time that appeared on your card on payday. I eventually ended up getting fired from that job. It happened the day I explained Aristotlian logic to him.

So it was seven o'clock when I climbed the fire escape to my crow's nest. I was feeling pretty good, even if I hadn't made my fifty bucks profit after all. I was down twenty. I don't earn much money as a cab driver, but I do sometimes get fixated with money, in the way that someone washing windows might get fixated by a tiny little speck of dirt that won't come off a pane of glass. You start concentrating so hard on it that you lose all sense of perspective. It becomes terribly important that you deal effectively with this teensy little minuscule thing—whether a speck of dust or your income. You start pressing so hard with the sponge that you accidentally break the glass or fail to make your daily profit. Then you look up and realize that it wasn't all that important to begin with, that there are more significant things in this world than dirt or money. But try and tell that to the man who hired you to wash his windows. He ended up docking me fifteen bucks. That was in Kansas City.

Well, not making my profits for the day due to giving twenty dollars to the hippies put things back into perspective for me and reminded me that my life wasn't about driving a cab. It was about making a million dollars off a best-selling novel. You might think that I wouldn't forget something like a million dollars, but it happens. So coming up short that Friday had the peculiar effect of making me feel sort of wild and free. Who cared if I hadn't earned fifty bucks? I wasn't dead. I wasn't starving. I wasn't anything at all. This was just another Friday like all Fridays. "Spring break" had arrived, meaning I was going to take off all of the following week, which totaled nine days of doing nothing—Saturday through the second Sunday on the calendar.

I do this only once a month though, prior to paying my rent. I have to work five days in a row to make enough money to pay the kid who manages the apartment building. His name is Keith. He's in his twenties, and in a way he is like a hippie. He attends a free school where he takes courses in Yoga and macramé and all the other stuff that was co-opted by the entrepreneurs who saw an opportunity to profit off the sorts of people who once had a sneering contempt for the concept of profit, i.e., hippies.

Every time I go to the supermarket, I always check to see if the latest issue of the free-school catalog has been placed on the rack near the front door where they put publications that nobody will buy. I like to peruse the "art" classes in the catalog to see what sorts of courses are being offered by the people who are trying to profit off art. I'm referring to the teachers, not the students. You can take classes in pottery and painting and photography and, of course, writing. There are all kinds of writing courses available, non-fiction as well as fiction. I like to read the descriptions of the courses on writing fiction, whether short-story writing or novel writing. There are also courses in screenwriting, but I kind of gave up on my ambitions to crank out screenplays after that business with the "murdered" girl.

Mostly I like to read the blurbs that describe how you can become a writer by getting in touch with your "inner shaman," or the classes that explore the concept of "writing to make sense out of life." What I'm really looking for is "writing to make a million dollars" but they never seem to offer that one.

Anyway, I had a little problem with this month's spring break because I hadn't made my fifty dollars on Friday. I had come up twenty bucks short. I tried to ignore this fact, but it's hard to ignore not having money. I live a sort of hand-to-mouth existence, although I will admit that I do it on purpose. I earn just enough money to get by, i.e., to pay for rent and food. My rent is cheap and so is my food, but when a person lives this close to the edge, he has to stay on top of things, which I don't like doing. But I once lived the life where you didn't have to stay on top of things and I learned that it has its own unique drawbacks. I once had a job where I made twenty grand a year, and I never had to stay on top of anything. That was at Dyna-Plex. I made so much money that I became like a big blob of whipped cream. I lost all ambition to become a millionaire writer. I sat at my desk week-in and week-out and never did anything. Once a month I did have to write a brochure, which took an hour. Then it was back to blobsville.

I know what you're thinking. How could he walk away from a sweet deal like that? It wasn't easy, believe me. From the outside it looked like I had everything I wanted out of life, which was to do nothing forever. But I didn't want to do nothing in an office, I wanted to not do it in Tahiti. I wanted to be a dissolute millionaire on a beach. Another version of the fantasy was to wander around in a mansion like Jay Gatsby. I wanted to drift down to the swimming pool, take a dip, towel myself dry, and mix a martini. I assumed that's what millionaires normally did. I didn't know because I had never been one, and the odds of my ever becoming one were nil as long as I was earning twenty G's a year. No, I had to get out of Dyna-Plex if I ever expected to make The Big Money. I had to find a job that paid so little that it would force me to think about money all the time, and cab driving filled the bill.

Now I spend all my time trying to think up novels that will become instant best-sellers and turn me into a blob again. Only this blob won't have to get up every day and put on a suit and "be" somewhere at eight in the morning. I don't think there is anything that annoys me as much as having to "be" somewhere. It seems like every bad thing that ever happened to me happened when I was somewhere.

But on that Friday night I had to face up to the fact that unless I worked one more shift I would come up short on the rent. It made me feel a bit blue. I had always looked forward to my spring breaks, so the fact that I would have to work at least one day next week put a damper on everything. But I wouldn't have to work a full shift. I just needed to make up the missing twenty dollars and everything would be copacetic. "Copacetic" is one of my favorite words because its origin is unknown. At least, it's unknown to people who write dictionaries. The fact that millions of people go around saying, "Everything is copacetic," without having the slightest idea what it means says something uninteresting about the human race.

I decided I would work on Monday. Just get it done and get it out of the way. Of course from a strictly utilitarian point of view, I could have worked on Saturday, or even Sunday, but that would have been an aberration of such monumental proportions that it actually made me laugh. Nobody works on weekends. Anybody who works on weekends has to be living a life of such pathetic desperation that he would be better off checking himself into a nut house.

With this in mind, I spent the rest of the weekend watching television. The next thing I knew, it was Monday morning.

CHAPTER 9

I was furious when the alarm clock woke me up on Monday. My body was used to waking up only three weeks in a row, so getting up on the fourth week threw a monkey wrench into my metabolism. But I dragged myself off to work consoled by the fact that my shift would be finished by noon.

"... Let's get it done and get it out of the way, let's get it done and get it out of the way ..." I sang softly as I drove to Rocky Cab.

When I walked into the on-call room, a lot of old pros standing in line at the cage did double-takes. I have a rep at Rocky. The old pros know I take the fourth week off every month, but they also know that if I show up on a Monday of the fourth week I've got a good reason, most often one that they would rather not know about. Actually their double-takes were more like furtive glances. When they saw me walk in they quickly looked away. They didn't want to get roped into an untenable situation. That sometimes happens to cabbies who are in my immediate vicinity when I show up unexpectedly. It happens to friends, enemies, and strangers, too.

Even Rollo did a double-take when I got to the front of the line. But he worked in the cage so he was sort of trapped. He couldn't look away because he had to hand me my key and trip-sheet. But I could see it in his eyes. My presence was stressing him out. He didn't dare make a snide remark because it conceivably could have left him wide open to entrapment. Rollo and I don't get along very well, but we do understand each other, sort of like Lex Luthor and Superman. We tread lightly around each other. If he had any snide remarks hidden up his sleeve, he would save them until the next week when I would be back on my regular schedule—I'm talking about Rollo's "Zone of Comfort" here.

"I'm pulling a short-shift today," I said. "Six hours."

Rollo nodded, then squinted at me ever-so-slightly. He knew what I was up to, I could tell. He understood that the only reason I was working was to make up for a shortfall on my income. I had done this before. There was nothing untenable in this, but he still refrained from "saying" anything. Best let sleeping dogs lie, as cab drivers and everybody else with half a brain say.

I paid thirty-five bucks for the short-shift, picked up my key and trip-sheet, and walked out of the room.

"… Let's get it done and get it out of the way …" I sang as I searched the parking lot for 123. I found it halfway across the lot, which meant it had been driven by a blooded newbie, meaning a cabbie who had been driving for at least a month and had somehow managed not to give up in despair and start looking for a real job.

The newest of the newbies always leave cabs parked way the hell out at the edge of the lot, like they're afraid to park near the on-call room after a night shift. Why they do this I do not know, but I did it when I was a newbie because I was afraid the old pros would get annoyed at me for taking a choice spot near the building. The fact that anybody can park anywhere he wants in the lot is something that the old pros keep under their hats. You don't get much opportunity to feel "special" when you drive a taxi for a living.

I made a quick check of the cab for dents, didn't find any, then hopped in and got to work. I decided I would take calls off the radio rather than sit in front of the hotels. In theory I could have cut two hours off my shift if I actually worked. The reason I rarely use the radio on a normal twelve-hour shift is because I like to have my cake and eat it too. Also Twinkies, joe, and soda, as well as reading paperbacks and listening to rock 'n' roll on the AM radio. Since I'm forced to work in order to get money, I try to make it as little like a job as possible. I had perfected listening to music surreptitiously when I worked at Dyna-Plex. Thank God for earphones.

I stopped off at a 7-11 but put only five dollars worth of gas in the tank, since I was driving a half-shift. I bought a Twinkie and a cup of joe and headed out on the road. It made me feel funny to drive to downtown Denver and not go straight to one of the hotels. I usually hit the Brown Palace first because it's the closest hotel on my route. And if the line of taxis at the cabstand is too long, I drift toward the Hilton or the Fairmont or whatever hotel where the cabbing looks good, like a fisherman looking for a choice spot up the lazy river.

On that Monday though, I averted my eyes as I drove past the hotels, but the temptation to simply pull in at a cabstand and park started to overwhelm me. Fighting temptation does not come natural to me but somehow I managed to keep driving. If you've ever sipped a beer, you know what I mean.

Pretty soon a call came over the radio for a fare on Capitol Hill. I grabbed it. It was an elderly woman who wanted to go to an address in Aurora, "To my sister's house," she informed me, even though I did not ask for the information. I try not to know as much as I can about my fares, and it practically never works.

A lot of people have a compulsion to tell cab drivers where they are going and why. The where is okay, but the why is irrelevant. Some people even seem apologetic about their reasons for going places, as if they are sorry to bother the driver by making him take them there. If this doesn't make any sense to you, join the club.

Then there are the people who talk about where they are going as if they are trying to convince themselves that they have made a correct decision and want some sort of affirmation. I always remain silent and just nod. The nod is the most useful and meaningless form of communication ever invented.

On the way to Aurora I played a little game as the woman talked about her sister who was either going into the hospital for an operation or had just come home from an operation. I tried to calculate how much the meter fare would come to. All cab drivers play this game. Newbies are terrible at it. It takes awhile for a driver to get used to measuring distances in terms of dollars rather than miles. For example, when I first started driving, the distance from the Brown Palace to Cherry Creek Shopping Center was five dollars and forty cents away. Every so often the PUC steps in and raises the mileage rates of taxicabs, so the drivers have to learn the New Math. It doesn't really matter though because the meter does your thinking for you. But when you get a fare going from central downtown to Aurora it's kind of fun to see if you—as an experienced asphalt warrior—have "the right stuff" and can calculate how much the meter will run to. In order to win the game your guess has to fall within a range of plus-or-minus twenty cents of the final tote—twenty cents being the smallest number a meter can display.

I guessed eight dollars and sixty cents that day, and I scored a bull's-eye. I can't begin to tell you how good this made me feel and I probably shouldn't. Pathos is pathos no matter how you gild it. The woman gave me a ten-dollar bill and told me to keep the change. That made me feel even better.

As soon as I pulled away, I caught a bell at a nearby King Soopers. An elderly black woman had done her weekly shopping and was waiting out front with a shopping cart filled with white plastic bags.

Her address was only two dollars and forty cents away, which was not unusual for a grocery run. I drove to her house and helped her carry the bags inside. She handed me a five-dollar bill and told me to keep the change. This made me feel good, too. I had grossed fifteen dollars in less than an hour. At this rate my shift would last only four hours. I needed forty-five more dollars to make my nut, so things were running smoothly.

And then I jumped a bell that broke my heart.

CHAPTER 10

I was just pulling onto Colfax Avenue and thinking about driving past Gino's Barbershop, where I go once a month for a free haircut. I always beep my horn when I drive past even if I'm not stopping. The beep is sort of like Carol Burnett tugging her earlobe. I get free haircuts at Gino's because I once did a favor for the nephew of the owner, and he won't let me pay to get my ponytail trimmed.

Gino is the barber who gave me my new "look," meaning the ponytail. Prior to that my hair was just sort of an unkempt explosion. Gino is an elderly Italian who has taken a proprietary interest in my ponytail because he designed it. He has forbidden me from ever using a comb. He gave me a special brush to use in the way that dentists give patients a special decay-preventing dentifrice for their choppers.

I was getting psyched up to make my run past Gino's when a call came over the radio, so I grabbed it. The house was in the opposite direction so I scotched the beep and headed toward the address.

It was a small, white clapboard house in a quiet neighborhood. I pulled up in front and waited, hoping the guy would be watching for me. I do not under normal circumstances beep my horn when I pull up in front of a residence. It's not illegal for a cabbie to beep his horn, but it is considered bad form. As someone who sleeps a great deal in the daytime, I am especially sensitive to the concept of infuriating noise. I waited for about a minute, then psyched myself up for getting all the way out of my cab and walking all the way up to the front door, which must have been a good thirty feet. The weather was nice, there was no snow, no rain, or hail, or wind, and no tornado warnings, but still, I would have to walk thirty feet.

I was just in the process of heaving a sigh of exasperation when I saw the front door open. I quickly changed it to a sigh of relief, which can be physically damaging if you don't know what you're doing.

The fare seemed to be having trouble getting out the door, then I realized he was carrying something large. He was hugging it to his chest. I quickly got out of the cab and hurried around to the rear to open the trunk. The distance from the front seat to the trunk was only seven steps, so I had no problem with that, even though there was a slight breeze in the air. Then I realized he was carrying a television set, a twenty-seven incher. I recognized the dimensions from a distance of thirty feet. I know my televisions. I've owned a lot of TVs in my life. I've shopped in Salvation Army stores from Atlanta to San Francisco. It's amazing the bargains you can get in those places, especially on color sets.

The sight of someone carrying a television like the Creature from the Black Lagoon carrying a gorgeous woman in a white bathing suit struck a deep chord in my chest. I immediately assumed there was something wrong with the TV. I forgot all about tornadoes and hurried up the sidewalk to see if I could give him a hand.

"Need any help with that?" I said.

"No, no, I think I've got it," he said. He was young, mid-twenties, husky, looked like he could handle the weight. I escorted him down to the cab, walking at his side and looking at the TV, which appeared to be in good shape. It was an ancient Philco model. The aerial wasn't bent, the screen was intact, and the wooden casing was clean and unscarred. I got a sinking feeling in my gut. I feared we were dealing with internal injuries here. When a picture tube goes out, you feel so goddamn helpless. I wanted to ask what had happened to it, even though it was none of my business, but it was a Philco fer the luvva Christ. I had a Philco in KC.

He gently laid the TV in the trunk. I lowered the lid but it wouldn't close tight.

"I'll have to tie the lid with a rope," I said. I keep a ten-foot length of rope in the trunk for emergencies.

"You don't have to do that," he said. "We won't be going very far."

His voice was kind of forlorn. Where were we going—to the city landfill? But I shook it out. Most likely we were going to a TV repair shop. When TVs actually die, they end up in alleys. Large-item pickup does the rest.

I hurried around to the driver's side, climbed in, and started the engine. I felt like a medic in a war zone. The kid didn't look like he could afford to own two TVs, and for one moment I saw myself sitting in my crow's nest with no television in the corner. I quickly put the image out of my mind.

"Where to?" I said, glancing back at him. I already had the shift in low.

"I just need to run down to Colfax," he replied quietly.

"Can you give me an address?" I said.

"No," he said. "I'm going to a pawnshop."

I froze.

"There's a lot of pawnshops on Colfax," he said. "Any one will do. This will be a round-trip."

I faced front and pulled away from the house. I barely remember the trip to Colfax. I was in a daze. It was the worst news imaginable. He was pawning his TV.

I drove in silence. I didn't know what the hell to say. Somehow I got us down to Colfax and turned right. There was a pawnshop in the middle of the block. The kid told me to pull up in front. I parked and got out and walked to the trunk. I held the lid open. The kid picked up the TV. There was nothing wrong with the TV at all. It was in perfect running condition. I closed the lid and followed him to the door and held it open for him but I didn't go inside. I went back and got into the driver's seat and just stared out the front window.

After a while the kid came outside. He wasn't carrying anything. He climbed into the backseat.

"You can take me back to my house," he said.

I got a lump in my throat.

I started the engine and pulled away from the curb. Neither of us said a word all the way back. When I pulled up in front of the house, the fare came to seven dollars. The kid leaned forward and handed me a ten-dollar bill.

I didn't want that ten-dollar bill.

I didn't want anything from the kid.

Based on my personal knowledge of hocking, I figured the kid had gotten maybe forty or fifty bucks for the TV—sixty tops. And here he was, handing a big chunk of that dough to a cab driver. But I took the money. Yeah. That's right. I took the money and stuffed it into my shirt pocket and pulled out three dollars and started to hand it to him, but he said, "Keep the change."

I tried to say, "Thanks, pal," but it caught in my throat. I nodded and forced a smile onto my face, then watched as the kid climbed out and trudged up the sidewalk.

To an empty shell.

A house without a soul.

I put the cab into gear and drove off.

I worked the radio the rest of the morning. I didn't pay attention to how much money I made. I took calls and answered them. The radio bounced me all over town. I just wanted to get this shift over with. I wanted to get back home and lock my door and sit down in front of my TV and forget I had ever made the decision to drive during spring break. For a lousy twenty bucks. Ten of which ... ten of which ... I couldn't bring myself to think about it.

And then, just before noon, I got an L-2.

An L-2 is a secret code that the dispatcher uses to tell a driver to return immediately to the cab company. You never argue with an L-2. It means the supervisor wants to talk to you face-to-face. Given the fact that nobody ever wants to talk to me face-to-face, I knew it meant trouble.

An L-2 in the middle of the day can be annoying if you are clear across town when the call comes in. But I was near Washington Park so I pulled onto University Boulevard and drove north. I didn't know how much money I had earned and I didn't care. I wished I had never driven that morning. But I wouldn't be going back out on the road after I spoke with whomever wanted to talk to me. I assumed it was Hogan, the managing superviser at Rocky. He's the only person who ever speaks to me when I get an L-2. He's the only person at Rocky who cares when I screw up—not counting Rollo. But "care" isn't the right word with Rollo. "Deviant interest" is apt.

It took fifteen minutes to get back to the motor. I parked as close as I could to the on-call room, then took a moment to fill out the blank spaces on my trip-sheet. It was then that I discovered I apparently had earned more than twenty dollars in profit, but I didn't count it. I just smirked with derision. I often do that when I surprise myself. I could have quit work a lot earlier. The thing is though, I hadn't been thinking about money for the past couple of hours. Times flies when I'm not thinking about money. Primarily I had been trying not to think about what it would be like to live without a television. But that's like hearing the word "caboose" and then trying not to think about it. Lotsa luck.

I grabbed my briefcase and climbed out of 123 and said au revoir. I didn't plan on working again until the Monday of the following week. I cursed myself as I crossed the dirt lot toward the door. As far as I was concerned I had wasted one whole day of spring break chasing the almighty dollar. What a fool I had been. I allocate three weeks per month to chasing almighty dollars, and now I had gotten obsessed with trying to pick up twenty almighty dollars just to round out the shortfall of the previous week, which time and experience had proven would have occurred anyway.

As I have stated, every April 15 I pay the same almighty taxes. I felt like one of those neurotic people who go around straightening pictures on walls or adjusting the flounces on their living room furniture so their guests won't think they're slobs. A "flounce" is the cloth fringe that runs around the bottom of a chair or a couch like a curtain. It prevents people from seeing the legs. Rich people often order flounces when they have their furniture reupholstered. I once delivered furniture for a living. I know my flounces.

There were a couple of cabbies hanging around the on-call room when I walked in. It was quiet. Midday. I could hear the clang of tools in the garage down the hall. A mechanic's job is never done. I walked up to the window to let him know I had come in for an L-2. He was smiling one of those smiles that reveal nothing—and everything. It was the "pinched" smile that he had ripped-off from Victor Buono. He obviously knew that I had been L-2'd. The man in the cage knows everything. It's part of his job description. That's one of the many things I hate about Rollo. Why can't I know everything?

"Hogan wants to see you," he said in a pleased and all-knowing tone of voice.

I nodded and turned away from the cage. I stepped into the hallway and made my way up the stairs to Hogan's office. The door was closed as usual.

I reached the top step and knocked. Hogan said "Yeah," which was the standard signal to enter.

I shoved the door open—and froze.

Two men were standing at Hogan's desk. Their backs were to me but I recognized their suits. They were the type of suits men buy off the rack in stores with names like J.C. Penny and Montgomery Ward. Suits that don't cost a lot, purchased by men who don't earn a lot, men who have more important things on their minds than fashion statements, men who don't read *Esquire* or *GQ* or even *Atlantic Monthly*. They were talking to Hogan as I opened the door. They stopped talking and turned to look at me. They were cops. Their names were Duncan and Argyle.

And then I did something that to this day strikes me as an inexplicable—if not a bad—move.

I pulled the door shut and began walking back down the stairs. I forgot all about Philcos and almighty dollars and spring breaks. I would have to say that, in truth, my mind was rather empty as I made my way to the bottom of the steps. I felt as if I was viewing a form of *déjà vu* so intense that it had become reality, and that my real life was just an illusion glimpsed from a corner of my eye. By "real" life I mean my childhood in Wichita, my stints in the army and college, and the past fourteen years of cab driving. It was a one-second dream experienced by a man walking down the stairwell of eternity.

"Murph!"

I was three steps from the bottom of eternity when my name snapped me out of it.

I stopped and looked back up the stairwell. Hogan was standing at the top of the steps looking down at me. Behind him stood Duncan and Argyle. They were looking over his shoulders, which made him look like a three-headed man.

"Where are you going, Murph?" Hogan said.

"Uh ..." I said, trying to collect my thoughts. "I don't know."

Duncan and Argyle glanced at each other, even though they couldn't see each other because Hogan's head was in the way. I had never seen a three-headed man before, not even in a monster movie, so I started wondering if I could write a horror novel about a three-headed man, which shows you how rattled I was. I often think irrelevant thoughts when I'm rattled, confused, or confronted by anybody.

"Did you get my el-two?" Hogan said.

I hesitated, then nodded.

"Great," he said. "Come on up. I need to talk to you."

I turned and began trudging up the stairwell of eternity. It didn't take long to get to the top. Maybe I had eternity figured wrong. I was always lousy at math.

CHAPTER 11

Why did I do that? Why did I shut the door and walk away when I recognized Duncan and Argyle? The explanation is two-fold, although I don't understand the first explanation myself, other than to say it was a knee-jerk reaction to seeing, once again, two detectives from the Denver Police Department—specifically, the Bureau of Missing Persons. The other explanation is that I had once given them my word that they would never see me again. The fact that they saw me again apparently triggered something in my mind. I would like to think it was a desire to be perceived as a person who kept his word, but I think it was embarrassment. I had really meant it when I told them they would never see me again. I had every intention of walking the straight-and-narrow, keeping my nose clean, maintaining a low profile, and doing all the other things that cops advise you to do after you've been cleared of kidnaping, robbery, homicide, etc.

Which is to say, Duncan and Argyle were the detectives who had been involved in the investigations of the murders of the eighteen-year-old girl and the homeless man, which I have tried to emphasize here were not murders at all and did not even involve actual dead bodies.

"Hello, Murph," Duncan said.

I nodded at him as I entered Hogan's office clutching my briefcase under my left arm.

"Hello, Murph," Argyle said.

I nodded at him, too, then tried to work up a noncommittal smile that would indicate to them that I had no idea why they were here, which was true. When cops show up, I never have a clue.

"Thanks for coming in, Murph," Hogan said. "Sorry to cut into your short-shift. When we're finished here I'll give you another hour on the road for free if you like."

"That's okay, Mr. Hogan," I said. "I … I … I … I …, what I mean to say is, I was just getting ready to come off the road anyway. I'm done for the day."

I swallowed hard. I had inadvertently stuttered—one of the top five things you should never do in front of a detective. Swallowing hard is on the list, too.

Hogan nodded. I glanced at Duncan and Argyle, who were standing next to Hogan's desk. They both had noncommittal smiles, which communicated absolutely nothing to me. I don't know why I would assume that my own noncommittal smiles mean anything to anybody. Probably hubris.

"Okay Murph," Hogan said. "You've met Detectives Duncan and Argyle before, so I guess we don't need to make any introductions."

I shook my head no, then abruptly stopped. I was afraid I might be communicating a "flippant" attitude.

"No need for introductions," Duncan said with a smile, looking me right in the eye. "We remember you quite well, Murph." He was being so affable that I felt like dropping to my knees and begging forgiveness for letting him see me.

"Have a seat, Murph," Hogan said.

I slowly sat down on a chair next to Hogan's desk. The two cops remained standing.

"Detectives Duncan and Argyle asked me to call you in," Hogan said in a businesslike tone of voice. "They want to ask you about a couple of ladies you might have given a ride to last week."

"Ladies?" I said, as if I didn't know what a lady was. I cursed my inflection.

"Two young girls," Argyle said. He wasn't smiling. "We received a report that these two girls may have gone to a music concert at Red Rocks Amphitheater last Friday."

Call me slow, but I finally caught on. The thing is, though, I get so many ladies and other types of people in my cab that they become a blur. But his mention of the two hippies cleared things up quickly. I smiled and raised my chin and nodded. "Oh yeah …" then I abruptly stopped smiling.

Bad move.

The reason I stopped smiling was because a number of thoughts suddenly occurred to me, one of them having to do with marijuana. I won't mention the other thoughts. They sort of dwindled in comparison.

"So you gave a ride to these two girls?" Argyle said.

I licked my lips and looked from Argyle to Duncan and back again. I did all sorts of things that I kept instantly regretting: lip licking, hard swallowing, throat clearing, eye flickering. And in between those maneuvers I kept thinking about marijuana.

"Yes, I did take two girls to Red Rocks last Friday," I said. Argyle nodded, then he reached down to Hogan's desk and picked up a trip-sheet.

"Mr. Hogan was kind enough to let us take a look at your trip-sheet from last Friday," Argyle said. "It appears from this that you forgot to write down the trip to Red Rocks." He held it vertically so that I could see it clearly. Adverbs and cops always come in pairs.

I looked at my scribbles that indicated the times and locations of pickups and drop-offs, as well as the meter costs. Tips are not included on the trip-sheets. That's just between the cabbie and the IRS. Some people call it "The Honor System."

But nowhere on my trip-sheet was a mention of the Red Rocks Amphitheater. If it had been mentioned, it would have appeared at the very bottom of the list, within one of the long, rectangular, blank boxes.

"I didn't write it down on my trip-sheet because it wasn't actually an official taxi ride," I said.

The room got awfully silent. I managed to avoid swallowing hard. I even managed to avoid glancing at Hogan. I continued to stare at the blank rectangle near the bottom of the trip-sheet as though all questions had been answered and I could now arise and go join a monastery in Tibet and never communicate with another human being as long as I lived.

"Why not?" Argyle said.

I looked up at him, and my Adam's apple took on a life of its own. It swallowed hard.

"I did it as a favor," I said.

Argyle nodded and set the sheet of paper on Hogan's desk.

"Are you in the habit of giving free rides to people?" he said, with a frown that, frankly, looked contrived.

"No," I said. "I rarely do anything for free."

He nodded. He seemed to approve of that. I pegged him as a capitalist. I breathed a sigh of relief. I was well on my way to Tibet.

"Tell me something, Murph," he said. "Prior to last Friday, did you ever give any other free rides to these girls?"

I started shaking my head no, then stopped abruptly. I wished I could stop stopping abruptly. The problem was, my body kept trying to give an answer before my mind had grasped the question. This was a problem that actually went all the way back to high school and involved lying to nuns about whether I had done my homework, but let's not get into that.

I raised a finger and said, "Oh yeah ... yes ... I remember now ... I did give a free ride to these girls once before." I was doing my best to give the appearance that I was "coming clean" and had nothing to hide. In all probability criminals do this, too—and are much better at it.

"When was that?" Duncan said.

I glanced at him. "On Thursday."

"What were the circumstances?"

"I saw the girls panhandling outside the Brown Palace Hotel," I said. "I gave them some spare change, then I advised them to move on down the road."

"Why is that?" Duncan said.

"I felt that panhandling outside a fancy hotel was not a good idea, and that they should find a better location."

"But why?"

"What do you mean?"

"Why would you care what those girls were doing?"

I shrugged. I had asked myself variations on that question hundreds of times during the previous fourteen years. I gave Duncan the only viable answer I had come up with.

"Because I'm a nosy parker."

Duncan nodded. "Were the girls alone?"

I nodded, then abruptly shook my head no. I decided to give up trying to control my body, except for the area around my mouth. "No," I said. "There was a boy with them."

Duncan and Argyle glanced at each other.

"Do you know his name?" Argyle said.

"No," I said. Then I abruptly nodded. I wasn't having any better luck with my mouth than with the rest of my body. "Yes, as a matter of fact I do know his name."

"What is it?"

"Billy."

"Do you know his last name?"

"No."

"How did you learn his name?"

"One of the girl told it to me when I was driving them to Red Rocks."

"Did you drive him to Red Rocks, too?"

"No."

Duncan glanced at Argyle, then nodded at him. It wasn't a brief nod, but rather an extended nod that went on, in my estimation, for three seconds.

Up until then I had been trying hard to remain calm and to cooperate fully and let them ask all the questions. But I finally had to ask:

"Are the girls missing?"

"Why do ask that, Murph?"

"Because you work for the Bureau of Missing Persons."

The cops looked at each other and nodded slowly.

There were two chairs set against the wall below a horizontal coat rack. Argyle went to the wall and grabbed one of the chairs and pulled it over near Hogan's desk. He sat down on the chair and took out a notebook and pen, then he looked me in the eye.

Duncan remained standing. He was, in fact, standing between me and the door. It occurred to me that if for some reason I went off my rocker and ran for the door I wouldn't make it. I don't know why that thought occurred to me. I don't have the temerity to guess why any thoughts ever occur to me.

"Let me tell you what's going on here, Murph," Argyle said. "On Saturday afternoon the mother of one of the girls called DPD to report that her daughter hadn't come home."

I nodded. I started to feel awful. Missing girls always make me feel awful. The only thing that makes me feel worse is being suspected of involvement.

"We've been interviewing people concerning the disappearance of these girls, and our investigation led us to believe that a cab driver had taken the girls to the concert at Red Rocks."

"How did you find me?" I said.

I didn't mean to say it quite that way but that's how it came out. I defy anybody to control their syntax in front of John Law.

"Witnesses," Duncan said.

Witnesses—the bane of my existence.

I gave Duncan one of my useful and meaningless nods, then said, "What witnesses?"

"We talked to Billy," Duncan said. "He told us that a cab driver picked up the girls near the intersection of Broadway and Colfax and agreed to take them to Red Rocks."

I nodded. Then I said, "But how did you know ... I mean ..." then I gave up a small chuckle. It was the kind of chuckle that a man makes when he has been "found out" by cops or nuns or anyone generally defined as an "agent of authority."

"Billy described your cab to us," Argyle said. "He told us that a driver had given a free ride to him and his two friends on Thursday, but he wasn't certain of the number of the cab. He told us that it was either Rocky Mountain Taxicab number one-twenty-eight or one-twenty-three."

I nodded. Rocky Cab #128 was driven by an old pro named Schmidt who had been driving for nineteen years. I looked at Hogan.

"We talked to Schmidt earlier this morning," Hogan said.

I looked at Argyle. "How did you find Billy?"

"The woman who reported the girls missing knows Billy. Billy is a high school dropout, but he had gone to school with one of the girls. We picked him up last night. He told us everything he knew."

I nodded, then waited for Argyle to drop the other shoe.

He did.

"Now we would like you to tell us everything you know, Murph."

I spilled my guts. I told them the details of the free ride from the Brown Palace to the D&F Tower. I told them how we didn't quite make it to the tower.

"They had never heard of the Beatles?" Argyle said.

"That's what they told me."

Duncan and Argyle looked at each other, then looked back at me.

I told them about seeing the kids again on Friday. I told them how I had decided to give them a free ride to Red Rocks. Here's the thing though. It's basically a violation of PUC rules to allow people to ride in a taxicab for free, meaning without dropping your flag and turning on the meter. So by telling Duncan and Argyle the truth, I was basically confessing to breaking the law in front of two cops. You can imagine how that made me feel. But given the fact that the girls were missing, I didn't think my violation had any significance in the larger scheme of things. Insignificance has always been my ace-in-the-hole.

"What did you talk about on the ride out to Red Rocks?" Argyle said.

"Just the usual cabbie banter," I said. "I asked them their names and where they were from and …" I abruptly stopped.

The image of Janet lighting up that joint sprang into mind.

"And what?" Argyle said.

I swallowed hard. I decided not to mention the fact that I had given them permission to smoke marijuana. Even though I had not deliberately and with volition expressly told them that they could smoke cannabis leaf in the backseat of my taxi, I still decided it might be best to skate over the whole subject. You know how prosecuting attorneys are—during intense cross-examinations they can take a simple declarative sentence and turn it into life without parole.

"I asked them how long the concert was going to last. I also asked them how they were going to get home from the concert."

Duncan and Argyle glanced at each other.

"What did they say?" Argyle said.

"They told me they were going to hitchhike home."

I told them about the twenty-dollar bill I had given to the girls in case they needed to call a cab.

"Are you in the habit of giving money to your taxi fares?" Argyle said.

"No."

"Then why did you give them the twenty dollars?"

The answer seemed obvious to me, so I started to get annoyed. I hate explaining the obvious. I prefer to explain things that are subtle and obtuse, which may have more to do with my ego than my desire to illuminate the human race. The best situation, though, is to give an explanation that cannot be disputed, refuted, or disproven. I win bar bets that way.

Before I could reply, Argyle said, "You gave these two girls a free ride out to Red Rocks, and then you gave them twenty dollars. And since you have stated that you are not in the habit of doing things like that, could you tell us why you chose to do that last Friday?"

My annoyance increased in size, but then I realized that the answer was not so obvious. I recalled the primary reason I had decided to give them the free ride out to Red Rocks. I looked Argyle in the eye and said, "I felt badly about the fact that I had yelled at them on Thursday when they told me they had never heard of the Beatles. I just wanted to make up for it, and I decided that a way to do it would be to give them a free ride. I was finished for the day anyway and I didn't think they would make it out to Red Rocks on a bus in time for the concert. So I gave them a free ride. That's all."

"Do you like the Beatles, Murph?" Duncan said.

"Yes."

"Who's your favorite Beatle?"

"Ringo."

Duncan and Argyle glanced at each other.

"You *do* understand, don't you, that the Beatles was John Lennon's group? He founded the band. He was the leader."

"I know."

"But Ringo is still your favorite?"

"Yes."

"I'd like to ask you one more question, Murph."

"Okay."

"Why did you drive a short-shift today?"

CHAPTER 12

I blinked. I don't mean that metaphorically, I literally blinked. It struck me as an odd question. I immediately wondered why a policeman would ask a cab driver why he had driven his cab. But rather than get balled up in hairsplitting, I decided to "play along."

"Because I needed the money," I said. I figured they would fall for that. To my knowledge, money is the only reason cab drivers exist.

"But why a short-shift?" Argyle said.

"Oh," I countered. "I came up a little short last week, so I wanted to make up for it by working today."

Argyle nodded. "Mister Hogan here informed us that you normally take a week off once a month, and that according to his records, this would have been the week that you took off."

"That's true," I said.

"How much did you come up short?" he said.

"I …" I said. Then I continued. "I came up twenty dollars short."

He nodded. "The twenty that you gave to the girls?"

I nodded.

He nodded again.

I didn't look at Duncan. There were enough useful meaningless forms of communication going on in the room.

"Let me ask you something, Murph," Argyle said. "If you work only three weeks out of the month, why would coming up twenty dollars short bother you?"

I looked him in the eye. "Because I'm a perfectionist."

"How do you mean?" he said.

"Well … I live on a fairly tight budget. I try to earn the exact amount of money I need to get by. I try not to work hard. Or … I guess another way of saying it is that I try to work as little as possible. I suppose technically they're the same thing. But the upshot is that I try to earn exactly fifty dollars a day. This gives me enough money to live on, provided I work two extra days a month in order to cover the rent, which means working five days in a row, usually on the third week of the month. This allows me to take three work-days off once a month, which actually gives me a total of nine days off in a row which I refer to as my monthly spr … not-working week."

Argyle stared at me. I quickly surmised that I might have given him too much information in one lump. This used to happen when I tried to explain my personal behavior to my friends, which I quit doing years ago.

"Do you always earn fifty dollars per shift?" he said, indicating to me that he understood my lump.

"Almost always," I said. "I've gotten pretty good at it during the past fourteen years. Occasionally I earn more than fifty dollars, but I just accept that as one of the pitfalls of working. But when I fail to earn my quota of fifty dollars I try to make up for it."

"So you worked today because you needed exactly twenty dollars?"

"Exactly."

"And last Friday you did earn fifty dollars, but then you gave twenty to these girls, so you were forced to work a short-shift today to make up for the loss."

"Exactly."

"Because you're a perfectionist."

"Exactly."

"What would have happened if you had not taken the trouble to drive today and earn the money back?"

I shifted uneasily on my chair. "Well I … I … I … I don't know. It might have caused me to buy fewer sodas or something. But I almost never encounter that problem. I always seem to earn more money than I need, rather than less."

"If you do earn more than fifty dollars per shift, does this motivate you to work fewer shifts later on? Or else drive fewer hours per shift?"

"Oh no, I never do that," I said. "That's a realm of higher mathematics that I'm afraid to tackle. It would be like trying to trim the legs on a table to make it level."

"That happened to my brother-in-law once," Duncan said, thank God.

"So let's see if I have this straight," Argyle said. "You earned fifty dollars last Friday, gave twenty of it to the two girls, then you worked today to earn back the twenty. Is that right?"

"That's right."

"How much did you earn today?"

I blinked again. Then I reached up and touched the breast pocket of my T-shirt. All my T-shirts have breast pockets. You wouldn't believe the trouble I have finding T-shirts on sale that have breast pockets.

"I don't know," I said. "I haven't totaled it up yet."

"Would you be willing to count it right now?" he said.

"Here?"

"Yes."

"I wouldn't mind," I said. I withdrew the wad from my breast pocket.

I was sort of embarrassed because the bills were all crumpled up. Old pros do not normally smooth out their bills until the end of a shift. Newbies are always smoothing out their bills. That's the mark of a beginner. It usually takes them awhile to fully comprehend the pointlessness of everything.

I laid the bills out on Hogan's desk one by one and tried to flatten them with a surreptitious maneuver involving the edge of my right palm. The situation made me feel like I had holes in my socks.

Pretty soon I had three stacks of tens and fives and ones. They weren't very flat. They rested upon one another like autumn leaves.

"Ten … twenty …" I began mumbling, as I counted up the take. It came to ninety dollars. I was astonished, but I tried to hide my astonishment by separating the money into two new groups. Then I looked up at Argyle and smiled.

"How much did you earn?" he said.

"Well, I grossed ninety dollars, but forty of that went to my short-shift lease payment and a half-tank of gas. So my net profit for the day is fifty dollars."

"That's thirty dollars more than you wanted."

"Yup," I said, trying to sound casual.

"Why didn't you stop driving when you earned twenty?"

I shrugged. "Table legs?"

I glanced at Duncan for reassurance. He seemed to understand what I was getting at.

"So even though you worked only six hours, you earned the same amount of money you normally would earn on a twelve-hour shift, correct?"

"Yup."

"Can you explain that?"

"Yup."

"Go ahead."

"I worked hard today."

"Even though you normally try not to work hard."

"Yup."

"Why did you work hard today?"

I hesitated, even though I knew the answer. I looked from Argyle to Duncan, then I realized I ought to tell the truth. Two girls were missing.

"Because one of my fares pawned his TV set. It made me feel so bad that I started working hard so I wouldn't have to think about it."

"Why would that bother you?"

"Because I hate the thought of someone not owning a TV."

"That happened to my cousin once," Duncan said, relieving me of the burden of trying to give Detective Argyle an in-depth analysis of my mental processes.

"So basically you accidentally earned fifty dollars today," Argyle said.

"Well, not entirely," I said.

"How do you mean?"

"I earned fifty dollars because I took calls off the radio. Normally I sit in front of hotels and read paperbacks. I don't make as much money working the hotels."

"So if you always worked hard, you conceivably could earn one-hundred dollars in profit during a normal twelve-hour shift?"

"Piece of cake," I said.

"But you don't work hard because you don't like to work hard."

"Exactly," I said. I felt we were making progress at last, although in what direction I didn't know.

"Let me ask you one more thing, Murph," Argyle said.

"Okay."

"Is there any other reason why you might have driven your taxi today?"

"What do you mean?"

"Aside from your pursuit of perfection, might there be another reason why you wanted to cover your … losses?"

I heard that ellipsis. Cops rarely use them. It indicated to me that he was hinting around at something.

I shrugged. "No. Not really. Whenever the tiniest little imperfection enters my life I try to smooth it over as soon as possible, except on weekends. I never work weekends."

"Why not?"

"Because when I was in the army they sometimes made us work on weekends, and I really got to hate it."

"You served in the army?" Argyle said.

"Yes."

"What rank did you achieve?"

"Private. Although I didn't really achieve it. I started out as a private and just sort of stayed there."

Argyle nodded and sat back in the chair. "One more question, Murph."

It seemed to me that he had been saying that with regularity during the past ten minutes, but I tried not to dwell on it. I couldn't tell if this was a subtle interrogation technique commonly used by policemen, or if Argyle was simply forgetful. There was also the possibility that he spoke what might be referred to as "sloppy" English. As you can see, I have trouble not dwelling on things. I have a tendency to parse things to death and often end up losing track of conversations. I have the same trouble when watching movies. An actor might say something funny or interesting, and I'll start dwelling on it and the next thing I know I've missed some critical dialogue which forces me to either rewind the tape and play the scene over, or else wait for the show to come on TV again, which can take forever.

"Did you?" Argyle said.

"Pardon me?" I said.

Argyle glanced at Duncan, then looked at me. "I asked whether or not you happened to notice if the two girls met anyone before they walked through the gate at the rock concert?"

"Oh," I said. "I'm sorry, I was ..." I stopped.

"You were what?"

I wanted to say my mind was wandering, but I didn't think he would buy it. It sounded like something a person would say if he was being evasive. But then I realized I may have given Detective Argyle the idea that I was, in fact, being evasive.

"I was trying to picture the scene in my mind," I said. "I once heard that if a person tries to picture something in his mind he can get a clearer ... picture."

I then realized that this was almost the exact same thing that Tony Perkins said to Martin Balsam in *Psycho*. I started to get nervous. If Argyle had seen *Psycho* he might "eye" me knowingly.

"As I recall," I said, "the girls just walked toward the gate. In fact, I believe they were trundling."

"Trundling?"

"Walking side-by-side so that occasionally they bumped into each other as they moved forward. To me, that's trundling."

"What did you do then?"

"I made a U-..." I stopped again. I almost said I made a U-turn, which is illegal. Of course I doubted he could have ticketed me right there in the office, but he was, after all, a policeman. Even if he didn't have a ticket book on him, he could have called in a black-and-white unit to write me up.

"Where did you go after you made the U?" he said.

I realized that he thought I had actually finished my sentence. I quickly picked up where I had left off. I didn't want him dwelling on the fact that I had whipped a u-ey on a public thoroughfare.

"I drove back to Denver."

"Was that the last you saw of the girls?"

"Yes."

He nodded, and said, "All right. I guess that about covers it."

On previous occasions, this was usually the point where I held my breath and waited for the cuffs to come out. But Argyle just closed his notebook and slipped his pen into his pocket.

Then he paused and looked at me.

For some reason I interpreted this maneuver as part of an "act" that he was performing, like the good-cop/bad-cop act that you see on TV shows. Except this was more like an epilogue. "Is there anything else you can tell us about the trip to Red Rocks, Murph? Something you might have left out? I know it's tough to remember the details of a situation that you never expected to be questioned about, especially when you have so many people getting in and out of your taxi. But sometimes in the course of a conversation something might be said that will shake loose a memory."

This made me think of the love beads I had found in my backseat. That in turn made me think of the pot smoking.

I frowned real hard. I didn't want to lie, so I looked to my left and back again, which I hoped would be misinterpreted as a negative head-shake. Is it my fault that he misinterpreted it correctly?

"All right," Argyle said. "Thanks for your cooperation, Murph. I'm glad we caught you at the end of your shift so you didn't come up short again." He smiled. "I wouldn't want to be responsible for making you work tomorrow."

Was that a dig, or was he being empathetic? It took all of my willpower not to dwell on it—although to be honest I think there was a smidgen of a dig in there.

"I was happy to cooperate, Officer Argyle," I said. "I hope you find the girls."

I realized my remark might have sounded banal but it wasn't as bad as a question I almost asked: "Do you think you'll find the girls?" I had known Duncan and Argyle long enough to know that cops are not issued crystal balls along with service revolvers. But my statement seemed like a polite way to bring the conversation to a close. An epilogue, you might say.

"So do we, Murph," Argyle said.

I won't describe the departure of Duncan and Argyle. I want to jump ahead one minute.

Duncan and Argyle's footsteps were still echoing in the stairwell of eternity when I turned to Hogan and said, "I know what you're thinking, boss."

Managing Supervisor Hogan sat back in his office chair, which creaked. He intertwined his fingers and gazed at me through the thick lenses of his glasses, and waited for me to reveal the secrets of my crystal ball.

CHAPTER 13

"I know I shouldn't have given those girls a free ride," I said. "I know it's a violation of PUC regulations to a haul a fare when the meter isn't running. I know you're going to have to report this incident to the top brass, and that they will take a dim view of my action. And I know that my desire to help out a couple of kids will be considered irrelevant by the insurance company and they will probably insist that you suspend me from driving until this case is resolved. So rather than going through all the rigmarole of having you call me into the office again and giving me the bad news, why don't we just do this? I wasn't going to work for another week anyway, so why don't I voluntarily put myself on suspension for the next six days. I will then come in on Monday morning at seven A.M. and if the case hasn't been resolved, you can officially suspend me."

Hogan raised his chin and said, "I'm glad you see it that way, Murph."

"Well … I figure there's not much difference between being suspended and pretending to be suspended, since they both involve not working."

He nodded.

"I'm sorry I had to do this to myself," I said, "but my hands are tied."

"I understand," he said.

"I'll go downstairs now and turn my key in to Rollo, and then I'll get started on not working," I said.

He nodded.

We left it at that. Everything that could have been said hadn't been said. Everything else would be said on Monday morning, when I intended to drive to the motor as usual and walk into the on-call room as if everything was copacetic, and then find myself trudging up the stairwell of eternity to hear the bad news handed down from the top brass and the insurance company and … and maybe even the Bureau of Missing Persons.

I went downstairs and entered the on-call room. A couple of old pros were standing in line at the cage waiting to pick up their keys. I took my place at the end of the line. When I got up to the window, Rollo still looked like Victor Buono, which was the only good thing I could say for him. I returned his self-satisfied smile with one of my own. I didn't say anything to him. Everything that Rollo and I had to say to each other had been said years ago, although we still said things like, "Hello." Even though I was mimicking his smile, my smile had nothing to do with Rollo. My smile was self-directed. It was the smile of supreme irony, for this was the first time in my life that I had fired myself.

I knew the chances were good that I would never be coming back to work at Rocky Cab. The top brass were probably tired of hearing my name, and the insurance company … well … their computer was probably tired of processing my punch-card. Plus, I had been seen by Duncan and Argyle once too often.

Strike three, pal.

I'm out.

But I figured as long as I had the smile, there was no point in wasting it. That's why I tossed it Rollo's way. There was a good chance it might baffle him. But even if he saw through it, the fact that I had gone to the trouble to baffle him might ruin the rest of his day.

Now you know the dark truth about me. When it comes to smiling, I can be a real bastard.

I gave him my key and trip-sheet and walked out of the room. I crossed the parking lot, climbed into my heap, and aimed the hood ornament at Capitol Hill. My '64 Chevy actually does have a hood ornament. It looks like a chrome-plated naked lady with wings being fired out of a cannon.

Before I got home I stopped off at a Burger King on Colfax. I didn't feel like cooking that day. The clerk behind the cash register asked if I wanted a soft drink. I said no. But what I didn't tell him was that I had plenty of sodas in my refrigerator at home. They're included in what I had loosely referred to as my "budget" when Duncan and Argyle were interviewing me about the missing girls.

I know what you're thinking. How could I have lied to Duncan and Argyle about the pot smoking and finding the love beads? The answer is simple: I'm only human.

Let me explain:

I felt that the pot smoking and finding the love beads in my backseat had no actual bearing on what had become of the girls. The smoking of the pot hadn't made them disappear, and the appearance of the love beads hadn't made them disappear. Consequently, why bring it up? Why mention it? Why tell the detectives that I had given two teenage girls permission to smoke pot while I was illegally driving them to a rock concert? The information couldn't possibly have helped the police find the girls. How could it?

That was what I kept asking myself over and over as I drove home on that pleasant afternoon in Denver, the Queen City of the West, the Mile-Hi City, the Home of the Championship Broncos.

How could it?

How could pot and love beads help anybody find anything?

I was pulling into the parking lot behind my apartment when the answer came to me.

If the girls possessed pot, maybe Duncan and Argyle could find out who they had gotten it from and pick up a lead from there. Also, the cops could conceivably pick up a lead from the person who had sold them the love beads. By the time I got up to my crow's nest and entered the kitchen, I saw myself pulling a nickel in Cañon City. I don't know the legal terminology but "withholding evidence" catches the gist. And "lying to law-enforcement personnel" is as good a layman's term as any.

So when I said, "I'm only human," I was really just saying I got scared. When I had gone to work on the previous Friday, I had expected it to be like any other Friday. But by the time the shift was over I had violated every moral law in the universe.

I walked into the living room and removed the cash from my shirt pocket and stuffed it into my copy of *Finnegans Wake,* then I carried my briefcase into my bedroom and put it in the closet, where I always put my briefcase during spring break. I don't like to see the briefcase when I'm on vacation because it makes me think of work. And I was especially sensitive to the fear of thinking about work that day because it would have made me think about looking for a job after my cab license was revoked.

The last time I had looked for work on purpose I ended up delivering flowers. That was when I was suspected of murdering that homeless man. I had also worked as a Santa Claus on two separate occasions, but I never got paid for those gigs.

At any rate, God only knew what kind of trumped-up charges I would be facing during the coming days. Two girls were missing and I was the last person known to have seen them alive. On top of that, when I was being interviewed by the police, I may or may not have appeared to be giving evasive answers to their questions. It was difficult to judge how I had looked to Duncan and Argyle. It would be nice if the police were required by law to give you a mirror along with your Miranda rights so you could see how you looked when you answered their questions, and thus be able to make the proper facial adjustments in order to enhance your appearance of innocence.

That seems not unreasonable to me.

I went back into the kitchen and started to grab a soda, but since this was the first day of spring break my hand grabbed a beer. Then I picked up the commercial hamburger and went into the living room and flopped down in my easy chair. I lethargically chewed my burger and stared at the blank face of my TV. I couldn't bring myself to turn it on. I didn't want to look at the two Gilligan girls: Mary Ann and Ginger. It would have made me feel guilty. I started to think that if I had been a castaway on the island, I probably would have ended up getting Mary Ann and Ginger hooked on skag. I would have made Gilligan himself look like the Professor.

Then I started thinking that the Professor probably knew how to make skag. As far as I could tell, he could do anything that could be done by any person who held lots of college degrees: biology, botany, astrophysics, etc. He was like Doc Savage. When I was a teenager I read the paperback reprints of the *Doc Savage* magazines from the 1930s. Doc Savage was sort of like the Green Hornet or The Shadow, a non-superpower hero. He was built like Hercules and knew everything there was to know about every branch of science. My dream was to grow up to be just like him. Unfortunately, I didn't own barbells when I was a kid and I hated homework, so I missed my goal by a million miles.

After I finished the hamburger I carried the wrapper into the kitchen and took pleasure in the act of tossing the waxed paper into the trash can rather than doing a dish. But it was a fleeting pleasure. It was over in an instant. I grabbed another beer from the fridge and walked back into the living room and flopped down in my easy chair.

Spring break had begun at last—although technically this was the third day of spring break because Saturday is the normal first day. By Monday I've usually worked myself into such a state of indolence that I've got a beach towel spread out on the floor and I'm reading a paperback while listening to a recording of Pachelbel's *Canon in D With Ocean Sounds*. I play it when *Gilligan's Island* isn't on. It makes me think of Tahiti, or a Tahiti-like island in the South Pacific where I had once hoped I would end up. Aside from being built like Doc Savage, another one of my youthful dreams was to be a novelist living on a desert island. Without belaboring the obvious, at the age of forty-five, I had ended up a million miles from everywhere.

Nevertheless, spring break was that time of the month when I always tried to follow through on my perpetual vow of getting started on a new novel. I didn't have to drive a cab for another six days, I had cleared the decks of all chores and responsibilities, and I was ready to start hammering the keys.

This is the dream of all cab drivers, or at least all novelists—I'm not sure what the distinction is.

But a monkey wrench had been tossed into my plans. Thanks to my obsession with perfection, I had already lost two days of writing time, meaning the weekend. I hadn't written anything on Saturday or Sunday because working a short-shift on Monday kept intruding on my thoughts, making it difficult to think up a book. This is the fear of all cab novelists—intrusive thoughts.

When it comes to thinking up a book, your brain must be completely empty, like a recently purchased fishbowl waiting to be filled with sand and colorful rocks and water and goldfish. They don't necessarily have to be goldfish, but you hardly ever see fishbowls that don't have goldfish. Sometimes you do see fishbowls that have little brown fish that aren't very pretty but are interesting in other ways, at least to people who find aquatic creatures interesting.

I once knew a guy in college who owned a piranha. It lived in a rectangular aquarium. I didn't know what he fed it, and I didn't want to know. I also knew a guy who owned a big turtle that sat underwater at the bottom of an aquarium and never seemed to come up for air. I used to worry about that turtle. My friend told me that the turtle didn't need to come up for air very often. He explained the physiology of turtles, but I didn't pay much attention. I once asked him if the turtle ever got thirsty. My friend said it was doubtful since the creature lived underwater. But it seemed to me that once in a while the turtle might open his mouth and take a quick gulp. I really did worry about that turtle. When I was ten years old my Maw bought me a small turtle at the five-and-dime. It lasted a week.

Now here it was Monday, and for all practical purposes I had lost another day of potential writing time. Tuesday would be my first full day of cleared decks to get to work on a book. This gave me only six days to write, rather than the usual nine, and the thought depressed me. Three days wasted, all because I had tried to make up for the twenty dollars I had given to the girls. If I hadn't given them the twenty I would have been able to start writing a new novel on Saturday, which meant I would now be three days into a book, which meant I could have written at least three thousand words. Whenever I write novels I try to write a minimum of one thousand words a day, although if I get hot I can write one chapter per day, which is another dream of novelists—a chapter a day. Novelists have a lot of dreams. I realized that if I had written a chapter a day for the past three days,

I would be starting on Chapter 4 tomorrow. This thought depressed me even further. I felt like I was chasing a caboose.

But I knew the solution to the problem. Sit down and start hammering. That's what I did back in college. That's what I did when I worked at Dyna-Plex. That's how you start novels, and ultimately complete them. It had been a long time since I had completed a novel. I've started more novels than I have completed. Then it suddenly occurred to me that if I added up all the starts, they would probably equal a dozen full-length novels in terms of word count. I wondered if I could link a bunch of starts together, and change all the main characters into one main character. Maybe I could cobble together a single novel from all the bits and pieces. Maybe I could make an avant garde novel out of the extraneous material scattered in my steamer trunk.

I began to feel a surge of the old excitement.

Then I realized that if I did manage to tape a novel together, I would still have to retype the entire thing in order to have a clean manuscript to submit to a publisher. And if I was going to do all that typing, I might as well think up a new plot.

It was too much to dwell upon. I'd had a bad Monday, and next Monday I would be going to Rocky Cab to see whether or not I would continue going to Rocky Cab. My time would probably be better spent reading the want-ads. All of a sudden the next six days began to seem more like fake days than real days. I began to feel like I was truly suspended—not from cab driving but "in time." I felt that time had literally stopped and the clock wouldn't start ticking again until Monday morning.

Under normal circumstances this would have seemed like a pretty good deal, since the whole point of spring break is to step outside of reality for nine days, which is like stepping outside of time. But now it gave me an unpleasant feeling.

Suddenly I wanted the clock to start ticking again.

But I knew the clock would start ticking only after I walked into Rocky Cab to find out whether I had a job.

The clock would start ticking only after I found out whether Duncan and Argyle had made progress in their missing-persons case.

The clock would start ticking only after I found out what had become of the two girls.

I knew I wouldn't be able to enjoy my trip outside of reality if bad news was waiting for me at the end of the track.

That's when I finally admitted to myself that I had been thinking about Janet and Vicky ever since I had walked out of Hogan's office. I'll be honest. I have a hard time admitting things to myself. But when I do, look out brother.

That's when the clock started ticking again.

CHAPTER 14

It was Tuesday morning and I was on the road. You heard me right: "on."

The road I was on was called Colfax. It was a long road. It started somewhere out on the eastern plains and sliced through the heart of Denver. It stopped where the mountains started. And somewhere in between the eastern plains and the mountains was a kid I wanted to talk to. A high-school dropout named Billy.

I wasn't driving my taxi that day. I was behind the wheel of a red-and-black '64 Chevy. The doors were red and the body was black. I had long ago given up hope of finding black doors for this make and model. I gave up when I realized it just didn't matter—the standard signal that it's time to give up.

I was sipping joe at the wheel. I had spent a restless night tormented by a vision of two young girls who had giggled their way to a jumble of rocks the color of the setting sun—I'm talking red. That's right. Red Rocks Amphitheater, a natural geologic formation heavy on the iron oxide that had risen out of the earth sixty million years ago and had been turned into an open-air performance venue during the administration of Mayor Benjamin Stapleton. You heard me right. Stapleton. Same name as the old airport that served Denver before DIA wrecked the cab business.

The girls had gone to a concert at Red Rocks and hadn't come home. I was thinking about the fact that I was the cab driver who had given them a free ride to the concert. I was thinking about the marijuana they had smoked during the ride. I was thinking about a class in Ethics and Morality that I had taken at the University of Colorado at Denver when I was twenty-six. It was an elective offered by the Philosophy Department. I was required to tack three hours of Philosophy onto my credits in order to earn an English degree, so I figured what the hell, I might as well take a gander at this ethics jazz. It looked like an easy A.

I should have stayed awake in college. If I had, maybe I wouldn't have let a couple of kids get away with breaking the law in the back-seat of my meal ticket. Maybe I would have told them to snuff the joint, or at least wait until they got out of my territorial imperative before they toked. Maybe I would have given them a lecture on the finer points of not getting into trouble. Maybe I would be enjoying my monthly spring break with a clear conscience instead of search-ing the mean streets of Denver for a kid wearing bell-bottoms and a headband, a high school dropout who once sat in the backseat of my taxi and said, "You can drop us off here," in a tone of voice so polite that I knew he didn't care for my company.

I wanted to find that kid. I needed to find that kid. I needed to know what he knew, and who he knew. I needed to know where to start looking for his two friends, Janet and Vicky, who referred to themselves as Sunshine and Moonbeam, two crazy teens who had turned their backs on contemporary social customs to embrace the styles of a generation that was all but dead. My generation. The Baby Boomers. The generation that had embraced a lifestyle dedicated to the proposition that all love should be free and so should rock con-certs like Woodstock, whose organizers gave up on the idea that they would make a bundle off the youth culture about halfway through the movie.

I pulled into a 7-11 parking lot on Capitol Hill to get a refill on the joe. I was feeling kind of rocky. I hadn't slept well the previous night. I had done everything I could to avoid doing what I do best, which is to succumb to guilt. But it hadn't worked. I tried logic. I tried denial. I even thought about sleeping pills, but I hate sleeping pills because they make me feel crappy the next day.

The moment my head had hit the pillow I started thinking about the two missing girls and wondering where they could be. A couple of runaways, that's what I told myself. The '60s had been full of runaways, so it made sense that they should disappear. That was the "logic" part of my inability to get to sleep.

The "denial" part had to do with me telling myself that the personal lives of the people who get in and out of my taxi are none of my business. But I had a hard time keeping a straight face when that popped into my head. I don't have time to explain why that excuse was laughable. It would take sixty million years.

I bought a fresh joe, went back to my Chevy and climbed in. It was getting on toward noon. I had spent the morning cruising Capitol Hill and checking out the intersections frequented by panhandlers. If you have ever been to Denver then you would know that this amounted to approximately ninety percent of the downtown area. But I needed a better plan. I was hoping I would spot Billy through sheer luck. "Sheer luck" has always been the driving force behind most of my plans.

I reflected on this as I sat in my Chevy waiting for the coffee to cool down. I won't bore you with a list of all the plans I had made since high school, the success of which was predicated on luck. Some of my plans did work out, but that was due more to the whimsical nature of mathematics than any volition on my part. This is in reference to that useful and meaningless phenomenon called "odds."

There are people in this world who can makes odds work for

them, usually during poker games, but I am not one of those people. My love of poker is based primarily on the opportunity it gives me to make wisecracks when I'm seated around an octagonal table. The sorts of people I play poker with are so hooked on the game that not even my presence is powerful enough to make them get up and walk away. How can I resist such a captive audience? Fortunately, I play so badly that any hostility that my poker buddies might feel toward my ceaseless prattle is compensated by my money. If I haven't lost at least thirty dollars before the last round of stud is dealt, I feel like I've cheated my friends.

In thinking about odds in general and poker in particular, I began thinking about Big Al.

Big Al is the Rocky Cab driver who trained me in the fine art of hacking fourteen years ago. The training consisted of myself sitting shotgun in his cab and riding around during a single day-shift. There was also a day of classroom training at RMTC, which involved watching movies about horrible traffic accidents. They also gave us overviews on how to operate the radio, how to work the meter, and how to perform all the other esoteric minutiae involved in driving a vehicle of public transportation. But like everything else in this world—high school mostly—we didn't really learn how to be cab drivers until we got out on the road. It was sort of like army training where they showed us movies about how to act if we got captured by communists. Then they turned us loose "in the field," which is military terminology for "mopping the latrine."

On top of being my taxi mentor, Big Al was also a gambler who had taught me everything I knew about staying away from the dog track. That's why I thought of him as I sat in the parking lot of the 7-11 blowing on my joe and thinking about poker and odds and my fruitless search for a hippie at-large on the mean streets of Denver.

There had been plenty of times during the past fourteen years when I had gone to Big Al for what I referred to as "further mentoring." He would refer to it as "last-ditch effort," but that's neither here nor there. We don't always view the world from the same perspective.

Whenever I am baffled by a personal conundrum of one sort or another, I find that a brief conversation with Big Al often has the effect of clearing the air, of showing me the way, of forcing me to admit that every decision I ever made was wrong. The funny part is, I always knew that. But that's the human brain for you. Sometimes you have to be told what you already know before you realize that everyone is on to you. That's when you realize you might as well start doing what you knew all along you ought to have done in the first place or he will keep badgering you and harassing you and threatening to call in all his IOUs unless you "get your head out of your ass."

That was one of the drawbacks of going to Big Al for advice. He seemed to have some deep-seated psychological need to reform me instead of just telling me what to do next. Fortunately, I have a deep-seated inability to take unasked-for advice, so I never hesitate to track him down and dump my problems on his head—unless the problems can be solved by simply ignoring them. That's always Plan A. Plan B is Big Al.

I started my heap and drove out of the parking lot. The odds of finding Big Al were much better than finding Billy because Big Al works the hotels when he gets tired of jumping bells, in the way that craps gamblers in Vegas take a break by sitting in front of slot machines. Unlike myself though, Big Al doesn't read paperbacks. He uses his "down time" to pick greyhounds at the local kennel club. He buys his daily racing schedules at 7-11 stores. I remember when I first discovered that you could buy tip-sheets at 7-11. I thought I had discovered a treasure trove, but I don't want to talk about my gambling days—seven to be exact—and my subsequent reformation by Big Al. Believe me, I expend enough energy keeping secret from him the fact that I still buy lottery tickets.

I headed west on Colfax, turned north on Lincoln, and made my way over to the Brown Palace. As I pulled around the corner at Tremont I slowed down to look at the cabs, but I didn't see Big Al's hack. It felt funny to be driving past the cabstand in my Chevy. I had the urge to park in line and wait for a fare. I wondered what would happen if I did that. What would happen if a "stranger" trespassed on the territorial imperative of a sullen breed of men? I pictured taxi doors flying open—drivers would leap from their seats, cries of moral outrage would fill the air, trembling fists would darken the sky, dire threats would echo off the brownstone walls. As I stated earlier, you don't have much opportunity to feel "special" when you drive a cab, and let's be honest, there is nothing quite as soul satisfying as moral outrage combined with actually being right.

As I cruised by I wondered if I could write a novel about a man who made the mistake of parking his civilian car at a cabstand. Upon realizing his mistake, he would then refuse to move, deciding instead to make a statement about society. By the time I got to the end of the block I had given up on the novel. I couldn't figure out what kind of a statement the guy would be making. This is one reason why I write commercial novels rather than literary novels. With literary novels the author has to "say" something. That's what the how-to books say anyway. I'll admit it. When I wrote my first novels back in college I tried to "say" things. It was hard though. I would spend hours sitting in front of my typewriter trying to think up something to "say." What I had in mind were "profound utterances." I figured that if I got good at profound utterances, the royalty checks would start rolling in. I blew an entire semester staring at a blank sheet of paper before I finally admitted to myself that I might not be profound.

This soured me on the whole concept of introspection. On the plus side, it did help me to stop admitting things to myself.

Then I saw it: Rocky Mountain Taxicab #61, the oldest cab in the fleet, the last of the two-digit taxis. Big Al was parked fourth in line at the Fairmont Hotel. I started looking for an empty parking space close to the hotel, preferably with a meter that still had some time left on it. As a taxi driver, I have an inherent aversion to using parking meters—I always make an extra effort to park in no-parking zones, but I wasn't driving 123 that day. It looked like I was going to have to swallow my pride and pull into a commercial parking lot, which is considered by cab drivers to be gauche. It was like a knife in my heart to pay a dollar. I ended up parking in a lot five blocks from the Fairmont. I could have parked closer but I didn't want any cabbies to see me skulking hurriedly away.

After I hiked to the Fairmont I found Big Al's cab still fourth in line. He was sitting in the driver's seat marking his tip-sheet. The dogs were running that night at the club. I walked up to his window and rapped my knuckles on the roof. He glanced out his open window and nodded. Then he did a double-take. It was Tuesday. It was the fourth week of the month. What was I doing at a cabstand? Big Al can read me like an X-ray. Before he managed to roll up his window and lock his door I said, "I need to talk to you."

I could see it in his eyes: surrender. As I said, Big Al is something of a realist.

"Hop in," he said with overt resignation, pointing his thumb at the shotgun seat. I rounded 61 and climbed in.

Due to the fact that Big Al always casts a jaundiced eye on preambles, prefaces, prologues, forewords, introductions, or any other attempt on my part to "soften the blow" through idle chatter about sports or the weather, I got down to brass tacks.

CHAPTER 15

"You want me to do *what?*" Big Al said.

"I want you to help me find a hippie," I resaid.

Big Al gently closed his tip-sheet and set it on the seat between us. He looked me right in the eye and said, "Does this request have anything to do with the two girls whose lives you ruined?"

"Yes."

He took a deep breath and sighed. He turned his face away and stared out the front window for a moment. Then he looked back at me and said, "I want to know as few details as possible, and that includes why you want me to help you find this hippie."

"Okay."

I took a deep breath in order to collect my thoughts. Then I exhaled a long sigh and said, "I don't think I can do that. I'll have to give you a little bit of the why."

"I was afraid of that."

"The thing is, on the day I gave the free ride to the two girls, the hippie boy was standing with them at a bus stop over on Colfax."

Of course there was no real need to explain all of this to Big Al. In the pecking order of those who know everything that is going on at RMTC, Big Al stands third in line behind Hogan and Rollo. But I went ahead and said it anyway as a kind of "back story." I didn't do it for Big Al's benefit though. I did it for my own. I always have trouble starting a story *in medias res.* I get confused.

Big Al closed his eyes and nodded impatiently, then opened them. I moved things along.

"I've been driving around all morning looking for the kid because I want to talk to him in person and see if I can find out anything about the girls that might help me locate them."

"And just what makes you think you can gather any more information from this hippie than Detectives Duncan and Argyle did?" Big Al said.

"Hubris?"

"Good guess."

"But I haven't had any luck spotting him. I figured he might be out panhandling somewhere and maybe I would run into him. I mean, last week I ran into him twice, once by accident, and once sort of on purpose."

"I assume it was the 'sort of on purpose' event that generated this appalling situation."

"Yes. I saw the boy and the girls at the bus stop, so I pulled over to …" I stopped abruptly.

"To what?" Big Al said.

I cleared my throat and said softly, "To help them."

"Louder please."

"To HELP them," I said.

"I see. And subsequently you set into motion a chain of events that has culminated in their disappearance from the face of the earth."

"I guess you could look at it that way."

"And now you have decided to follow up on that smashing success by attempting to help them even further."

"Something like that."

Big Al nodded. Big Al's nods are among the few nods that actually are not meaningless—they speak volumes. After nodding, he sighed and said, "The fact is, Tenderfoot, I approve of your tactic."

"You DO?"

"Yes. Given the inherently hostile relationship that historically has always existed between bohemians and the police, it is doubtful that Duncan and Argyle were able to pry the entire truth out of our young rebel."

"His name is Billy."

"I know. And given the fact that you sport a ponytail and hold a vague resemblance to the remnants of that diminishing breed of humans known as hippies, you just might be able to incur his trust and get him to open up. Thus, there actually is a slim possibility that you might inadvertently stumble across a nugget of worthwhile information through sheer ineptitude."

"That's what I was counting on."

"What's the 'plan'?" he said in quotes.

"I want you to pass the word along to the other drivers to keep a lookout for the kid. That way we can cover the entire city. If they see him on the street, they can tell you where he is, and then you can tell me."

Big Al pondered my plan for a few moments, then said, "Why drag me into this any further? If one of the drivers spots the kid, he can contact you directly."

I swallowed hard. Once again I felt that I had been put in the annoying position of explaining the obvious. But then maybe the X-ray was a bit blurred. Doctors aren't always perfect—and even a broken clock is wrong only 22 times a day. I cleared my throat and laid out my reason as clearly and concisely as possible. "The other drivers wouldn't do it if I asked them to," I said.

"Why not?" he said.

"Well … I prefer to think it's because they don't like me, but it runs deeper than that. The other drivers are afraid of getting involved in *any* situation connected with me."

"I see you are making satisfactory progress in the self-awareness department."

"What's that supposed to mean?"

"I know full-well that there is not a driver at RMTC who would hook his wagon to your falling star. I just wanted to find out if it was a mystery to you."

I started to call him a bastard, then abruptly stopped. I should do that more often.

"So are you willing to do this for me?" I said.

"'Willing' isn't the word, but yes. I will pass a request along to the other drivers to keep an eye out for Billy."

"Thanks."

"But there is one caveat," he said.

Damn.

"What is it?"

"I will perform this favor provided that you swear to me right now that as long as you possess a taxi license you will never again get involved in the personal lives of your fares."

A nervous smile sprouted on my lips. I began nodding. I kept at it until I almost started weeping. I bowed my head and looked at my toes. "I can't promise you that, Big Al."

"I know," he said. "I just thought I'd give it a shot."

Then he asked me to give him a fresh description of Billy. As I was finishing up, a man with a suitcase came out of the Fairmont and climbed into the first cab in line. The other drivers at the stand started their engines in preparation for pulling forward one space. The sound of the engines firing up and the odor of exhaust fumes filling the air made me wistful. What simple lives were led by cab drivers who did not get involved in the personal lives of their fares.

"Given the fact that scores of drivers will be keeping an eye out for Billy, you might as well go home and wait for a call from me," Big Al said, seeming to take charge of the situation. He should do that more often. Come to think of it, he does.

I climbed out of 61 but didn't leave right away. I stood on the sidewalk and watched as Big Al put his gearshift into Drive, pulled forward one space, and shut off the engine. I would have given anything to trade places with him right at that moment. I would have given anything to be living the uncomplicated life of a man unencumbered by guilt, responsibility, or hubris. It seemed like I had wanted that all my life, but it was only since high school.

I headed back toward the parking lot where my Chevy was waiting for me. I glanced over my shoulder a couple of times to make sure there weren't any cabbies watching me. After I climbed in and started the engine, I slunk down as low on the seat as I could and drove out of the commercial lot. I pulled onto 13th Street and cruised toward the intersection that links up with Colfax. When I sat up straight and looked around I saw two taxicabs behind me and one on my right side. But they were only Yellow drivers, so I didn't care. It was like I had burped in a restaurant among people I would never see again. It made me feel brave.

I drove back to my crow's nest measuring the relief I felt at having drafted Big Al to my cause. I hadn't been certain he would go for it so I had made a few backup plans to win his sympathy, but then who doesn't do this when looking for undeserved help? I was hoping that the mere fact that two girls were missing would motivate him to help me, but if that didn't do the trick I intended to communicate to him through a variety of sad facial expressions that I was burdened by a sense of guilt that no man should be forced to endure. I don't know why I thought that would do anything except make him laugh.

I was back in my apartment within fifteen minutes of having slouched out of the parking lot, and the first thing I did when I got inside was rush to the telephone and take a look at the answering machine to check for messages. I had never done this before. Rush to the phone I mean. I usually "notice" messages on my machine when walking through the living room on the way to the beer. The machine has little red numbers that blink on and off. If there is nothing good on TV, I will play the messages. I hate telephones, but I am ambivalent about my answering machine. It was a gift from a rich man whose daughter I did not kill. The machine's only saving grace is that the messages are recorded, which means I do not have to actually talk to the people who call me. Again, we're back to the burping-in-a-restaurant scenario. I have no fear of listening to recorded messages. In fact, I rather enjoy listening to them. They make me feel like the invisible man.

There were no messages on the machine. Back when I first hooked up the machine, I would get dozens of messages every day, but as time went by they became fewer and fewer. I was pleased to find that the callers were giving up. It made me feel unpopular and lonesome, two of my favorite adjectives.

I went into the kitchen and opened the refrigerator and started to grab a beer, then I realized I had better not drink because I might have to hop into my heap and head back downtown within the next few hours.

It was with bitter reluctance that I reached for a soda. Not that I'm reluctant to drink soda, it's just that on a typical Tuesday afternoon during spring break I'm usually lying on my imaginary beach listening to Pachelbel and downing some "brewskis," as the young and the hip say nowadays. I've often wondered if young people in the 1880s thought in terms of being "hip" and "cool." I doubt if they used those words, but I'm talking about the general concept of acting "groovy" and being "with it" while walking down cobblestone streets covered with horse manure. The streets I mean, not the kids. Were there Bob Dylan or Jim Morrison or Marlon Brando types back then? I'm talking the Marlon Brando of *The Wild One,* not *Sayonara.* Did kids back then bob their heads and talk jive-ass lingo? These are the kinds of thoughts I have when not engaged in productive labor, so as you might surmise, I have them a lot.

In fact, when I was fifteen years old I spent a lot of time fantasizing about going back in time and hanging out with teenagers of the 1950s. All the kids with their DA haircuts and engineer boots would be flabbergasted at how cool I looked in my white Levis and Beach Boy haircut. They would be astonished by my knowledge of rock music to come. They would idolize me and crown me "The King Of The Teenagers" and … well … perhaps it's best I not speak of these things.

I carried my soda into the living room and sat down in my easy chair, and then I did something I never thought I would ever find myself doing twice. I looked at my telephone again. I expected it to ring at any second. I couldn't believe my life had come to such a turn. This was supposed to be spring break, and here I was sipping a soda and staring at a telephone. I felt like I was waiting for my life to begin, which was a familiar feeling. The first time I received a rejection slip from a publishing company was the first time I experienced that feeling. When I unfolded the slip paper-clipped to the cover letter of my manuscript and read the words, "Sorry, not for us," I immediately felt as if my life had been put on hold and wouldn't begin again until I read the words, "Your novel has been accepted for publication." I was twenty-three years old at the time. You do the math.

I thought about turning on the TV, but I was afraid I might get swept up in the plot of a sitcom and then the phone would ring and I would have to wrench myself from the TV and rush out the door. I could not believe what I had done to myself.

You heard me right. "What I had done to myself." That's what I said and that's what I meant. A year earlier I would have said, "I could not believe what had happened to me," as if external forces were throwing monkey wrenches into my life. Big Al was right when he said I was making progress in the self-awareness department. Don't ask me how it happened. Maybe it was all those murders and kidnapings and missing persons in general. Maybe my subconscious was "fed up" with me. But as I sat there in the silence of my living room sipping a soda and staring at the telephone, I knew that I had brought all of this on myself, although I did spend a minute trying to pin it on someone else. It's hard to break old habits.

CHAPTER 16

The phone rang.

I thought I was hallucinating. I thought my ears were playing tricks on me again. I mean, how many times in your life do you want badly for something to happen, and then it happens? Like … never?

Thus, I made the mistake of hesitating to pick up the receiver, as if afraid I was the target of a cosmic joke and the phone would magically disappear. Instead, the answering machine kicked in. I had forgotten about the machine. I possessed so little practical experience with telephones that I had botched it thoroughly, and the next thing I knew Big Al was saying, "Stop being paranoid, Tenderfoot, and pick up."

I grabbed the receiver. "Sorry," I said. "I was in the bathroom."

"I'll ignore that and move on," he said. "Billy has been spotted."

I looked at my watch. It had taken approximately thirty minutes to find Billy.

"Where is he?" I said.

"He was seen entering The Bop Shop at Thirteenth and Grant five minutes ago. Jacobson is keeping an eye on him."

Jacobson is an old pro who drives Rocky Mountain Taxicab #101. He's been driving almost as long as Big Al.

"I'll be there in five minutes," I said.

"Are you absolutely certain you won't make that promise to me now?" Big Al said.

I swallowed hard.

"I heard that swallow," he said. "Never mind. Just promise me something else."

"Okay." If Big Al wanted to go on playing The Promise Game, I wasn't going to stop him. He knew what my promises were worth.

"Promise me that this is the end of my involvement in this affair," he said.

"First let me check my crystal ball," I replied.

"*Touché*," he said.

We rang off.

Promises.

Give me a break.

The Bop Shop was a used record store eight blocks away from my apartment building. It was in a red brick storefront next to a laundromat and two or three other shops that I had never patronized—office spaces where businesses came and went, opened and closed, lived and died. Only the laundromat survived. I didn't hold much hope for The Bop Shop's survival, except that its clientele consisted of the kinds of people who had always inhabited Capitol Hill: young, broke, college-age kids on their own for the first time, living with roommates and making the transition from youth to suburb.

I was out the door in less than a minute. If Billy had been seen entering the store, then I wasn't too worried about losing him. The Bop Shop is the kind of place where kids waste hours leafing through stacks of used records and listening to headphones planted all over the store. It has the atmosphere of what used to be known as a "head shop." The place was kind of a last vestige of the hippie days. It also stocked incense, strobe lights, and movie posters, i.e., the junk of youth. That's where I got my poster of Brando in *The Wild One*.

I pulled onto 13th Avenue and headed west. Parking at the western edge of Capitol Hill can be tough because it's made up of apartment buildings that don't provide garage space. I got there in one minute, but then spent nine minutes driving around looking for an empty curb space. I found one three blocks away from The Bop Shop and pulled in. Fortunately there are no parking meters in that part of town, since there aren't enough private businesses nearby to support a government program designed to help tax people to death.

I climbed out of my heap and made my way to 13th Avenue. I slowed when I got to the corner so I could surreptitiously peek down the block to see if Billy had come out of the store. I didn't see Billy, but I did see Jacobson's taxi parked across the street from The Bop Shop, which meant Billy was still inside. If Billy had left the store, Jacobson would have followed him. The power that Big Al wields over RMTC cabbies is both awesome and enviable. Everybody likes Big Al and would do anything he asked. I wield no power at Rocky or anywhere else.

I turned left at the corner and sauntered down the block as if I was an unemployed man killing time on The Hill, which maybe I was because I didn't know if I would be going back to work on Monday. I glanced at Jacobson. He was feigning sleep with the bill of his cap pulled low over his eyes. I came to the entrance of The Bop Shop and pushed the door open. There was a tinkle of bells like the temple bells where the dawn comes up like thunder. The Bop Shop sells Eastern philosophy books, too.

I quickly scoured the room utilizing the field training I had undergone in the army. There were perhaps fifteen young people in the store. I divided the room into twenty-foot quadrants and gave my full attention to the customers within each quadrant. This technique took too long, so I just looked at everyone regularly. I saw Billy standing on the left side of the store near the rear.

I casually made my way to the right side of the store and moved up an aisle, glancing around as if I was looking for the used albums of one rock group in particular, which I was: the Beatles. I was winging it. I was playing it by ear. I was making it up as I went along. This was also how I wrote novels, and it never worked. But whether making a million dollars or stalking a hippie, I didn't know what else to do.

My plan was simple: find a Beatle album, carry it over to Billy and say something like, "Ever heard of these guys?" He might or might not recognize me, but I would make a point of introducing myself, and maybe—just maybe—incur his trust and get him to open up. That's about as far as my plan went. I usually abandon my novels at that point. But the fate of runaway girls is never determined by my inability to think up happy endings. This was reality, and because there are no happy endings in reality, I was hoping the denouement of this scenario would write itself.

It did.

I stopped at the section where Beatle albums were stacked. My eyeballs almost popped out of my head. I saw an album recorded live in a nightclub in Hamburg, Germany, before the Beatles became international celebrities. I almost reached for my billfold, but then I remembered why I had come here. Instead I reached for the album. I held it close to my face. I glanced at Billy. My eyeballs almost popped out of my head again. He was standing at a section that displayed 45 rpm records, and at the very moment I glanced at him he leaned forward and begin leafing through the disks with his left hand while his right hand surreptitiously slipped a platter inside his shirt.

I slowly rotated my eyeballs until I was looking at the cashier. He was engaged in a conversation with a girl dressed in black and sporting a haircut composed of short spikes. I eyed Billy again. He was now letting the fingers of both hands do the walking across the stacks as if he was just an average teenager curious to see what sorts of corny tunes his pop used to stack on the hi-fi when rock was young.

The kid knew his business. I could tell that he had done this before. He didn't vacate the immediate vicinity after secreting the record under his shirt. He played it cool. I knew quite a bit about the techniques of shoplifting.

I know what you're thinking.

But you're wrong.

Me ol' Dad had managed a retail store called Kresge when I was a kid. If annual profits were down, his Christmas bonus was small. If profits were up, my Christmas improved dramatically. So when shoplifters walked out of my father's store with loot hidden up their shirts, they were not stealing from some faceless corporation, they were stealing from my father—but more importantly, they were stealing from me. I'll never forget the year I asked Santa for the deluxe edition of the L'il Mad Scientist chemistry set, but got a plastic Slinky instead.

You heard me right.

Plastic!

I set the Hamburg album back on the rack and casually made my way toward the front of the store. The clerk didn't even notice me as I walked by. He was too busy admiring a golden safety pin attached to the girl's lip. I opened the door and stepped outside. The temple bells sang their farewell. I looked across the street and noted that Jacobson's taxi was no longer there. Mission accomplished. Now I owed him one. I hate to owe people, but favors between asphalt warriors can often be settled by a free cup of 7-11 coffee. We are a simple folk.

I didn't move down the sidewalk. I stayed where I was. I stood with my back to the door in the recessed entryway, and waited. I waited for the tinkle of temple bells. I waited for the quiet voice of a guilty man saying, "Pardon me," as he tried to step past my body, which was blocking the exit. I didn't feel very good about what I had to do. When I thought back on all the reasons I never got promoted past private in the army, I felt a twinge of hypocrisy. Who was I to play First Sergeant?

The temple bells spoke.

"S'cuse," a muted voice said.

I glanced over my left shoulder and saw Billy trying to edge past me sideways. His head was bowed. His shoulders were hunched. He was making himself small and inconspicuous. I was familiar with the stance, the demeanor, the body language—he looked like a private sneaking out of a latrine after I hid my mop in a toilet stall.

I glanced down at his feet and saw that he was still wearing sandals. This made me feel good. I turned and faced him, still blocking his way.

"What do you have under your shirt, Billy?" I said.

This was a double-whammy. I was telling him that I knew he had stolen a record, and that I knew his name. Some people call this "the ol' one-two."

He stopped trying to get past me and raised his face. His eyes were in the process of emerging from his head. I took advantage of his lapse of cool, and hauled back for a roundhouse-right. "If I escorted you into the shop and asked the cashier to look under your shirt, would he be proud of you?"

His expression changed. He was entering Phase 2 of what is known as "getting caught." It's kind of like the emotional stages a person goes through when faced with impending death: "shock, denial, anger, etc," but I wanted to bypass as much of that as possible and get right to "acceptance."

Billy frowned at me. "Do you work in the store?" he said, his eyes flitting left and right, seeking an opening around my beer belly.

"No, I don't work there," I said. "But I saw you take that record."

"If you don't work there then what the hell do you care?" he said, trying to finesse me with the sort of logic that impressed me when I was young.

"I don't. I have no intention of squealing on you, Billy. "

This brought him up short. All expression fell away from his face, then he frowned. "How do you know my name?"

"Janet and Vicky told me your name," I said. I braced myself to grab him in case he tried to split.

But he didn't. All of a sudden he looked scared.

"Who the hell are you?" he said.

"We've met before, Billy," I said. "Twice."

He gave me a quick scan cap to toe but it didn't register. Not surprising. It was possible that he might have recognized the back of my head, but I wasn't about to turn around. "I'm the cab driver who took Janet and Vicky out to Red Rocks last Friday night."

I could see it in his eyes, the pieces of the jigsaw puzzle assembling on their own. The fear on his face changed to recognition, then bafflement, then to something resembling curiosity, but the curiosity of someone wondering what that "thing" was, standing in the middle of his backyard at midnight during a lightning storm.

He must have figured out what it was because a look of contempt spread across his face.

"What do you want from me?" he said, glancing past me.

"We need to talk," I said.

"Let me go, man, I don't have anything to say to you." He tried to edge past me but I moved in front of him.

"Let me explain reality to you, Billy," I said. I almost choked when I said that. I had been trying to explain reality to myself since college. "First of all, you're wearing sandals and I'm wearing tennis shoes. You can't outrun me. Second, some friends of mine followed you here and told me where to find you. Even if you do get away from me, they'll keep following you. And third, you can come with me to a coffee shop for a little talk, or I'll escort you back inside and let you talk to the manager of the record store where you've been shoplifting on a regular basis."

There you have it. That's my explanation of reality.

Billy's shoulders and facial muscles relaxed, and the fire in his eyes faded as if Smokey the Bear had walked past with a bucket.

"What do you want to talk to me about?" he said.

"I want you to help me keep my job as a cab driver," I said.

"What do you mean?"

"Duncan and Argyle think I had something to do with the disappearance of your friends."

Fear seeped back into his eyes. I liked the fact that there was no need to explain who Duncan and Argyle were.

"They told me you gave them the number of my taxi, number one-twenty-three." I let this statement hang in the air for a moment, then said, "Telling those cops my cab number was sort of like squealing on me, wouldn't you say?"

I could see it in his throat: he swallowed hard.

He had arrived at last.

Acceptance.

CHAPTER 17

Let me say right off—it was not a Starbucks. It was a Starbucks imitator that sold expensive yuppie coffees with names that only my barber Gino could understand—latte, cappuccino, etc., which made me think of Capucine, the French movie star, who in turn made me think of the wild opening scene of *Never on Sunday*, where all the young fishermen leapt into the sea out of love for Melina Mercouri. But let's stop right there and get back to Billy, although my mind certainly didn't. It was already moving on to Federico Fellini. I'll be the first to admit that I have trouble focusing on matters at hand after I start contemplating European films. This is ironic because I do not like watching subtitled movies. Movies are supposed to be stories told in pictures and yet when you watch most European films you end up staring at the bottom 20 percent of the screen throughout the entire show. Nevertheless I like the films partly because a great many were shot in black-and-white, which may have been due to economic conditions following the end of World War II and the exorbitant cost of ... well, I seem to have lost focus again.

The coffee shop was at the far end of the block.

"Do you like coffee, Billy?" I said, as I escorted him inside the store.

"I dunno," he said sullenly. I liked that. He presented no mysteries to me.

"Have you ever drank espresso, Billy?" I said, as I led him to a table over in a corner near a picture window that gave us a view of the street.

"I dunno," he said.

"Espresso was made famous by the beatniks," I said. "They used to drink espresso in coffee shops that looked like this place."

I studied his face as I said this. We were still standing. He was looking at me the way bored students look at history teachers. I was ambivalent. I won't claim I invented the look in high school, but I did uphold the tradition.

"Why don't you take the record out of your shirt, Billy," I said. "You might break it when you sit down. I promise I'm not going to squeal on you."

For one moment his sullen demeanor cracked. But why not? He was only human. I'd been there. He was being asked to acknowledge through body language that he had committed a crime. I wasn't sure if he had committed a felony or a misdemeanor—I hadn't kept tabs on which criminal activities had been federalized during the past few years. But it didn't matter. Deck chairs, Titanics, it's all moot when you live below the poverty level.

Billy pulled the record out of his shirt, then sat down at the wooden table with his back to the wall. I sat down opposite him and held out my hand.

"May I take a look at the record?" I said.

He shrugged and handed it over. I squinted at its dark purple label.

"Holy cow," I said, mostly to myself. I read the title out loud. "Seaman by Lolita." I looked at Billy. "I haven't heard this record since I was a little kid."

Billy had the history/boredom look again. I quickly became baffled by this mystery. Why would Billy shoplift such an obscure record? It wasn't even a rock 'n' roll tune. It was more like a Norse folk song.

I asked.

Billy shrugged. He did this frequently during our conversation. I won't bring it up again.

"I sell them to this guy I know."

"What is he, some kind of record collector or something?"

"I dunno." Billy shrugged here, too. I mention it once more just so you'll understand how often he did it. He was like a junkie with the heebie-jeebies.

"How much will you get for this?" I said.

Billy got tight-lipped for a moment. His eyeballs latched onto the record in my hand. Possession is ten-tenths of the law. Even two-year-old kids know that.

"Did you bring me here to talk about records?" he said.

This was a delicate moment. The kid was getting sarcastic. Which meant he was scared, I could tell. He was scared that I might not give his record back, but he was also scared about other things. This spoke in his favor. I always feel uneasy around people who don't get scared. I consider fearlessness the first big step on the road to the Intensive Care Unit.

I reached across the table and handed the record back to Billy. He took it and held onto it.

A waitress showed up and asked what we wanted. I ordered two lattes.

"I'm just curious," I said. "I can't imagine that the markup on a stolen record makes it worth risking jail time. What does this cost at The Bop Shop, two bucks?"

Billy looked down at the record, then looked up at me. "This guy once gave me a list of records and told me that if I ever saw one of them in a used record store, I should buy it and he would pay me double whatever I paid for it."

"So two times zero is four?" I said.

He blinked twice. Then grinned. "Sort of."

The waitress brought our cups. I paid, and then made a big show of handing her another dollar and saying, "This is for you."

She thanked me and walked away.

"That was a procedure I call 'giving a tip to a waitress,'" I said to Billy.

He blinked again, but I think it was just bafflement. I didn't press the issue. I believe the best way to teach is through example, which as I have said, was how I learned to speak English. Let the kid see a tip in action rather than try to explain giving away money when you don't have to.

"I don't care what you do to make bread," I said. "But this is interesting to me. You say a guy gave you a list of records, and you look for them in used record stores, and then he buys them from you?"

"Yeah," Billy said, raising the Italian joe to his nose and giving it a sniff.

"Has this guy ever paid you a lot of money for an especially rare record?"

Billy shook his head no.

I was instantly infuriated. The only thing that annoys me more than the naiveté of communism is the ignorance of capitalism. By this I mean that Billy obviously did not have a solid grasp of the nuances of free trade, and therefore was being taken advantage of by the collector who had discovered a treasure trove in this street kid who was virtually giving away valuable records.

"How old are you, Billy?"

He mulled this over for a moment, then said, "Seventeen."

"Too bad," I said. "You're not old enough to drive a taxi. That's how I make money. When you get old enough, Billy, I recommend that you become a cab driver. It's easier than breaking the law. I make fifty bucks a day sitting down."

His expression now was just sort of blank. He had probably never held a job in his life. Something deep inside me wanted to keep it that way. "Cab driving is the best job I ever had," I said, "and I've had a lot of jobs. I handed out handbills in Pittsburgh. That wasn't too bad, except I had to walk around all the time. But that's what you do, too, don't you?"

He nodded. This was preceded by a shrug, but I swear I won't bring it up again.

"The thing is, Billy, I'm kind of worried about my job. Those two cops grilled me on Friday because I was the last person to see Janet and Vicky alive."

I threw in the "alive" part just to give Billy something to think about. It was the same thing I had been thinking about ever since I talked to Duncan and Argyle.

"If the taxi company thinks I was involved in some way with their disappearance, they might take away my license, and then I would have to find a real job. And let me tell you something, Billy, I don't want a real job. I want to drive a taxi."

I was trying to let Billy know that he and I had something in common. Objectively speaking, I would have to say that the only thing we did not have in common was youth.

Billy looked down at his cup. "I told the police everything I know."

"That's what I heard," I said. "They told me you gave them my cab number, which was how they tracked me down and brought me into this missing-persons case. And now it looks like I might get fired."

He looked up at me with a new kind of fear, the fear a person experiences when he is responsible for getting someone else in trouble.

"I'm kinda scared, Billy. I'm forty-five years old and I have no marketable skills. If I lose my cab license, I don't know what I'm going to do for a living. I might end up panhandling on the street. That's why I tracked you down, Billy. I need your help."

Another delicate moment, and about as underhanded as you can get. If you can give another person the impression that he is helping you, if you can tap into his compassion, if you can diminish his overall sense of uselessness in any way, then maybe—just maybe—you can take him to the cleaners.

"Do you have any idea what might have become of your friends?" I said.

"No," he said.

I looked him in the eye, then took a deep breath and sighed. I shook my head as if I had reached the end of my rope and there was no use continuing this conversation and I might as well get up and walk out of the coffee shop and never see Billy again.

Instead, I leaned back in my chair, reached into my jeans' pocket, and pulled out the string of love beads.

"Do you recognize these?"

Billy froze.

Then licked his lips and said, "Where did you get them?"

"Do you recognize them?" I said.

He nodded.

"Who do they belong to?" I said.

His eyes flitted from the necklace to my eyes, to the necklace, to my eyes, etc. …

"Duncan and Argyle don't know I have this necklace," I said. "I didn't see any reason to mention it to them. I found it in my taxi after

I got back from Red Rocks. I didn't think anything about it until Duncan and Argyle brought me in for questioning. But I was afraid to say anything about the necklace. I thought it might look bad, ya know? A couple of girls turn up missing, and I have in my possession a necklace belonging to one of the girls. The cops might think it was funny, and I don't mean ha ha funny, I mean suspicious funny. It was like a necklace that might have gotten broken during a struggle, ya know? I started to get scared. I didn't know what to do. I was afraid to tell them about the beads. I didn't want be held on suspicion of murder. So now I have these beads and I'm scared to throw them away because the cops might be watching me. What if they see me throw these in a trash can? That's as good as a confession to a cop. I might get the chair."

As I wove this tapestry of nonsense, Billy raised his cup to his lips and stared at me as if he was watching a cop show. Then he set his cup down.

"They belong to Janet," he said.

CHAPTER 18

I lowered the beads into my left palm. They rattled, but I tried not to like it. "There's no reason for the police to know I have these. Right now you and I are the only people on earth who know I have them and I'd like to keep it that way. I doubt if Janet knows I have them because she lost them while she was smoking marijuana."

Billy gave me a furtive look. I ignored it.

"Janet and Vicky asked me if they could light a joint on the ride out to Red Rocks, and I said it was okay," I lied. "It didn't bother me," I lied. "But when I found the beads in my backseat I wanted to drive back out to Red Rocks and return them. I would still like to return this necklace to Janet, only nobody knows where she is. Nobody knows where Vicky is. Duncan and Argyle don't know, and they told me you don't know either."

Billy started to get nervous—I could tell by the way he started pretending to act casual. Pretending to act casual when you are starting to get nervous is something that I myself have not gotten very good at, mostly in the presence of cops. But I was familiar with the moves, the casual folding of the arms, the casual glances around the room, the casual curling of a corner of the lip, the casual sigh. There are plenty more busy/casual moves that I could list, and they are all dead giveaways, because innocent people don't move at all. They stare at you with their jaws wide open.

But Billy was acting casual so I decided to probe. "Do you have any idea where Janet *might* be?"

Admittedly that wasn't very subtle. But then I'm not a trained law-enforcement officer—yet.

He raised his chin but at the same time glanced down at his cup. Dead giveaway. I waited for him to get to the point.

He didn't.

"I know it's tough to talk to cops," I said. "I got arrested a few times when I was in my twenties. I was kind of a drifter, traveling around America looking for something, although I didn't know what. I got arrested one night in Wichita for streaking. I was running naked down the middle of main street." Billy cracked a smile for the first time, which didn't surprise me. Creative writing often does that to audiences. But the truth is, the cops never caught me on the night I streaked Wichita. I took refuge inside a taxi. It's a long story. Let's move on.

"I was hoping maybe there was something you didn't tell Duncan and Argyle that you might be willing to tell me," I said. "I just want to give Janet back her beads and keep my job."

Billy shifted uncomfortably on his seat. I could read him like an X-ray. He began tapping the sides of his coffee cup with his fingertips. He wanted to talk.

"I know it's hard to squeal on your friends," I said. "And maybe you want to protect Janet from the cops. But Duncan and Argyle told me that Janet's mother reported her missing. So I thought, even if you knew there was something you didn't want the cops to know, you wouldn't want her mother to worry, would you?"

"Her mom doesn't like me. She's never liked me."

"I know the feeling," I said. "No girl's mom ever liked me. You know how moms are. They want their daughters to grow up and marry men who are mature and responsible. I never had a chance."

Billy smiled. "There's this guy ..." he said, tapping the cup. I waited.

"He's the guy that ... that gave Janet and Vicky the free tickets to the concert."

"Janet did say a man was handing them out at the bus stop."

"Yeah," Billy said.

"What about him?" I said.

"Janet and Vicky are with him."

The hair on the back of my neck prickled. I lifted my cup and took a sip. I was "acting casual."

"How do you know they're with him?"

"Janet called me at my place and told me. The girls met him again at the concert. After it was over, they left with him."

"When did Janet call you?"

"On Saturday."

Janet's mother had reported Janet missing on Sunday. Duncan and Argyle had interviewed Billy on Monday. Suddenly I understood fathers.

"How come you didn't tell the cops this?" I said.

I started to lose Billy then. He gave me an "angry" glance. "It was none of their business."

I felt like a desperate fisherman reeling in an angry marlin. I gave the line some slack.

"Yeah," I said, a word that when placed in the proper context can be as useful and meaningless as a nod.

"And anyway ... Janet made me promise not to tell anyone who she was with. He's kind of a strange dude. Sort of a guru."

I let the beads spill onto the table. "Well, you've already blown that promise. But the only thing I care about is keeping my job, so here's the deal. If you tell me where Janet and Vicky are, I'll go there and give Janet back her beads and talk to her myself. I won't tell her you told me. You won't be involved in this anymore. You can go back to shoplifting records for the guy that's ripping you off. I just want to ask Janet to call her mom and let her know she's alive so I can keep my job."

"What do you mean, ripping me off?"

"I don't have time to explain free enterprise to you, but you could get a lot more for your stolen merchandise than you're currently receiving, and from the same collector, too."

Billy frowned.

"Where is she?" I said. "Where is Janet?"

He picked up his record and turned it over, then looked at me. "She's at this place up near Boulder. It's kind of a ranch in the mountains. I guess you would call it a 'hippie commune.'"

By now I felt exactly like a father. It wasn't a good feeling. "Have you ever met this guy?" I said.

Billy nodded. "I've seen him around."

"What does he do, come to Denver and give out free tickets to concerts?"

"He does that sometimes."

"What else does he do?"

Billy shrugged. "I dunno."

"Does he sell pot?"

Billy didn't reply.

"Did he sell you guys some pot on the day he gave you the free tickets?"

No reply. But that was all right. I understood. I was transporting Billy from the realm of misdemeanor to the realm of felony.

"All I want from you is an address," I said.

Billy looked at me with his eyebrows raised.

"I'm going up to Boulder to visit Janet and Vicky," I said. "I need the address of the ranch."

"I don't know the address."

"If I took you along with me, could you show me the place?"

"Hey man, you said I wouldn't be involved in this."

"You're right," I said. "But can you tell me how to get there?"

He nodded. "It's a couple miles west of Boulder on Flagstaff Road. It's called the Smith Ranch. That's what the sign on the front gate says. I've been up there before."

"What were you doing there?"

He looked down at his record, and said quietly, "Me and some friends were scoring."

"Did you go inside the commune?"

"No. We just met some guys at the gate. They sold us the stuff."

"This guy who owns the ranch, what's his name?"

"I don't know his real name, but he calls himself Brother Chakra."

"Brother Chakra?"

"Yeah."

"How old is he?"

"Real old. He's your age."

I took the blow but hung on. I had learned long ago not to blame reality for everything. I had known for the past fifteen years that I was older than thirty, but I tried not to think about it. "Why didn't you tell Duncan and Argyle that Janet and Vicky are alive? Couldn't you at least have told them that?"

"Janet asked me not to."

I was going to ask Billy why he didn't tell Janet's parents, but I already knew the answer: the Generation Gap will never die.

"All right," I said. "A deal's a deal. This ends your involvement in this as far as I'm concerned. If Duncan and Argyle pick you up for more questioning, I want you to know that it won't be because of me. Cops just do that."

There were a lot more things I wanted to say to Billy but didn't. A line from a Bob Dylan song came to me: "The next time you see me coming, you better run." But I lifted the needle from the platter. Billy was of no consequence. The only thing I cared about now was Janet and Vicky. I wanted to see them alive and in person. I wanted to know what they were doing at Brother Chakra's ranch, and how long they intended to stay there.

"Thanks for the information, Billy," I said. "I'm gonna split now."

"Wait a minute," he said, with the uncouth charm of youth.

"What?"

"What did you mean when you said I could get more money for this record?"

I hesitated. Even though Billy was a street person, he was a young person, which indicated that he didn't have the same smarts as the record collector who was taking advantage of him. Billy's ignorance generated a kind of impatience in me, the impatience of someone who used to be stupid, too.

"Let me put it this way," I said. "Tell your collector friend that you met a guy who will pay you ten dollars for that record. This is what is known in the world of free enterprise as 'competition.' Competition makes the price of things go up."

"I thought competition made the price of things go down."

"It does that, too. It's a weird concept."

He frowned with bafflement. I liked that. But then he said, "I don't think he would believe me. Who would pay me ten dollars for this record?"

"I would," I said. I pulled ten dollars from my billfold and held it out to him. "I never hear that song on the radio anymore."

Suddenly he looked scared. This is what happens to people who have something to sell. They're afraid of getting ripped off. Writers have the same attitude toward plots.

Billy shook his head no. "I don't think so," he said. "I think I'll just stick with my dealer."

"Fair enough," I said. "That's a valid part of free enterprise even if it's … well … never mind."

I tucked my ten dollars into my shirt pocket and stood up.

"One last word," I said. "You're not a good shoplifter. I would hate to see you do time for stealing a record. If you want to get rich ripping people off, go to college and become a lawyer."

I left him mulling that over. I mulled it over myself as I walked out of the cafe. Given the fact that I possess a Bachelor's Degree and I'm broke, I guess I have a lot of nerve telling kids to go to college.

CHAPTER 19

It was Wednesday. It was nine in the morning. I was on the road. Not the taxi road but the Boulder road. I was paying for it out of my own pocket. I was driving my civilian heap northwest along what had once been a toll road when it was built in the 1950s: the Denver/Boulder Turnpike. People still call it that. It's hard to break old habits. Imagine the energy it would take to not say "Turnpike."

The sun was up and the sky was clear. Anybody who didn't know me would have mistaken this for a beautiful summer day. But there was nothing beautiful about what I was trying to do. I was looking for beautiful people. That was a euphemism for "hippies" back in the sixties, although me ol' Dad always said, "When I was a boy we called 'em bums."

The road from Denver to Boulder is hilly. I topped a hill and saw the Flatirons in the distance. They're located southwest of Boulder. The Flatirons are rock formations similar to Red Rocks, except they're not red, they're gray, and triangular in shape. Thus the name. The man who had named the orange was on a roll that year.

I've never visited the Flatirons. Don't intend to. I've been told that rock climbers practice their craft on the faces of the Flatirons. Don't ask me why. I steer clear of people who do stuff. But rock climbers especially baffle me because after they finish what they set out to do, there's nowhere to go but down. Hell, I've been there all my life. Why spend money on pitons when there are so many six-packs looking for a home?

The city of Boulder is located in a kind of valley set between the foothills of the Rocky Mountains and the hilly plains. But don't let me mislead you. The "hilly plains" are just the last vestiges of Kansas. By that I mean the flatlands. I grew up there. The hills that lead into Boulder are like swelling waves lapping against the shore of the mammoth island of the Rockies, like the island in that Bugs Bunny cartoon where two shipwrecked sailors get stranded and Bugs makes a marionette out of a plucked chicken and scares the sailors and ... well ... my analogies are getting a little strained here, but maybe that's because I was feeling a little strained myself that Wednesday morning. I was looking for two teenage girls whose lives I had probably ruined. Word on the street said they had run away from home and were living in some sort of hippie commune ruled by a mysterious guru who called himself "Brother Chakra." Let's see Bugs Bunny do something funny with that.

My favorite Bugs Bunny line is, "So long, screwy, see ya in St. Louie." I sometimes say that when I'm alone ... I hope.

I was in a foul mood as my heap made the long run down the last big hill that leads into Boulder. The girls had been missing since Friday night, which meant they had been in the clutches of this holdover from the sixties for almost five days, long enough for anybody to become brainwashed. I had spent a restless night trying not to imagine what it would be like to live in a "commune" run by a guy who referred to himself as a "major energy center of the human body." That's the definition of a "chakra."

I had been forced to leaf through the counterculture section of my bookshelves to find that word. It isn't in the *American Heritage Dictionary*—not in my 1969 edition anyway. I bought the dictionary at a flea market fifteen years ago. It replaced my old *Webster's Collegiate Dictionary*, which I had begun using as a snare drum after a taxi fare left a pair of drumsticks in my backseat. I do realize that using a book as a snare drum to play along with rock 'n' roll records might be viewed as blasphemy by writers, English majors, and book lovers in general, but man oh man, dictionaries make a righteous thud. You oughta try playing "Wipeout" on a copy of … well anyway, my *Webster's* was worn to a frazzle so I bought the *American Heritage.*

I finally found what I was looking for in one of my hippie books: "*Chakra,* a Sanskrit word referring to the seven major energy centers within the human body." I was forced to conclude that I do not possess any chakras.

I pulled onto Baseline Road and headed west through Boulder. I passed the campus that I think of as my step-mater, in that CU Denver is an extension of CU Boulder but is not the real thing, insofar as college is real. The Boulder campus has a national reputation as the "biggest party college in America." I suppose that mathematically speaking the title has to fall on somebody. After all, I was the "oldest" student in my creative writing class at UCD. A kid named Leonard was the "youngest." He aspired to write techno-thrillers. All the intellectuals in the class thought he was a chump. I desperately wanted to ask him how to write techno-thrillers, but I was afraid he would think I was a chump.

I passed through the city and came to a narrow two-lane blacktop road that led up to a place called Flagstaff Mountain. That narrow road is all business, take my word for it. It's a steep winding snake of a road that feels like it goes damn near straight up before you get to the top. By "top" I mean where the road levels out a bit, since you don't really get to the top of any place in Colorado until you come to the Continental Divide. The Divide eventually feeds you down into California, but California doesn't play a role in this, thank God. The last time I was in California, I had just dodged a murder rap. It's a long story. Let's move on.

I followed the road past a scenic point that overlooked the city of Boulder. The last time I had stood on a scenic overlook I was getting set up for another murder rap, but that's a long story, too. Let's stick with this one.

I kept driving. I was looking for a fence. The fence would end at a gate that had a sign on it that said "Smith Ranch." That was the word on the street anyway—the street of Denver, not of Boulder.

Then I was there. The Smith Ranch. The home of the hippies. The site of Brother Chakra's commune. It made me sick. Wait a minute. I was wrong. This was the Smythe Ranch. The Smith Ranch was another mile down the road. I put my sickness on hold and kept driving. Pretty soon I was there. The gate blocking the entry to the property was made of galvanized steel. There was a metal grate on the ground designed to keep cows from wandering out onto the road. I pulled up at the gate and looked beyond it toward the ranch property.

I didn't know if it was a real ranch or if they just called it that. People tend to call things stuff. I couldn't imagine raising 10,000 head of cattle on that terrain. The ranch was in a small valley. There were hills to the left and right. I could see a building a hundred yards or so into the property. It looked like a large house. I could see the roofs of a few other buildings. Maybe barns, stables, mangers, whatever ranchers own. I didn't know. I was never a big fan of *Bonanza,* although I felt bad when Dan Blocker died.

Then I saw it. A cloud of dust. It was coming my way. I got out of my heap and stood by my open door to get a better look. I got it. A green pickup truck was coming down the dirt road that led to the gate. Suddenly I had the feeling I was about to be greeted by the welcoming committee. I was wrong. Whatever kind of committees they had in the social structure of the commune, "welcoming" wasn't one of them.

The truck came up to the fence and made a left turn so the side of the truck blocked the road. Two men climbed out of the cab. A third was seated in the bed of the pickup. Although I had no conclusive evidence, I got the funny feeling that secreted somewhere in the bed was a gun. Possibly a shotgun—maybe a rifle.

The men looked like hippies. They had long hair, headbands, and sunglasses, but they were wearing denim jackets and jeans. One of the guys had cowboy boots, and the other had moccasins. I couldn't see the footgear of the hippie in the bed. He was sitting down. He was staring silently at me. He never once took his sunglasses off me and never cracked a smile. Hence the belief that he was armed. Or maybe just stoned.

One of the men approached me and smiled. "What can we do for you?" he said. He was lean, and his teeth were very white, which indicated to me that he was middle-class, possibly upper. He reminded me of Peter Fonda. I'm talking *Easy Rider,* not *Futureworld.*

I smiled back. "I'm looking for somebody who might be here."

"Are you a cop?"

"No, I'm a cab driver."

"Where's your cab?"

"In Denver. I'm not working today."

He nodded then glanced at his hippie partner, who smiled at me. His partner said, "If you're a cop, you have to tell us."

The three of us were within a hair's breadth of hostility. I could sense it. When you've driven a taxi as long as I have, you develop a radar for hostility. I know my hostility. But we weren't there yet.

"I'm a friend of two girls who are here," I said. "I came up to visit them."

The three men stared at me for a moment, then the taller one came closer to the gate.

"I think you came here to score," he said. "Strangers come here all the time. People in Boulder tell other people that they can buy things here, but we don't deal in drugs. This is a health ranch. We deal in health. So you might as well turn around and go back to Denver, stranger."

I nodded. "I understand," I said. "But I didn't come here to buy anything. I came here to visit my two friends, Janet and Vicky. They call themselves Sunshine and Moonbeam. They came here last weekend. They were at the Plastic Infinity concert at Red Rocks. I drove them there in my cab. I just want to talk to them."

"Hey," the shorter of the two said. The tall one looked around. The short one motioned to him with a finger. The tall one walked back toward the pickup and they had a discussion that lasted thirty seconds. They both kept glancing at me. Then the tall guy came back.

"You drove them to Red Rocks in your cab?" he said.

"That's right."

He nodded. "That doesn't sound right to me. They're your friends but you made them pay for a cab ride?"

"No. I gave them the ride for free."

"How long have you known these women?" he said.

We stared at each other in silence. The guy could read me like an X-ray. I suddenly realized that I had made a mistake. I had come here armed with half-truths. I had intended to bluff them, had wanted them to get the impression that I knew Janet and Vicky and was concerned about their welfare. Have I ever told you about my "expertise" at poker? I realized that I should have been lying to them from the start instead of bluffing on the fly. I should have told them I was Janet's brother—or father.

"There aren't any women here by the name of Janet or Vicky or Sunshine or Moonbeam," the guy said with a smile. "You must have the wrong place. Maybe you should try the Smythe Ranch a mile back down the road. People sometimes make that mistake."

"Listen," I said. "Can I come into your ranch and talk to some of the people? Maybe Janet and Vicky are using different names than Sunshine and Moonbeam."

"I don't think so, man."

"If this is a health ranch, can I join?" I said. "I'm not very healthy."

The other guy spoke up. "You'll stay a lot healthier if you go away, pig."

The tall guy turned and made a "hush" hand signal. The hostility had arrived. He turned back to me and smiled. He reminded me a great deal of Peter Fonda. I could see why he was the gatekeeper. He had the diplomatic personality of a good bouncer. His friend, on the other hand, reminded me of Dennis Hopper.

"Really sorry, man, I can't help you," Peter said.

He was a smart bouncer. He had created a polite wall between me and what I wanted, which was to enter the ranch and snoop around. It's a lousy feeling when you want something badly and it's right there in front of you and you can't get your hands on it. Children know what I'm talking about. Between every kid and a candy bar stands a mother.

I had the sudden urge to jump the gate and shove the hippies aside and walk into the commune, but I was forty-five years old. So instead, I said, "I want to talk to Brother Chakra."

CHAPTER 20

The smile faded from Peter's face. The air got chilly. Dark clouds flooded the sky. Lightning crashed. Okay, I'm kidding about sentences two through four, but that's what it felt like. The hippie in the pickup sat up straighter. I expected to see the barrel of a long gun appear. Come to think of it, I wasn't kidding about sentence number two. The air definitely got chilly.

"Maybe you better leave," Peter said.

"I was told that this place was run by a guy who calls himself Brother Chakra," I said. "I'd like to speak with him."

"Hey man, why don't you hit the road?" Dennis said, striding toward the gate with his arms held away from his sides like a gunslinger.

Maybe it was the fact that I had served in the army and had almost thirty minutes of judo training under my belt—or maybe it was the fact that there was a gate between us. But for some reason I wasn't intimidated by his sudden approach. To be honest, it was probably the fact that he was skinny. I'm not exactly skinny. "Exactly" is the operative word there. I was being honest when I said I wasn't healthy. My beer belly alone could underwrite a health ranch.

"There's nobody here by that name," Peter said, smiling that winning *Race With the Devil* smile. Or maybe I'm thinking of *Dirty Mary, Crazy Larry.*

My Univac went into high gear. I realized they were holding all the cards. Janet and Vicky were there, I was certain of it, which meant if I threatened to call the police, or even got into a scuffle with the Hopper hippie, it could mean trouble for the girls. The chill of the Rocky Mountain air began to seep into my heart. I realized I had made a truly terrible mistake. I had come to this place thinking I could contact two teenage girls utilizing the sort of bluffs I had perfected as a cab driver to increase the size of my tips. Which is to say, I had come here without a plan.

There was a moment of impending violence. All of us were connected by violin strings stretched so taut that the slightest pluck could result in a calamitous version of "Flight of the Bumblebee."

I smiled.

"Okay," I said. I realized now that I should have just passed my information along to Duncan and Argyle and let them handle it: Janet and Vicky are at the Smith Ranch in Boulder. What made me think it was my responsibility to talk the girls into coming home? Am I responsible for every life I ruin?

"No problem," I said. "I'm leaving. I just wanted to make sure Janet and Vicky are all right."

Peter raised his chin ever so slightly. He gave me a brief and friendly wave. Was he trying to tell me that the girls were all right, or was he just nudging me along? It didn't matter. I didn't need a nudge. I stepped back to my heap and climbed in.

I closed the door, started the engine, and whipped a u-ey. The trio watched me silently. I looked at them in my rear-view mirror as I drove down the road. They remained at the gate, staring at my car. When I got far enough away so that I was certain they couldn't see me, I hammered the steering wheel with a fist and shouted, "I blew it!" I do lots of things when nobody can see me, and admitting defeat is at the top of the list.

I passed the Smythe Ranch and began heading downhill, the only direction I was good at. Somebody once told me that the downhill ride was so much fun, but that was long ago and on another mountain. By the time I passed the scenic overview on Flagstaff, I was analyzing to death everything I had done wrong, starting with getting out of bed. From there I moved on to the concept of "winging it." When—I asked myself—had that ever worked?

Okay, there were a few times in my life when I had managed to extricate myself from terrible situations by winging it. But most often I found myself solving problems through a technique that I refer to as "doing nothing." I couldn't begin to list all of the phenomena that seemed to have solved themselves due to an absence of effort on my part. The common cold comes to mind.

Then it occurred to me that what I ought to have done that morning was sign out my cab and driven to the Smith Ranch and told the hippies that two teenage girls had called for a taxi. Maybe the presence of a motorized vehicle authorized by the Public Utilities Commission would have given me an aura of legal authority that might have intimidated the hippies.

"Damn!" I said, pounding the steering wheel.

Have you ever done that? Not pounding, but doing something and then wishing you had done something else? It's practically the guiding philosophy of my life.

I made it to the bottom of the mountain and drove back through Boulder. CU is a pretty campus. A few scenes from *The Glenn Miller Story* (1954) were filmed there. A scene was also filmed a couple blocks from the state capitol building in downtown Denver. I'll admit it. Whenever I see Jimmy Stewart standing in the fake phone booth on Colfax Avenue making a call to June Allyson, I get excited.

That's why I own a Glenn Miller record. I listen to "In The Mood" when I'm alone in my crow's nest and nobody can see me. Sometimes I jitterbug. Let's move on.

I headed to Denver feeling hollowed out. I didn't know what to do. Janet and Vicky were obviously in the clutches of a group of surly hippies, one of whom had adopted the pleasant persona of an actor who had become the living icon of rebellion in the late sixties. Marlon Brando held the title in the fifties, i.e., *The Wild One* (1954). Nineteen fifty-four had always been a big year for me. That was the year me ol' Dad bought our first TV.

By the time I got off the turnpike and onto Interstate 25 headed south toward Denver, I knew what I had to do. I had to call Detectives Duncan and Argyle and tell them everything I knew, except the name of the immature kid who had told me where the girls were. I wanted to keep my promise. I wanted to salvage what was left of my honor. Which is to say, I wanted to keep the worst promise I had ever made in my life.

"Let the police handle this situation, pal," I snarled like a reporter in a movie. Again—nobody could see me.

I got off the highway at Speer and drove down into the heart of Denver. I turned up Colfax and headed for the Denver Police Department headquarters building at 13th and Bannock. I had decided to park at a meter and go visit Duncan and Argyle and come as clean with them as I ordinarily get with cops.

I was a few blocks west of the place when I kept driving until I was a few blocks east. I did this for two reasons: (#1) cab drivers hate to use parking meters, and (#2) I couldn't face the detectives. It would be almost the same thing as "facing the music," something I have never gotten good at. Call me a coward, but confessing terrible truths to people who carry handcuffs has never seemed wise.

When I got home I trudged up the fire escape to my back door and entered the kitchen. It felt strange to be returning to my crow's nest after a Boulder trip without a T-shirt full of money. I went to my easy chair and sat down and stared at my telephone. The only thing I hate worse than answering a call is making one. I'm a firm believer in the audio version of The Golden Rule, which states, "Don't call me, and I won't call you." Yet here I was, breaking another one of my rules, vows, codes, dictums, guiding philosophies, or whatever you want to call the counterfeit money that finances my existence.

I picked up the phone and poked "O" for operator.

A minute later the phone rang at DPD HQ. I asked to speak with either Detective Duncan or Detective Argyle of the Missing Persons Bureau.

"Argyle," a voice said.

I swallowed hard. I had never spoken to Detective Argyle over the phone. His voice sounded funny, if you think of Woody Woodpecker as having a funny voice.

"Detective Argyle? This is Brendan Murphy? I drive for the Rocky Mountain Taxicab Company?"

I often use the lilt of a question in the tone of my voice when I talk on a telephone. I don't know why. Maybe I'm hoping somebody has some answers.

"Hello, Murph," Argyle said.

I won't bore you with a protracted account of the details of our conversation. You've been there. I told him I had tracked Janet and Vicky to the Smith Ranch west of Boulder.

"We already have that information," Argyle said in his flat, level, and occasionally reassuring cop voice.

"You do?"

"We brought that kid Billy in. He told us where they were." My hair almost stood on end.

"Did he mention my name?" I said.

"Why would he mention your name?" Argyle said.

I froze.

I thought fast. Believe it or not, this is one thing I am good at. "He was with the girls before I drove them to Red Rocks, so I just thought maybe he mentioned me."

"No, he didn't mention you."

"Why did you pick him up?" I said.

"He was caught shoplifting records," Argyle said. "When the arresting officer found out he was connected with our case, he brought him to our office for a follow-up."

This made me feel bad. Billy was now an official JD. "I'm a *JD*," Sal Mineo said with a scowl to James Dean in *Rebel Without A Cause*: "JD" means "Juvenile Delinquent" for those of you who aren't hip to outmoded slang.

"Is Billy going to jail?" I said.

"That's for a judge to decide," Argyle said.

"Are the girls all right?" I said. "Are they coming home?"

There was a moment of silence at the other end of the line, then Argyle said, "We appreciate your interest and your help with the situation, Murph, but I'm not at liberty to discuss the details. Yes, the girls are all right. But our department has dropped the case. Since both of the girls are over eighteen, it's basically a family matter. It's between the girls and their parents."

The phrase "Generation Gap" popped into my head. I don't know why that phrase isn't used anymore. Has there ever been a period in history when there was not a gap between the generations? We Baby Boomers probably ran the label into the ground. We get criticized for a lot of things, most of which we weren't responsible for, like being born in the suburbs, and wearing Davy Crockett hats— neither of which I got to do.

After Argyle and I said goodbye and hung up, I experienced a number of emotions. One was embarrassment. I was embarrassed by the fact that I had phoned Argyle thinking I was bringing good news, only to learn that he already possessed the information. For one moment I had felt like a hero, then I felt like a fool. Another emotion was chagrin. I was chagrined by the fact that even though the girls were okay, they were still at the ranch.

I was so depressed by the fruitless events of that day that I decided there was only one thing to do: cheer up.

I have various techniques for doing this: downing a six-pack of beer is a standby, but beer is so sacred to me that I hate prostituting it. That would be like writing for money. I have never drunk beer for money, and I saw no reason to start debasing the medium now. Beer should never be used as pancake makeup to camouflage the blemishes on the mottled surface of a twisted soul. That's what television is for.

You're probably way ahead of me by now.

In less than a minute I was out the door and on my way to a video store.

CHAPTER 21

I passed a number of giant video franchise stores on the way but I didn't stop at any of them. When you walk into one of those mammoth operations you know you're going to find the latest Hollywood releases, but the kind of movies I prefer to view are not necessarily stacked on squeaky-clean shelves.

The store that I regularly patronize had been a head shop back in the days when small mirrors and rolled dollar bills were still legal. But after the *video revolution!!!* came along, they got rid of all their hippie stuff and filled the store with VCR tapes. Included in this were the sorts of tapes that you can't find at the big franchise outlets, i.e., art films, avant garde, European, and just plain weird movies. I found the place after visiting a similar store at Venice Beach in Los Angeles, called The Cult Hut. I had visited the place when I was tracking down the girl I didn't murder.

But back to Denver.

I lost myself in the video store for a while, wandering the aisles looking at all the offbeat tapes. This will probably mean nothing to you, but the store has one copy of a movie called *Summer Kicks.* I once met the female lead of *Summer Kicks.* She lives in Denver. It was her daughter that I supposedly "murdered," which I did not do because the girl is still alive and goes to college and everything.

Anyway, as I browsed the shelves I began to realize what I was really doing there. I was looking for hippie movies. It had been a long time since I had seen *Easy Rider.* Not to mention *The Trip.*

Even without the aid of a nickel psychologist, I understood why I was doing this. If you stick around, it ought to become clear to you, assuming you are more insightful than I am, which I assume about everybody.

I didn't know exactly when I decided to get further involved in the personal lives of two fares who hadn't even paid me for a trip to the concert at Red Rocks, but I knew that guilt is thicker than my head, and if I didn't make an effort to bring Janet and Vicky home from Brother Chakra's love ranch, I would never be able to sleep at night. Call it enlightened self-interest, but I'll do anything to avoid guilt.

As I was plucking tapes to rent from the shelves, I came across a choice plum titled *Psych-Out.* Jack Nicholson as a hippie—I'm talking pre-*Five Easy Pieces.* And get this: soundtrack by Strawberry Alarm Clock. Oh baby, if the cops pulled me over on the way home and saw my tapes they would call in the drug-sniffing canines.

Around five o'clock that evening, after recovering from *The Trip* and bracing myself for *Psych-Out,* I suddenly realized that this plan had begun forming the moment the Hopper hippie strode toward me with his hands hung like a gunslinger and snarling, "Hey man, why don't you hit the road?"

I watched a half-dozen movies that night but not all the way through. To be more precise, I couldn't watch them all the way through. I sort of skimmed them like books, and then studied the relevant scenes. "Relevant" was a word used a lot by anti-establishment protesters back in the '60s, but you never hear it much nowadays. Maybe everything is relevant now. It made me feel kind of good, though, to bring the word back to life, if only for one evening. Sort of a nostalgia trip. I first heard the word "trip" used euphemistically during the 1960s while watching *The Merv Griffin Show.* It was uttered by a singer named London Lee, who was talking about an event he had taken part in. "It was a real trip," he said.

Merv was baffled.

By the time I finished watching the movies, the original glimmer of an idea had grown into a viable notion, and the more viable it became the more depressed I got because I knew where all of this was headed. Ideas were coming to me faster than they did when I tried to write a novel. When I tried to write a novel I would sit in front of my RamBlaster 4000 and stare at the blank monitor, which was a reflection of my mind. And now here I was, dodging ideas like bullets because I didn't want to do what I knew I had to do. Maybe I would get some acceptance slips if writing was as dangerous as cab driving.

By the way, I didn't drink any beer that night. Some spring break huh? But I knew I had to stay clean and sober if I was going to follow through on my self-imposed mission. I knew this was the proper approach because whenever I did not want to do things I would normally get drunk. It always worked. Except in the army—they still made me do things. Ironically I didn't do them any worse than sober.

At midnight, I finished with Phase 1 of what I had come to think of as my preparations for "going in." I felt like James Bond in *Live and Let Die* when he spent a week jogging on the beach in preparation for his pursuit of Mr. Big "under the critical, appraising eyes of Quarrel." Quarrel was a Cayman Islander who helped James Bond get into shape and plan his assault on Mr. Big's network of terror. Quarrel later died in *Dr. No.* It made me feel bad.

I shut off the TV without rewinding my rental tapes. I staggered into my bedroom, kicked off my Keds, and collapsed into bed.

I opened my eyes.

It was six A.M. fer the luvva Christ—and during *spring break!!!* I cursed as I dragged myself into the kitchen for a quick meal of scrambled eggs. That's what James Bond always ate after a hard night of doing this or that, usually with women.

It was now time for Phase 2. As I tied my tennis shoes I started thinking that I ought to jump ahead to Phase 3 and get that over with. Or even Phase 4. This plan had a lot of phases, and it occurred to me that I should combine some of them and reduce them to a manageable lump. But I quickly put a stop to that sort of thinking. It was right up there with jotting notes on a "Things To Do Today" tablet instead of just doing them. No, I would take each phase one at a time. I knew myself well enough to know that juggling phases was the first big step on the road to confusion, followed by giving up, and then celebrating my defeat at Sweeney's.

It was time to hit the books. I won't bore you with the details, I'll just bore you with the titles. *Electric Kool-Aid Acid Test* by Tom Wolf. *Revolution for the Hell of It* by Free, who I think was Abbie Hoffman. I intended to read my copy of *Steal This Book* by Abbie Hoffman but someone stole it. I skimmed *The Stoned Apocalypse* by Marco Vassi and *Do It!* by Jerry Rubin. I accidentally spent three minutes skimming *The Greening of America* by Charles A. Reich, then I looked at *We Are The People Our Parents Warned Us Against* by Nicholas von Hoffman. I tried to read *Tarantula* by Bob Dylan but couldn't get past the first word. Then I dove into the classic J. Anthony Lukas book, *Don't Shoot—We are Your Children!*

There were other books, too. I own a lot of books that most people wouldn't. But you get the picture. I picked up where I had left off the previous night, immersing myself in the "sixties" like a method actor who wanted a pool of verisimilitude to draw from when the time came to go onstage. I knew I had taken my studies far enough when I started leafing through books by Seymour Krim. He wrote about beatniks.

It was high noon when I made "the call."

It was the bravest phone call I ever made in my life.

I dialed Detective Argyle's office.

Why did I call him? I wanted to find out if Janet and Vicky had come home from the Smith Ranch. By "wanted," I meant "hoped."

"No," he said. I asked if Billy was in jail. No, he was out on bond. I suppose I had sort of built that call up in my mind and had blown it all out of proportion. I had been hoping the gods had taken pity on me and had done magic things to make Janet and Vicky go home. But it was no-go. I don't know what makes me think the gods care what I do. Possibly hubris. You be the judge.

That evening I made "the call."

This was a different "the call."

It was a call to a guy who didn't owe me any favors.

He was a friend named Wally from my college days who owned a beat-up Volkswagen mini-van. I wanted that van. I wanted him to loan it to me. But I hadn't talked to him in fifteen years. It was one of those wistful situations where you lose touch with a pal. He got married, had kids, found a real job, and stopped going to Sweeney's. I felt embarrassed calling his house. His wife had never liked me. None of my friends' wives ever liked me. They viewed me as a bad influence on their husbands. This opinion had been formed at parties before they got married. My nickname in those days was "Howling Wolf."

"Hello?"

"Hi Wally, this is Howling Wolf."

"Hey Murph, what's up?"

"Can I borrow your van?"

"Sure."

That is a verbatim transcript of "the call" I made to a man I had not seen in fifteen years. Yes—he was still me friend, me buddy, me pal.

CHAPTER 22

I won't bore you with detailed descriptions of the other preparations that I made before implementing my "plan." I know what you're thinking. Why did Murph put the word "plan" in quotation marks? What is it about quotation marks that absolves people of responsibility for the things they try to do? I don't know the answer. All I can say is, thank God for quotations marks.

Late Friday morning I was driving toward Boulder. I was seated in "Doctor Lovebeads Cosmic Wonderbus and Mobile Mercantile." That entire phrase was printed in psychedelic colors on both sides of the van. But I had left out the possessive apostrophe on "Lovebeads[']" in order to show my contempt for bourgeois conformity. The phrase was printed in water-soluble paint. Don't tell Wally, all right? He had somehow been led to believe that I would be hauling boxes to a storage shed.

And who—you might ask—was Doctor Lovebeads?

I was Doctor Lovebeads.

I looked the part. I looked like a refugee from the sixties. I had even sacrificed my ponytail to The Cause. Did I cut it off? Worse. I combed it out. Earlier that morning I stood in front of my mirror and grabbed the rubber band that I used to gather those follicles into a whisk-broom that you might see draped over a horse's ass, and yanked it off. Then I grabbed a brush and went to work.

Hey, wait a minute.

Am I boring you? Is this a detailed description?

Let me put it this way: I am going to feed you the details randomly as I go along. That's a technique I read in a how-to book. How to write that is, not how to trick hippies.

As I stood before the mirror I bowed my head and combed my hair forward until I couldn't see a thing, then I parted the hair like a curtain and proceeded to make a tent out of it with my eyes and nose peeking through the opening. If I had known ahead of time what my plan was, I would have avoided shaving in the days preceding this ruse. I didn't shave that morning, but I didn't have much to show for it. I'm Irish-Catholic. There are not that many Irish-Catholic bolsheviks in the people's history. But at least I didn't look respectable. Fourteen years of cab driving had seen to that.

I dug out a bleached muslin shirt I had bought that time I woke up hung over in Tijuana. Did I ever tell you that story? No? Good. It was a pullover shirt with a bright red band around the neck. I went with blue jeans. I would be going with sandals as soon as I got near the perimeter of the Smith Ranch. I had a van full of sandals.

Doctor Lovebeads Cosmic Wonderbus and Traveling Mercantile carried sandals, video tapes, cassette tapes, vinyl records, flutes, necklaces, scarves, headbands, paperback books, and a stack of R. Crumb comics that I prayed to God nobody would buy because they came from my private stash. I'm not being disingenuous when I say that my entire life was packed into the rear of the van. I have structured my life so that I am prepared to get out of town fast.

I came to the base of Flagstaff Mountain. Like an experienced Coloradan, I immediately began to wonder if Wally's beat-up van would make the climb to the top. Driving an old vehicle up a steep mountain road is like tiptoeing past a sleeping grizzly. It makes you think stuff.

I got to the top okay. I pulled over to the side of the road where picnic tables were scattered about, including ancient stone fireplaces where people used to cook hotdogs in the days before the government outlawed fun with fire.

After I parked, I crawled into the rear of my mercantile and dug through the collection of sandals that I had picked up for a song at a Salvation Army store. It's amazing the things you can find at SA— and the prices! It's too bad I don't need plastic bags filled with stuffed animals or I would do all my shopping there.

I bought a dozen sandals at SA and a rack of women's blouses that were so flowery and ugly that I was sure the women at the ranch would interpret them as an in-your-face refutation of middle-class values. I had done what any ambitious entrepreneur would do: I had made a conscientious study of the marketplace and zeroed-in on my target focus group: troubled youth.

The same with the stack of LPs and cassette tapes. I also had a box of 8-track tapes. If you're not old enough to know what 8-track tapes are, then you do not have a "need to know." Let's move on.

I tossed my Keds under the driver's seat and strapped on a pair of huaraches that I had picked up for fifty cents. Then I did something that I didn't want to do, something that gave me the—for lack of a better word—"willies." I draped Janet's love beads around my neck. I did it to remind myself why I was here and what I had done to arrive at this juncture in my life. I did it so I would feel their weight around my neck when the time came to enter the realm of Brother Chakra. I did it to give me strength. I did it so I would not falter in the clutch. I had no doubt that I would be granted permission to enter the ranch. I believed this because if there was one thing that I had long ago learned to have absolute faith in, it was my ability to make really bad decisions.

The closer I got to the ranch, the farther away I wanted to be.

The word "Farther" was painted on the front of the van above the windshield. For those of you in-the-know, I had looked up the word "furthur" in my *American Heritage Dictionary* only to discover that Ken Kesey had completely misspelled it. Proof that LSD is dangerous? You be the judge.

When I looked up the word "further" in the dictionary, it sent me to the definition of "farther." The word "farther" means "to or at a more distant or more remote point in space or time." Whereas "further" means "at or to a more distant point in space or time." Fer the luvva Christ—which word should I paint on the van? I would be driving through a college town and I didn't want any English professors snickering at me. I got enough of that after my PSAT. I was ready to throw away my paintbrush and stop trying to be clever when I noticed a sub-paragraph on "Usage." It said that in terms of physical distances "80 percent of the Usage Panel specify *farther* as the preferable choice." But when it came to the figurative use, such as *further from the truth*, 66 percent prefer "further."

On the upside, I finally found out who is in charge of the English language: the Usage Panel, whoever the hell they are. Who put them in charge anyway—the Supreme Court? I sure as hell didn't remember voting on that one. I was ready to write an angry letter to a newspaper, but then I remembered what I was supposed to be doing: rescuing girls. I tell ya, getting lost in dictionaries is one of the seven warning signs of an English major. I decided I might as well go with the 80 percent crowd and just paint "Farther" on the van. Conformity, baby, that's my bag. Come the Revolution, I'm siding with _____ (insert winner here).

Inhabited mountaintops are sort of funny in the sense that they are more like hilly farmland. The asphalt road wound around hilltops and rose and fell as if on ocean swells. I always notice the details of my surroundings when I'm doing something out of the ordinary, such as getting into traffic accidents. I've never had an accident as a cab driver, but I've been involved in a few fender-benders as a civilian. The world slips into slow motion, the crash takes forever, broken glass and hubcaps float around like cheap special effects. You may have experienced this yourself. I might even have been the guy who rear-ended you somewhere near Salinas while you were waiting for a train. At any rate, there was a special clarity to the mountain air that day. Everything seemed in tight focus. The colors were vivid. It was like the difference between Kodak film and Fuji film.

I passed the Smythe Ranch. A few minutes later I came around a bend in the road and could see the entry gate to the Smith Ranch farther ahead. It was the same bend I had hidden behind while traveling in the opposite direction on Wednesday, the bend where I had pounded the steering wheel and recited my soliloquy about "Man and Failure."

When I saw the horizontal bands of galvanized metal blocking the path, something came over me, as I knew it would.

Let me explain.

Whenever I drive a taxi, I cease to be me the moment a customer climbs into my backseat, whether the fare is a soldier, statesman, milliner, bum, college student, baker, housewife, nun. At that moment I become whatever the fare wants me to be. Which is to say, my demeanor changes. Does the fare want a jolly driver? A curmudgeon? A philosopher? A clown? The first ten seconds of any cab ride are crucial because a tip hangs in the balance. That's when an asphalt warrior's internal Univac steps to the fore and makes instantaneous calculations determining the personality and attitude of the man or woman sitting in the backseat. The mirror provides the visual data in conjunction with a quick glance into the backseat and a snappy,

"Where ya headed?" The ears provide the audio data. "DIA," most businessmen say. "Cherry Creek Shopping Center," a lot of women say. But I do not wish to mislead you. The majority of fares have a similarity about them that relieves a driver of having to draw deeply upon his acting talents in order to maximize his profits. But the next time you watch the movie *Psycho,* note the voice of Norman Bates' mother the first time you hear her crabbing at Tony Perkins.

That woman is me.

I'm speaking metaphorically of course. It's highly unlikely that I will ever be allowed anywhere near a Hollywood soundstage. I'm the guy who predicted that *Titanic* (1997) would BOMB. Leonard Maltin gives it three-and-a-half stars. Let's move on.

The moment I saw the Smith Ranch I ceased to be Murph the taxi driver and was transformed into a free spirit from the land of enchantment—New Mexico—who went by the name of "Doctor Lovebeads," a self-taught philosopher on wheels, itinerant peddler of hippie paraphernalia, and guidance counselor to the young and lost. I had fourteen years of matriculation through the urban educational facilities of the Rocky Mountain Taxicab Company to thank for this. That's where I earned my Herdic Degree—summa cum laude, which is Latin for "Old Pro."

Lying next to me on the shotgun seat was an 8-track tape by Led Zeppelin. I picked it up and popped it into the machine. Yes—Wally's van had an 8-track dashboard player. "Whole Lotta Love" blasted from the speakers. "In-A-Gadda-Da-Vida" had been my original choice as the prologue for my entrance but I vetoed it for two reasons: (#1) the song lasts seventeen minutes and I was afraid I would find myself padding my intro just to carry the song to the end, and (#2) "Gadda" had always been a party-killer when I was in college.

By the time it was over the kids were exhausted and just wanted to go home and crash. You may have experienced this yourself.

My windows were rolled down, music was blasting from the speakers, the van was painted in psychedelic colors, the word "Farther" was blazing above the windshield, and a hippie was at the wheel. I was no Neal Cassady but I was hitting every mark laid down by Ken Kesey when he blew into New York City in his magic bus to take part in the publication party for *Sometimes A Great Notion,* which a few critics dismissed as "overwritten." I had thought about skimming it last night but the book was six hundred pages long and wasn't about hippies anyway. Too bad the movie didn't do well at the box office. But let's face it, ten minutes of watching Richard Jaeckel drown was a bit much.

CHAPTER 23

My flamboyant entry didn't do well at the box office either. There was no one at the gate to witness it. But this didn't really surprise me because the gate had stood unguarded on Wednesday, too.

I took advantage of the solitude to set up shop. I parked parallel to the gate, then hopped out and hurried around to the port side and threw open the sliding door so the merchandise could be seen by my customers, who were approaching in a cloud of dust.

Obviously there was some means of watching the front gate for visitors. My guess was a telescope, perhaps perched on a roof, the sort of arrangement you might expect from people who were perpetually "up to something." This coincides with my belief that the two most powerful forces in human nature are money and paranoia—and you know what "they" say about pot smoking. It's my theory that paranoia gave rise to the invention of the telescope so that people could see what was over there without actually going over there.

I turned the sound down a bit on Zep, then pasted a madman grin onto my face. This was a technique I had picked up in a single's bar. It never worked. But I wasn't looking for love that day. I was just pretending to look for love—or "luv" as they say in the Haight.

I used the present tense in the second half of the previous sentence because as far as I was concerned on that Friday afternoon, I was now in the sixties.

"Was now" is a peculiar phrase. It's practically an oxymoron—maybe I'll write a letter to the fascists on the Usage Panel.

The green pickup truck was moving fast. It swung around and parked parallel to the gate. Peter and Dennis climbed out. The third unidentified suspect was sitting at his place in the bed of the pickup, the lower half of his body obscured. This was the moment of truth. Would they see through my mask of fraud? The fate of two teenage girls hinged on my ability to trick these men, unfortunately.

I raised my right hand and began jingling the tiny bells attached to my fingers. Like I said, I won't bore you with the details of my preparations. I'll feed them to you like popcorn to pigeons. Did I mention that I was wearing a leather headband? Fasten your seatbelts, hipsters, it's going to be a spontaneous ride.

"Greetings from the land of enchantment!" I hollered like a barker outside a strip joint on Columbus Avenue in San Francisco—take my word for it. *"Doctor Lovebeads Cosmic Wonderbus and Mobile Mercantile is open for business!"*

Peter and Dennis were walking toward me, but they stopped when I started talking. They both squinted, but there was a faint hint of smiles on their faces. I took quick note of that. It was the squint/smile of uncertain curiosity, as opposed to the squint/frown of certain disgust that rich people toss at hobos. Peter and Dennis were sniffing the bait. By the way, just so you know, I mix my metaphors with abandon, so don't panic. You won't get graded. I will.

"Howdy," Peter said.

"Doody," I replied with a bow. My hair dangled in front of my face. My sunglasses almost fell off. I poked the nosepiece and stood erect.

Peter stepped up to the fence, his eyes scanning the van. He looked me up and down. His hippie Univac was running full blast, reading and analyzing the vibes non-stop, I could sense it. Who was Doctor Lovebeads? Where did he come from? What did he want? "What are you selling?" he said.

"What are you buying?" I replied. I stood aside and held a palm toward the open door of the van so he could view my wares. "I got incense, I got sandals, I got songs and dances, T-shirts, dresses, records and tapes. If you don't see it, you don't need it. Prices are negotiable!"

The squint/grins transmogrified into normal/grins, but neither of the men made a move toward the van. They weren't buying—yet.

I sensed Dennis was both pleased and dazzled by the traveling carnival that had shown up out of nowhere on this quiet afternoon in the dull, eventless Rockies. He was grinning like a kid. I pegged him as the potential heart of my focus group. I made a mental note to milk him if need be. Peter, on the other hand, would not be so easy. He seemed intelligent.

The guy in the pickup bed continued to stare at me without expression as he had done on Wednesday. I pegged him as a strong-arm man. His job description? Intimidation. Or maybe he was just stoned.

Peter lifted a looped rope that held the gate firmly to the fence, the only kind of lock you need when dealing with cows. He pushed the gate open just far enough so he could slip through, but he left it open, possibly so he could rush back.

He raised the brim of his cap a bit to get a better look at the interior of the van. "Mind if I step inside and browse?" he said. He was hip. He was playing the game. He was sizing me up.

"Open twenty-four hours," I said, doing a little buck-and-wing and making my finger-bells sing.

Peter eased himself into the van, knelt on the cheesy throw rug that I had laid down so I wouldn't bruise my weak Irish knees. He started leafing through the blouses, then picking through the boxes, searching here, searching there, looking for FBI wires everywhere. Thank God Wally hadn't taken very good care of the van. The dirt, the rust, and general shabbiness of the interior added to the verisimilitude that I would need to make Peter think I was me.

He even leaned into the front seat and took a casual look at the dashboard. He was thorough. I wondered if he had ever been rousted by the Feds, but then who hasn't?

He emerged from the van and stood erect, raised his chin and looked me in the eye.

"Interesting items," he said. "How did you find your way to this place?"

"I didn't," I said. "This place found its way to me. Doctor Lovebeads' cosmic head-office is located in Taos, and all kinds of good people been passing through my head shop ever since Terry Southern wrote *Easy Rider*. Kids from the East, kids from the West, kids from the Bronx to Manhattan Beach, and some of them even passed through Boulder. They told me about your ranch."

I paused to gauge his reaction.

He was watching my eyes and listening to my words with a noncommittal expression.

"You might have gotten the wrong idea," Peter said.

"How's that?" I said, holding tightly to my madman grin.

Peter turned a few degrees to the left and gazed up at the sun and squinted. He began scratching at a three-day growth of unshaven chin. "Oh, you know, people talk. You mighta got the idea that we sell things, too. Maybe you got the idea that you might be able to … score."

He turned back and looked me in the eye. "Know what I mean?"

I nodded. "I'm a seller, not a buyer." I hiked a thumb toward the van. "This is what I do to make my bread, man. I am a private entrepreneur, an independent contractor in the mobile world of tax avoidance." I smiled. "If I want to score I can do that on any street in Denver, Boulder, Taos, Earth, Moon, or Saturn. Remember, dude, the federal government is in charge of controlling substances, which makes it all so easy, doesn't it?"

There was a frozen moment when nobody moved and nobody spoke. Peter and I were looking each other right in the eye. He had the type of intense pupils that can mesmerize young people who are easily manipulated by authority figures. In other words, he had Drill Sergeant eyes.

I dropped my grin. "I need money for gas, man," I said. "I'm trying to get back to Taos. I thought maybe I could pick up enough bread here to carry me home, that's all."

He gave me one last study from my headband to the toes of my dusty feet.

"Welllll, you got some interesting products here," he said with a nasal sigh. "We don't get too many traveling salesmen at this altitude, so I'll tell you what. Why don't you follow us inside and we'll let you set up shop in the front yard and see if you can hustle some bread. We'll even give you a free feed. It's getting on toward lunch."

"Oh wow, that would be groovy, man," I said. "I've been eating Twinkies ever since I arrived in Denver." This was true.

I slammed the door shut and hurried around to the driver's seat while Peter began walking the gate open. His buddy rushed up next to him and began holding a whispered conversation, but Peter kept shaking his head no and saying, "It's cool, it's cool."

I could sense that Peter was the man in charge here. That was cool, too.

I started the van and pulled around and waited until Peter and Dennis climbed into their cab. They waved me forward and I drove ahead of them onto the property. And because my mind is my mind in all its raging glory, I suddenly thought of the scene in *Deliverance* when Burt Reynolds raced the hillbillies to the river. I got nervous. I hate it when my brain eggs me on. But I just pretended I was Jon Voight and managed not to floor it. Let's be honest. Deep down inside, we're all Jon Voight.

I scanned the landscape as I drove. Large house to the left. Smaller structures to the right. Farther ahead the road rose up the side of a hill toward what appeared to be a tree lying across the path, a mammoth thing, the trunk eight feet in diameter at least, but it had been chopped through to allow vehicle passage. I couldn't see much beyond that. The road curved left and out of sight.

The big house was sort of surprising, and reminded me of the types of structures you can still see in places like Central City: gingerbread houses, two-story affairs built back in the nineteenth century when people didn't have televisions and were forced to build interesting things out of wood. I have a theory that the outrageous fashions you see in pre-twentieth century culture came about as a result of the lack of television. I'm talking wild hats on women with lots of feathers, pelts, sequined dresses with long trains, as well as top hats on the men, with long-tailed coats. I figure that life in those days was so dull that people themselves became televisions. I'm still working on the theory. I include European royalty in this construct, but let's move on.

The house was three stories tall, a Victorian structure, the kind of place you might expect a rich man to have built for a wife who read romance novels and mooned about the property wishing like hell she had never left New York City and married a gold miner. I develop theories rather quickly, even when a tip doesn't hang in the balance.

The house had a wide front porch where young people were lounging about. "Hippies," if you get my drift. I drove toward the "front yard," which was just a level patch of earth in this small valley. The kids started rising and stepping down off the porch. I turned Zep up a bit and pulled into the middle of the yard and shut off the engine.

Peter slowed his pickup, nodded at me and pointed at the kids, then drove on up through the fallen tree and out of sight. This was unsettling. But hey, wasn't I in a place that had rejected the values of bourgeois society, which surely included long-winded explanations? Long-winded explanations had been my stock-in-trade for fourteen years, so I knew I would need an attitude adjustment. I was now in a milieu where everyone lived "in the moment" and went "with the flow," which I had tried to do many times in my life without much success.

Suddenly I got nervous. I was no salesman. When I was ten years old I tried to earn money selling American Seeds door-to-door so I could get rich and move to Disneyland. I don't want to talk about it.

"Go with your strengths," I muttered, as I placed the shift into Park. "Don't merely think like a fraud—BE a fraud." Suddenly it came easy. I realized that the long curtain of hair hanging in front of my face, and the groovy shades, and the bleached muslin, and the beads and huaraches, were so much decorative dross. I knew that when it came to not being me, all I had to do was be myself.

"Hey!" I chirped, as I shoved open the driver's door and hopped out. As far as I was concerned, I was climbing out of #123 in front of the DIA terminal at Christmas while a crowd of desperate airline passengers charged my taxi screaming, "Get us outta here!"

Dragging open the side door to my emporium was like raising the lid on my taxi trunk. I stood back grinning at the kids.

Did you ever see *Village of the Damned*?

If not, I guess it doesn't matter. It's just that the kids didn't crowd around the van hopping on their toes to see inside. They stood in a cluster staring at me. Their faces were expressionless.

They also reminded me of Eloi.

If you don't know who Eloi are, I guess that doesn't matter either.

CHAPTER 24

I heard a screen door open. It clattered shut. I looked up at the porch and saw—for lack of a better etcetera—Earth Mother. She was standing at the top of the steps with her arms folded. She was a biggish woman, maybe thirty, wearing a loose blouse and a long skirt. She was barefoot—I could tell because she didn't have any shoes. Her hair reminded me of my own. It was longer though, dark brown, and hung clear to her waist. I'm not entirely certain if there is a direct cultural connection between hippie women and the women's liberation movement, but I suspected that she wasn't wearing a bra. She was wearing a smile though.

"Are you hungry, stranger?" she said in a voice so softly timbred that I almost couldn't make it out. It was as if she was imitating the hippie men who were famous for talking in breathy whispers during the sixties. But this sounded like the real thing. She confirmed it after she took her time coming down the steps and walking among the kids and approaching me. She reached out with both hands and took my right hand in hers. "If you are hungry, we will give you food. If you are thirsty, we will give you water. You are welcome to share in everything we have."

I got rattled. I had been psyching myself up to break into a sales spiel, but she threw me for a loop. I couldn't remember the last time anybody had welcomed me anywhere. However, there was the possibility she was playing *mind games* with me, so I decided to "go with the flow."

"The guy in the pickup truck invited me to lunch," I said, pointing off toward the fallen tree where the dust of the passing vehicle was settling.

She turned and looked that way, raised her palm above her brow and studied the empty landscape. Then she looked back at me. "That would have been Otto," she said softly.

There you go. Not Peter but Otto. I don't think I'm giving anything away by telling you that Dennis turned out to be named Brent. Otto and Brent—the gate guards. I never did learn the third guy's name. But I did find out that he wasn't a strong-arm man. He was just a kid who liked to ride in the bed of the pickup.

"Then you'll join us?" she said.

A red flag went up in my mind—a rather worn and tattered flag, I might add. Any time I hear the word "join" I get edgy.

"Right on," I chirped.

If my brain was going to start interrupting me every five minutes and parsing every damn word it heard, I was just going to have to ignore it, the way wild teenagers ignore teachers. I was going to be here only long enough to find out where Janet and Vicky were and see if they would be willing to flee for their spiritual lives.

"What have you brought us?" Earth Mother said, looking toward the open door of the van.

Again—a red flag, this time at the word "brought." I did not "bring" them anything. I was a salesman.

"Knickknacks, trinkets, books and toys, clothes for girls and records for boys."

I was winging it, all right?

Earth Mother's placid smile broadened, and she stepped toward the van. At this point the kids began crowding around the van, too, and I noticed that there were now smiles on their faces. Some sort of "okay" signal seemed to have been given. That sickened me. People shouldn't have to wait to be told to smile, especially free spirits who have turned their backs on the anal retention of the uptight middle-class. I was really starting to get into this.

"Feel free to crawl inside and browse," I said. "If you see something you like, make me an offer. Doctor Lovebeads does not believe in price-fixing."

I walked to the rear of the van and opened the back door. Ingress and egress, that's how I live, that's how I love, that's how I increase my customer base.

"What's this?" a boy said, holding up an 8-track tape.

"Oh my goodness," Earth Mother said with a friendly chortle. "I haven't seen one of those since the seventies."

"But what is it?" the kid said.

"That's an eight-track tape," Earth Mother said.

The kid got a questioning frown on his face.

I grew embarrassed. I should have just left the damn things at the Salvation Army store. But for some reason I had been expecting the hippies to be older than they turned out to be. Okay. I'll admit it. Half of the 8-tracks were mine.

"It's like a cassette tape, man," I said, leaning into the rear where the kid was kneeling. "They don't make them anymore. That's what's playing on my stereo right now."

The kid glanced into the front seat, then looked back at me. "This is kinda neat," he said, fingering the plastic box. "How come they don't make them anymore?"

I sighed.

"I … don't … know," I said, which was true. Why did they stop making Fizzies? Why do people stop doing anything?

By now the girls were plucking blouses from the racks and draping them in front of each other. The boys were fingering the paper-backs and lifting LPs and examining the titles. A cold fear gripped me. What if they asked me to explain what a record was?

A bell started ringing. It sounded like one of those triangle things that farmers rap on to call the hired hands in from the fields, like at the start of *The Real McCoys* TV show. If you're not familiar with *The Real McCoys* I won't press the issue. It starred Richard Crenna though. He later became Rambo's commanding officer. If you don't know who Rambo is, I might as well resign from the human race.

The kids who were inside the van suddenly began shuffling out. I noticed that they also put back whatever they had been examining. The girls re-hung the blouses, and the boys slid the LPs back into the working-class cardboard boxes that I had used in lieu of uptight mahogany shelves.

Another signal had been given, obviously by the metal triangle. The Eloi gathered in a silent group, no longer smiling. They weren't surly though, they just weren't smiling. But to me that has always meant "surly." If people aren't smiling at me, I get worried. It's an ego thing.

"Let us now go to the feasting place," Earth Mother said, and began herding the kids like chickens up the road toward the fallen tree. I stood there staring after them. Earth Mother turned to me and said softly, "The feasting place is on the hill. Come."

"Let me close up the van," I said.

"No need," she said. "Your possessions are safe."

This made me feel good. Not the "safe" part, but the fact that she described them as MY possessions.

"Groovy," I said. I walked away from the van with the doors standing wide open. This normally would have bothered me, but for some reason it made me feel wild and free. It made me feel like I could run around in circles in the front yard and nobody could stop me. It wasn't a good feeling.

Nevertheless I went with the flow. I did feel a bit uneasy about the van itself though. After all, it belonged to Wally. Ever since I had borrowed it the previous evening, my Univac had been filing away excuses that I could draw upon to explain any damage to the van, whatever that would eventually turn out to be. I had faith in my Univac. It generates all-purpose excuses even when I'm sleeping. It's sort of like the print-spooler on my RamBlaster 4000.

The group walked in a loose formation up the dirt road. I stepped alongside Earth Mother and made a point not to march in-step with her feet. She might interpret that as conformity. I had to keep looking down at her skirt to time her footsteps so we would be out of synch, but then I noticed she was looking over at me, and all of a sudden Catholic guilt jumped out of a tree and landed on my shoulders because I was staring at her skirt—and I think we all know what's underneath skirts.

"Did you make that dress yourself?" I said, thinking faster than I had ever thought except when suspected of murder.

"Yes. We make many of our clothes here. Some of the boys man-ufacture leather belts that they sell in the city."

"What city?"

"Boulder. Sometimes Denver."

I scrambled to keep this conversation going. Thank God we were drifting farther away from the subject of legs. Farther! I was beginning to understand the works of Ken Kesey in a new light.

"Maybe we can do some bartering," I said. "I'm into the trade trip, too. Money isn't everything."

"It isn't anything," she said. "It's nothing."

I nodded, but it took some effort, given the fact that I had spent the past fourteen years rising at dawn in order to collect a whole lotta nothing.

We were approaching the felled tree, and I readjusted my estimate of its girth. The trunk was more like ten feet in diameter. It rested directly across the road. I'm talking a ninety-degree angle, if you think of a crossbar as an angle. I know mathematicians do, but if it isn't on a diagonal, it isn't an angle to an English major. Anyway, I was astonished by the sight of the tree blocking the road, and I wondered how it had gotten there, beyond the obvious laws of physics.

I wanted to ask, but I refrained. I didn't want to come on like Mister Ask-A-Million-Questions until I had gotten to know these people better. I was trying hard to not completely be myself. I don't know if I've mentioned this, but fighting temptation does not come natural to me. Refraining from succumbing to instant gratification takes at least one set of unusual circumstances, and I was dealing with a couple right at that moment: a hippie commune high in the Rockies, and missing girls. So instead of asking how the tree had gotten there and who the hell had chopped a path wide enough for a pickup truck to pass through, I simply stared at the age-rings as we walked between the high walls. I felt like Moses.

The land leveled out after we passed through the tree. To our left was what appeared to be an adobe cabin. Parked next to the cabin was an ancient trailer-house. Not as ancient as the trailer in *The Long, Long Trailer* starring Lucille Ball and Desi Arnaz, but more of a mid-sixties model, squarish, smaller, pre-RV (road vehicle). Who do you suppose the genius was who named the "road vehicle"? I don't know about you, but I never did buy into the ending of *The Long, Long Trailer*. Why would Desi go back to a woman insane enough to hide a ton of rocks inside their trailer? Did she really think she was going to get away with that crap? She could have gotten them killed on that mountain pass fer the luvva Christ. Talk about *foreshadowing*. I pegged their marriage as doomed from the get-go. Thank God for Fred and Ethel Mertz. They saved the sitcom as far as I'm concerned.

Thirty yards farther along, the land rose to another plateau, and from the top edge trickled a small stream, which meandered down the hill past the small, small trailer. As we walked along I kept scanning the landscape, which I had learned to do in the army. But I wasn't just sizing up the terrain and noting escape routes, which had become habitual with me during KP. I was looking for Janet and Vicky. I hadn't seen them so far. But I did see something that sort of freaked me out. A few naked people were walking along the rim of the farther plateau.

"What's that?" I said, pointing at the naked people.

"That's the pond," she said.

"The pond?"

"It's a man-made pond," she said. "We use it for swimming."

I almost said, "Who made it?" but caught myself in time. I was relieved though. At least a bunch of free luv wasn't going on up there. Or was it? I felt guilty squinting at the naked people, but I wanted to know if Janet and Vicky had shed the last remnants of civilization, i.e., clothes. I didn't see them. I counted three males and three females wandering around. They appeared to be gathering up and putting on their remnants. It was lunchtime.

The group stopped in front of the adobe cabin. The good odor of something cooking drifted from the jerry-built front door of the cabin. A wisp of smoke rose from a chimney. The cabin was very saggy-looking. I figured it was man-made. By that I mean as opposed to machine-made. Then it occurred to me that everything that isn't natural is man-made. This place was starting to make me feel insightful. Booze does that, too.

"This is the feasting place," Earth Mother said.

There was the imprint of a large circle engraved in the dirt. The kids began seating themselves on the circle. I figured the circle was butt-made. The stream that trickled from higher up bisected the circle. I didn't know if this bisection was a coincidence or if it was an element of a symbolic ritual, like candles lined up along a table where rich people eat. The primitive rituals of the wealthy fascinate me.

But it was kind of cool to have a "river" running down the middle of the dining room table. I sat cross-legged on the ground next to Earth Mother and waited to see how this feed would play out. All of the boys sat in the circle, but a number of girls went into the adobe and began bringing out bowls of soup and plates of beans.

Uh huh.

Sexism!

June Cleaver could have written that script.

Rebellion.

Give me a break.

CHAPTER 25

"What's your name?" Earth Mother said.

"Doctor Lovebeads," I replied.

"Is that your real name?"

"It's as real as it gets. What's your name?"

"Tammy."

I almost choked. I immediately knew how old she was. "Tammy" was a popular name when I was eight years old, thanks to Debbie Reynolds. During the late fifties, America became overrun with Tammys. By the late seventies, America was overrun with Heathers. I don't know what actress was responsible for that atrocity.

"But I am now called Windsong," Tammy said.

"After the perfume?" I said.

"No," she said. "I was named after the music the wind makes when it passes through the treetops."

I cursed myself. I don't know how it is that my mouth is able to ask questions before my brain gets in gear. It's almost as if I have two brains, The Idiot and The Snoozer. I crossed my fingers and hoped I had a third brain in there somewhere that could keep an eye on the others. It was plain to me that a tripartite-intellect was my only hope of succeeding at not being me.

"These are great beans," I said. "Do you grow them here?"

"No," Windsong said softly with a smile. "You can't grow beans up here."

Tell me about it.

"Good bread," I said. "Do you guys make it yourself?"

"Yes."

I nodded as I chewed. I was out of my element when it came to dinner conversation or anything else you can name. The thing is, I hate eating. By this I mean that making a ritual out of eating gives me the willies. What's the big deal about food? Get it in and get it out, that's my motto. I suppose that back when cavemen roamed the earth, eating was a big deal, since searching for food was the only reason for living. So making a sacred ritual out of eating was understandable. But thanks to fast-food joints, we no longer have a reason for living.

I have a theory though. I think most people are embarrassed to eat, primarily because they like the taste of food. They're so ashamed of their "secret vice" that they try to talk as many people as possible into doing it with them so they won't feel like outcasts as they pop that last French fry down their gullet. They gather friends and even strangers together to take part in a shameful debauchery that is transmogrified by unspoken consent into socially acceptable behavior. Okay. I'll admit it. That's why I buy drinks for people at Sweeney's—although we never say grace before we get blotto.

"Where are you from, Doctor Lovebeads?" Windsong said.

"Den ..." I said.

I gripped my Adam's apple with a thumb and forefinger and pretended to choke on the homemade bread. "Excuse me," I said. I had almost said Denver. "Penn," I said. Then I said, "Sylvania. Also Georgia, Ohio, and California. I lived in San Francisco for a year. I've been all over. But I live in Taos now. I dig it there. It's very mellow."

"I know," she said. "I lived there for three years back in the seventies."

I gripped my throat again. I wasn't pretending. I began choking so hard that two boys came over and began pounding my back. I could barely breathe, I was dying, and yet their pounding felt good. It must have been the de Sade I read in college.

After the crumb of bread was dislodged from my gullet, I wiped a few death tears from my eyes and nodded to the boys. "Thanks, dudes." I looked at Windsong. "I guess I'm just not used to eating rich food. I eat at a lot of fast-food joints when I'm on the road selling my stuff."

Windsong shivered noticeably.

"But ..." I continued, examining the slice of brown bread which had lumpy bits of healthy crud in it, "... we live in a plastic society where even the food has been co-opted by greed-head conglomerates, so it's hard to find a cafe that doesn't sell meat."

Specious reasoning was one aspect of myself that I clung to.

"How long have you lived in Taos?" Windsong said.

I want to emphasize here that whenever Windsong spoke, it was almost as if she was singing. Her voice rose and fell softly like someone who was idly humming—as for instance, a woman alone at a river washing clothes. It gave me the creeps.

I shook my head and idly waved my right hand. "The day I arrived in Taos I threw away my wristwatch and my calendar," I said. "And do you know what? I didn't die. Ever since then I've let the sun and moon keep track of time. I'm too busy living."

"It sounds like you've lived there a long time," she said.

"Probably."

"In what part of Taos do you reside?" she said.

I finished up swallowing the last bit of bread. I'll admit it. One thing I do like about eating is that you can use chewing time to make up answers without appearing to be stalling. But I was out of bread.

"It's a place east of town."

"Does it have a name?"

"Home," I said.

Everyone nodded.

"I lived near Pilar," Windsong said. "Were you ever there?"

"I passed by it a few times," I said, which was true. I had been to Taos in my mid-twenties. This was during a spring break when I was in college. I don't really want to talk about it, except to say that getting there involved a quart of tequila and possibly a Greyhound bus.

The girls began rising and collecting the plates and spoons from the boys. I felt foolish handing my plate to a girl. Nobody had done dishes for me since I left home, unless you count KPs.

"Would you care to join us up at the pond now?" Windsong said to me.

"I can't swim," I said so fast my teeth rattled.

She smiled sweetly. "We're not going to swim. Not so soon after lunch. We gather at the pond each afternoon for our self-criticism moment."

I swallowed hard. I couldn't decide which was worse—swimming nude or being honest.

"Sounds groovy," I said. "But if I start criticizing myself we'll be there all day."

"It's not quite like that," she said. "We don't tear ourselves down, and we do not tear each other down. Rather, each individual describes one aspect of his or her personality that he or she dislikes, and then we discuss how he or she might improve himself or herself."

I never thought she would make it through that sentence alive. As an English major I didn't know whether to applaud or denounce her deft use of pronouns. But I did know one thing: I wanted out.

Two girls were missing though. I smiled at Windsong. "Let's

do it," I said. "If there's one thing I never get enough of, it's self-improvement."

As we rose, I began dusting off the seat of my pants and looking around the commune. I was "acting casual." I was secretly looking for the pickup truck. It was nowhere in sight. I noticed that the road continued on up past the pond and into the trees.

"Is this everybody?" I said, waving at the kids as they began to form into a loose platoon for the short hike. "Or will there be more people at the pond?" This was my casual way of trying to find out how many people lived at the ranch.

"There are others," Windsong said. "They won't be joining us now." That was all she said. She motioned me to follow.

I noticed that every step I took in this place seemed to be in the direction of up.

We made it to the top of the next plateau. The pond was large but I couldn't see the source of the water. The sky, I supposed. The pond was three feet deep, very clear, no fish. "Can you drink from this pond?" I said.

Windsong smiled at me. She smiled at everything I said. "That's not advisable."

"But what if you were dying of thirst?" I wanted to say. I like to explore the parameters of everything. I want to know just how far I can go before free will turns into a mistake.

There was another circle on the ground at one edge of the pond. I didn't know whether it was the east edge or west edge. After a person gets into the Rocky Mountains, everything is pretty much west. The kids began sitting on the ground, although a few logs were placed here and there for people who had not entirely weaned themselves from the bourgeois concept of chairs. I sat down on a log next to Windsong.

There was a bit of chatter, but after everyone got settled they went silent and looked at Windsong. She smiled at them and clasped her hands together like Miss Jeannie on *Romper Room*.

"Everybody," she said, "I want to introduce our guest to you. This is Doctor Lovebeads, a salesman from Taos, New Mexico. As all of you know, I lived in Taos for many years, so I would like all of you to personally welcome him as a brother."

"Welcome, brother," the kids said in unison.

It swept over me like a warm wave. Everyone was smiling at me. I felt like I "belonged."

"Well thank you very much, I appreciate that nice welcome," a voice said. It was mine. I felt completely disembodied. It was exactly like driving a taxi. "And I want to thank you for sharing your food with me. The beans were excellent, and I have never tasted such fine home-made bread. But that's what I like about traveling around our country as free as a bee. Meeting new people, eating new foods, and …"

I paused. Suddenly I found myself searching for a denouement to this prattle. I was choking in the clutch. Where were those four-teen years of cab driving? My Univac advised me to stop lying—I had never liked anything about traveling around the country as free as a bee. I had lived in cities both big and small during my checkered past, but I never stayed too long in one place. I called it "itchy feet," although my lawyers called it "flight to avoid prosecution."

"… and spreading the message of love," I quickly finished.

The kids all hollered "Yaaay!" in unison. Some of them clapped their hands. I felt like Robert Preston. I'm not kidding. I submit as proof the things I proceeded to say during the next five minutes.

Windsong raised a palm. "Why don't we begin by taking hands and singing a song?" she said. She posed it as a question but I could tell it was SOP.

It felt good to take Windsong's hand in mine, but I wasn't as thrilled about holding hands with the hippie boy seated on the ground to my left. For some reason it made me think of my army physical. But I focused on that thought because I instinctively knew it was the only way I was going to get through their rendition of … yes … "Kumbaya."

By the time the last verse faded into the trees, the army doctor was telling us to put our pants back on.

We released hands, then Windsong turned to me with a smile and said, "Maybe Doctor Lovebeads has a song he can share with us before we begin our self-criticism moment."

I went through a lot of changes during that sentence. When she suggested I offer a song, I crawled into the retreat mode, but then, when she mentioned the self-criticism moment, I dashed back into the clearing.

"The fact of the matter is, I do have a little song I'd like to offer," a voice said. Again, it was mine. This was the first time in my life that I wasn't annoyed with my vocal chords. Rather than try to control them, I just sat back and watched the show. I saw myself rise from the log and begin speaking to the kids while moving my forearms like Professor Harold Hill. He was a by-god spellbinder.

"Let me tell you kids a little something about what it's like to travel alone through this great land of ours," my voice said, as I stepped to the middle of the circle. "A man gets lonesome."

I paused and looked around.

"When you're out there with nothing but a thousand miles of empty road, you get *mighty* lonesome. You start asking yourself, What am I doing on the desert or in the mountains or on Highway 1 along the coast of California with no one to talk to? You just can't help but notice that the road is mighty empty. But then you start thinking—Hey, somebody built this road. Somebody cleared the rocks and leveled the ground and drove the stakes and carved a path out of what had been wilderness. A path that allowed tired and disillusioned and even scared people to leave the cities and look for something better. Those people built themselves a friendly road. If you look real hard as you travel down the road, you can see the ghosts of the working men who laid down the sand and asphalt, and you realize that you're not alone after all. As long as you travel that road, you'll never be alone and you'll never be lonely. And you know what happens next?"

I looked around, looked into the kids' faces, looked into their eyes. Objectively speaking, I would have to say I had them spellbound—although I am willing to admit that they might have been flabbergasted.

"What happens next?" a girl said.

"You start singing," I replied. "You start singing the old songs, and the next thing you know, the ghosts of the road start singing along with you. The men laying down the asphalt stand tall and wipe their brows, and the women bringing them water pause in their labors to join in. You sing the songs of the open road. And when you run out of old songs, you make up new songs. That's what happens to me when I'm driving Doctor Lovebeads Cosmic Wonderbus and Mobile Mercantile. I make up songs. And there's one particular song that I've never shared with anybody before. But since there's so many of you here, I was thinking it would be nice if I could get you to sing it along with me. It's a simple song, and I could teach it to you real fast. Whaddya say?"

They began nodding eagerly. This was a new one on me. I grew frightened of myself.

"Teach it to us, Doctor Lovebeads!" a girl hollered.

"Yeah, teach it to us!" they chanted.

After everyone quieted down I said, "It's called 'Parking in a No-Parking Zone.' I made it up when I was driving from Memphis to Saint Joe four years back after I bought my van and headed west looking for something the city didn't offer. It's kind of a political song. Sort of anti-establishment. I hope that's all right with you. It's no 'Kumbaya' but it does express my deepest feelings about the phoniness of crass commercialism."

They applauded wildly.

I commenced singing:

"Um um um,
ya know,
really,
like, like, like.

"Um um um,
ya know,
really,
like, like, like."

I paused in mid-song and said, "That's sort of the chorus. That's the part I want you kids to sing. While you're singing that, I'll throw in the anti-establishment part."

The next thing I knew, two-dozen kids were singing the chorus of "Parking in a No-Parking Zone." I actually did make up this song, but I had lied to the kids. I made it up while deadheading to the Brown Palace from DIA.

"Um um um,
ya know,

really,
like, like, like.

"Parking in a no-parking zone!
Parking in a no-parking zoooooone!"

I sort of yelled my lines. It was more like a rap song—or maybe "Subterranean Homesick Blues," although not in terms of quality and genius. I rarely do things like that.

"Um um um,
ya know,
really,
like, like, like.

"I wanna get a job in retail sales!
I wanna get a job innnn retail sales!"

"Um um um,
ya know,
really,
like, like, like."

"The number you called!
It cannot be reached!
The number you called!
It cannot be reached!

"Parking in a no-parking zone!
Parking in a no-parking zoooooone!"

This went on for a minute-and-a-half although it seemed like two. I was swinging my hands up and down like Professor Harold Hill and the kids were following the beat with a precision that would have amazed Mister Delonatta, my sixth-grade music teacher. Did I ever mention that I played the trumpet in grade school? I wanted to play the drums but Maw nixed that dream. I don't want to talk about it.

I brought the song to a halt. The kids gave themselves a big hand. I avoided looking Windsong in the eye. I was afraid she might have noticed that the song had nothing to do with the phoniness of crass commercialism. I had taken a risk. But it was the only song I ever made up that could be sung in mixed company. Most of my songs consist of what I refer to as "colorful" lyrics. I sing them only when I'm alone, or else at Sweeney's.

CHAPTER 26

"That was *wonderful*," Windsong sang, applauding from her log seat on the organic mezzanine. "Thank you *so* much for sharing your creative imagination with us, Doctor Lovebeads."

Too bad she wasn't a book editor.

I walked back to the log and sat down, flush with paranoia. Any time I do something that draws attention to myself, I worry that someone might recognize me. But this had nothing to do with being on a hippie commune. It had more to do with small personal loans.

"All right now, why don't we get started on the meeting?" Windsong said. Suddenly I was back at Dyna-Plex where I had heard that same sentence every Monday morning. It made me nauseous.

"Does anybody have any personal criticisms they would like to share with us?"

A boy raised his hand.

"Yes, Donovan, what would you like to share?"

The boy stood up. He looked twenty years old or so. He pointed at me and said, "How come you invited a capitalist to the pond?"

Bummer.

I sat perfectly still, but I kept the smile of musical victory pasted to my face.

"Doctor Lovebeads is our guest," Windsong said.

"Yeah, but he *sells* stuff. He just wants our *money.* He's a capitalist *pig.*"

A murmur arose from the crowd. I couldn't tell if it was good or bad. I'll bet the Usage Panel couldn't either.

A hand shot toward the sky. "Yes, Miranda?" Windsong said.

A girl stood up. "Donovan isn't following protocol. He's supposed to say something bad about himself."

Another murmur. It sounded good.

Miranda looked eighteen. It was then that I realized Janet and Vicky weren't the only people I ought to be concerned about. For some reason I hadn't questioned the presence of these other kids. They just seemed to belong here, and now I began to wonder if they had parents who were worried about them, too. Did their parents even know where they were? Did their parents go to sleep at night wondering if their children were lying dead in a ditch? That's where my Maw figured I was whenever I failed to come home from school on time.

"I agree with Miranda," another girl said. "I think it's wrong for Donovan to violate the agenda."

Again, Dyna-Plex.

Then a boy stood up and said, "I think Donovan has a point. Buying and selling is what *they* do out *there*."

I had no doubt as to who *they* were and where *there* was. His meaning was clear. Talk about minimalism. This kid was a regular Hemingway.

I slowly stood up. I kept the smile taped to my face. I had the feeling that if I didn't play my cards right, I would be 86'd within the next minute. "I know I'm not a part of your group," I said. "I'm just a guest, so I don't know if I'm out of place in saying this. I don't want to disagree with anybody or create any bad vibes but I would like the opportunity to explain myself, and if you're not impressed with my explanation, then Doctor Lovebeads is ready and willing to pack up his van and hit the road."

Silence.

Eyes.

Young eyes.

Suddenly I had the feeling that I was more articulate than anybody here. I was older than thirty, so it was going to take every trick in the book to win the trust of these kids. Tricks were my only hope. I gave up on the truth when I turned seven.

"What we have here is a misunderstanding of the word 'capitalism,'" I said. "We're all capitalists here. We were *born* capitalists, because capitalists ain't nothing but traders." I pointed at Donovan.

"Did you ever trade baseball cards when you were a kid?"

He was giving me a sullen look, but I pried a nod out of him.

"Well, shoot, that's all capitalism is. It's just trading. Baseball cards, marbles, even sandwiches. Did you ever trade a baloney sandwich for a peanut-better-and-jelly?"

I scrounged a few smiles with that one.

"When I was a little kid I used to go to the theater and trade a quarter for movie. I traded a dime for a box of Milk Duds. It's all trade. It's just paper and metal. We've fooled ourselves into thinking its something called 'money,' but there's no such thing as money. It's just marbles and peanut-butter."

Everybody was smiling now. I felt evil, but I've never let that stop me.

"Windsong here tells me that some of you boys make belts out of leather. I could use some leather belts. I've got a whole van full of peanut-butter, so if any of you boys would like to sit down and calculate how many sandwiches your leather straps are worth, maybe we could come to an agreement. That's all I do for a living. I travel around the country trying to get people to agree with me."

I looked directly at Donovan. He seemed to agree with me. He shrugged and sat down. I sat down next to Windsong and secretly breathed a sigh of relief. I try to do most things in secret.

"Does anybody else have anything they would like to share?" Windsong said.

A girl raised a hand.

"Yes, Hope?"

"I have a character flaw that I'm having issues with."

"What's that, Hope?"

"I always feel ashamed of myself whenever I criticize others for not doing their share of the chores around here."

She was good.

I took mental notes.

The self-criticism moment at the pond eventually degenerated into a shouting match. But I had the feeling that this was SOP, too. According to Murph's Second Law of Human Behavior, no two human beings can occupy the same space without snarling. My First Law states: avoid people. My Third Law has to do with prenuptial agreements.

Windsong sat on her log serenely smiling while the kids complained about whose day it was to milk the cow or carry buckets of water or do all the chores that it takes to live the way the pioneers lived, which these kids apparently wanted to do.

I was dying to explain to these kids that our ancestors lived the way they did because they *had* to, and that as soon as Tom Edison invented the light bulb and motion pictures, Ma and Pa Kettle turned their backs on rustic living faster than a Texas tornado. Add to that mix the technological innovations of Henry Ford and Thomas

Crapper and you could kiss the nineteenth century goodbye forever, pardner.

But I understood. These kids were romantics. Jack Kerouac spent his adult life talking about finding a little cabin in the woods where he could carry buckets of water and chop wood and write novels and invite his friends out on the weekends for wine parties. And yet every time Kerouac went off to the woods alone it was a disaster—Ferlinghetti's cabin at Big Sur, or sixty days as a fire lookout in Washington State—he couldn't wait to get home to his mother's French-Canadian cooking and Westinghouse ironing. He was a city kid, like these kids, like me. My own personal dream is to own a cabin on a mountaintop with a 52-inch color TV. By "cabin" I mean a fully equipped robot house.

Windsong turned to me.

"Doctor Lovebeads, would you like to make a contribution to the discussion? Is there any special personal problem you would like to share with us?"

I froze.

But Doctor Lovebeads dove in. I was astonished.

"I guess my biggest problem is that I don't want to solve any of my problems. I'm afraid that if I solve my problems I might end up normal, and who wants to be normal? I tried that once and found out that normal people have jobs. I ended up crawling out of bed at six o'clock every morning and going to work. Fortunately, I solved that problem by getting myself fired. I've had nothing but problems ever since, and I couldn't be happier."

Doctor Lovebeads put a lid on it and sat back down. It was only when the log hit my ass that I realized the Eloi were laughing. I glanced at Windsong. She was older than these kids, and not so much younger than myself. I was afraid she would take offense at the fact that the substance of Doctor Lovebeads' recitation had amounted to overt criticism of self-criticism. But she was applauding. The whole group was applauding. I felt monstrous.

Windsong stood up and raised her hands. Everybody else stood up. This was more like Blessed Virgin Catholic Grade School than *Romper Room*. When I was a kid, the nuns wielded a variety of hand signals outside the classroom to keep us students organized whenever we moved in groups to the lunchroom or the playground. We were like attack dogs.

The hippies began walking back down the hill, following the path of the trickling stream. Nobody spoke. I assumed this was SOP, too, the quiet collecting of thoughts and the contemplation of new resolves after being reamed out by friends.

But I was starting to get worried. I had not yet seen Janet and Vicky, the gate guards had disappeared, and I didn't see any of the other people who supposedly lived here. So far everything was going the way they usually go when I make plans. I had learned nothing.

"Are you expecting the rest of the people who live here to come back soon?" I said. "I intend to head back down to Boulder and then to Denver if I don't make any sales in the next hour or so. I have friends in Denver who live on Capitol Hill. They're gonna let me crash in their pad tonight before I split for Taos in the morning."

Windsong shook her head no. "I don't expect the others back until evening."

Fer the luvva Christ. It was like pulling teeth.

Then I heard the sound of a motorized vehicle. I glanced back and saw the green pickup emerging from the pine trees. It wasn't moving very fast. It idled its way down the slope past the pond, then rolled on down the hill and came toward us.

Otto was at the wheel. The shotgun seat was empty. I noticed that the bed of the pickup was empty. Otto pulled over and stopped the truck and grinned and me. "How's business?"

"Kinda slow. I did have some customers looking over the merchandise but they stopped for lunch."

"Doctor Lovebeads broke bread with us," Windsong said. "Then we invited him to join us at the pond for our self-criticism moment. He taught us a song and told us some funny stories."

"Right on," Otto said. "Singing and laughing, that's where it's at."

"Check it and dig it," I said.

"I want to take a closer look at your cassette tapes," Otto said. "Maybe I'll buy some tunes."

"Feel free to browse," I said.

Otto gave me a one-fingered salute. There are various forms of one-fingered salutes, but his had a military bearing. He touched his forehead and said, "Keep the faith, baby," and put the truck into gear.

I gazed at the departing pickup, then looked at Windsong. I was going to ask where Brent and the other kids were, but instead I turned and looked back toward the pond. "Does the pond freeze in the wintertime?" I said.

Windsong smiled and nodded.

"Do you ice skate?"

"Nobody here has skates," she said.

"Well, maybe next time I pass through I'll bring some blades," I said.

Windsong glanced at me with a look that bordered on inquiry, as if she wanted to ask why I talked about things that didn't have any relevance to the moment. I do that a lot. I sometimes do it to cover up something else I'm doing, such as looking not at the pond but at the road and wondering where it led, and where the other two gate guards were, and where Janet and Vicky and all the other inhabitants of the Smith Ranch might be.

We came to the fallen tree and passed between the sections. The ground was littered with chips, but they were not fresh. Time and weather had aged them. The sight of the chips scattered all over the ground gave me the willies. It indicated a mind-boggling amount of manual labor.

"How did this tree get here?" I said.

"It fell over," Windsong replied.

I wondered if she was from New England. What could be more annoying than a straight answer? But I decided to play along with her insidious little mind game.

"Why did it fall over?" I said.

"It died."

Drat.

"Did somebody here cut the tree in half?" I said.

She nodded.

"Why?" I said.

She turned her head and looked me in the eye. "It was lying in the middle of the road."

The ball was back in my court. "Oh," I said.

Game. Set. Match.

Victory was hers.

CHAPTER 27

After we passed through the tree, I looked toward the big house at the bottom of the hill. The doors of my van were still wide open but nobody was browsing. The green pickup was parked in front of the house and Otto was stepping onto the front porch. He opened the screen door and went inside. By now most of the kids were approaching the porch. They followed Otto into the house. I wondered where the cow was. I had never wondered such a thing before.

When we arrived at my van, I tried not to make it too obvious that I was inventorying the merchandise to see if anything had been shoplifted. As I said, my father had managed a Kresge store when I was "growing up" so I knew a few things about "shrinkage," as thievery is called by businessmen. But everything appeared to be there. I felt guilty for not believing Windsong when she said my stock would be safe. Why didn't I trust people who believed in sharing everybody's wealth? I should have brought that up during the self-criticism moment.

Windsong went into the house, nobody was at the van, and I still hadn't seen Janet and Vicky. I might as well have been asleep in my crow's nest for all the good I had done. I decided it was time to make my next move. That was unfortunate because I didn't have one.

Then the screen door opened and all the kids came trooping out, followed by Windsong. They were smiling. They marched down to the van and started browsing again. Otto came out the door, strolled down the steps, sauntered right up to me with his hands shoved into his jeans pockets, and said. "So what are your plans now, Doctor Lovebeads?"

"After I shove off from here I'm gonna head down to Boulder and set up shop on the hill until sunset," I said. "Then I'm cruising down to Denver and crashing at a friend's pad. He lives on a hill, too. Capitol Hill."

Otto nodded. "Well listen here. If you want to stay over for tonight, we're having a solstice celebration tomorrow. Brother Chakra told me to pass on his personal invitation to you."

I started nodding. Then it hit me—Otto himself was Brother Chakra!

As usual, I was wrong.

"Does Brother Chakra know I'm here?" I said, even though Otto had made that clear. But saying stupid things on purpose is one of my taxi techniques for getting people to "open up."

"Yeah. I told him we had a traveling salesman down at the house."

"Oh," I said, raising my chin the way people do to emphasize the fact that they understand. My chin was lying of course. But I had found that overall it was much safer to utilize body language when lying, since reflexive twitches are inadmissible in court.

"It would be wonderful if you could stay," Windsong said. "Tomorrow will be the longest day of the year."

Brother, she didn't know the half of it.

"Groovy," I said.

"We'll be greeting visitors tomorrow," Windsong said. "Old friends always show up for the solstice festival."

"Sounds like a gas," I said, wracking my brain for far-out expressions. If I was going to stay overnight and take part in a hippie festival, it looked like I would be up all night cramming. It occurred to me then to separate some of the hippie books from the rest of the items in my cardboard box. I seemed to recall one of the books having a dictionary of hip lingo collected by a sociologist who apparently had a lot of spare time on his hands. My work was cut out for me. Suddenly I wanted No-Doz. I used to eat those things like M&Ms in college. During finals weeks I mean. I am generally opposed to the concept of staying awake in college, but the VA insisted I pass the tests.

I almost asked Windsong if they had any No-Doz around, but then it occurred to me that they might have stay-awakers a lot stronger than caffeine. Ergo, I decided not to ask. A buddy in college once slipped me a heart-shaped stay-awaker, and I not only stayed awake much longer than I desired, I managed to pass a Spanish 301 final, and I wasn't even registered for the course.

"What's this?" a voice said from inside the van.

I turned and looked into the rear. A hippie boy was holding a lava lamp that I had stowed with a lot of other things I had hoped to throw away before I got home.

"That's a lava lamp," I said.

"Okay, but … what is it?"

A crooked smile shaped my lips, the kind of smile that people get when they can't *believe* you've never heard of, for instance, Pepe le Moko. Parents mostly. I thought he was kidding. I thought the cheesiest symbol of commercially co-opted hipness was known and loved throughout the land, along with the beanbag chair. The crooked smile faded when I realized that I had come face-to-face with the brutal reality of the Generation Gap.

"It's a reading lamp," I said, deciding to educate him. "You plug it into a wall socket and this globby stuff inside the base heats up like pancake batter. They designed it so the stuff would float up and down inside the water like … like … ummm …" I couldn't think of anything else that floated up and down.

He was frowning at me, but not like a surly student so much as someone who truly wanted to learn, but wasn't sure he wanted to learn this.

"Why did they design it to do that?" he said.

I stared at him silently for a moment then said, "Because it's cool."

He shrugged. "How much do you want for it?"

How much did I want for it? How much did I want for it!!! Did Theo ask Vincent how much he wanted for *Starry Night*???

"I'm sorry, but that's actually not for sale," I said reaching for it. "I use it as my reading lamp when I'm camping along the road. I plug it into the cigarette lighter on the dash. I guess I should have separated it from the sale items."

He handed it to me with another shrug. I backed away from the van and stood gently cradling the lava lamp in my arms. I had intended to get rid of the thing after someone left it in the backseat of my taxi three years earlier. But now … well … now I was just going to take it home and set it up in a corner of my bedroom.

The boys and girls began picking out the items they wanted. They handed me dollar bills that were so new and crisp they appeared uncirculated. It occurred to me that they might be counterfeit. I always think that about brand-new American dollars. A lot of economists are in line with my thinking there.

I waited curiously to see if any of the boys would bring me belts for barter. After my little free-enterprise speech at the pond, I expected to be overwhelmed by young men wielding leather straps. But everybody was dealing in paper currency. That was all right with me, although I was tempted to explain the tax advantages of avoiding cash transactions in favor of barter.

In the end, I sold no 8-track tapes. But I did sell a handful of cassette tapes, a slew of blouses, some odds and ends, and not one book. I needn't have worried about my sacred texts. But this made me feel bad. What's the matter with young people today? Don't they understand that reading is one of the best forms of escapism ever invented? I blame our school system of course. It has alienated our nation's youth by programming them to believe that books were made for learning.

After the kids drifted away gazing at their treasures, I closed up the van. Windsong was still there. Otto had gone into the house. Now that I was staying overnight, I decided I was in a position to ask-a-million-questions.

"When I was down in Taos some of the people passing through told me about this place, and they mentioned Brother Chakra," I said. "Am I going to meet the good brother?"

"I'm sure you will," she said enigmatically.

Was the game afoot again?

"When?" I said.

She smiled at me. "He will be presiding over the solstice festival tomorrow."

"Do you celebrate every year?" I said.

"We hold a celebration twice a year," she said. "On the longest day of the year and the shortest."

I wanted to ask Windsong if two new recruits named Janet and Vicky—alias Sunshine and Moonbeam—had arrived recently at the hippie compound. But given the fact that I had asked the same question of Otto on Wednesday, it might have blown my cover. I thought about asking a generic question, i.e., how often do you get new arrivals here? But again—Wednesday. I wished I hadn't come here on Wednesday. I started to feel like a novelist who had written half a novel and then wished he hadn't. My problem basically was that I couldn't see into the future. Think how much easier life would be if we could see into the future. It would be dull, but easier.

The screen door opened. I heard bootsteps. I turned and saw Otto standing at the edge of the porch. He crooked a finger. "Windsong, could I talk with you?"

"Yes, Otto."

She went up the steps, and together the two of them entered the house.

I was alone now in the front yard. Everybody had disappeared. I wasn't sure what to do. As much as I dislike crowds, when I'm not in one I feel completely disconnected from humanity. It's a good feeling.

I waited a few minutes for Windsong to come back out. When she didn't show up I started to feel like I was on some kind of alien planet. The planet was silent but for the wind soughing through the trees. Anybody here know how to pronounce "soughing"? I decided to climb into the front seat of my van. It was like an escape pod. I started thinking about Part 3 of *2001: A Space Odyssey*. As you probably know, I hate to nitpick, but it seemed to me that if a Keir Dullea really was fired like a bullet through the total vacuum of outer space, he would have exploded like a hand-grenade before he got halfway to the airlock. And not just Keir Dullea, but anybody. That was one part of *2001* that I didn't buy into. Also Part 4. What the hell was that ending about? It was as if Jackson Pollock had invaded Shepperton Studios, locked Stanley Kubrick in a dressing room, took over the cameras, and told Arthur C. Clark to amscray with the typewriter he rode in on.

After I got settled in the pilot's seat, I felt okay. The sunlight was streaming through the windshield and the heat felt good on my bleached muslin. I hadn't realized how cold it was outside until I got inside. Not winter cold but where's-my-jacket cold. The doors were shut tight, the windows were rolled up, and the silence was reassuring. I felt safe. I knew that I could start the engine and drive away if I chose. I could abandon Janet and Vicky to a fate they had voluntarily embraced, return to my crow's nest, and wallow in guilt for the rest of my life. It was a tough call. Not the wallow-in-guilt part. I often use that as a substitute for action.

But even if I didn't have guilt to look forward to with eager anticipation, I still wanted to see Janet and Vicky alive. Then a thought occurred to me. I could start the engine, drive up past the pond, and follow the road to wherever it led. I was certain of one thing: the kid who had been riding in the rear of the green truck was up there, so I felt that other people would be up there, too. Maybe even Janet and Vicky.

Deductive logic led me to believe this. Normally, most of my logic is *inductive,* which is why I never seem to get anywhere. But inductive logic is safer than deductive logic because deductive logic is based on facts, whereas inductive logic is based on a desire to have a convenient excuse when I'm wrong, as in "Hey, it worked those other times I tried it!"

I pulled out my key, inserted it in the ignition, turned the key clockwise—and tapped the accelerator.

To my surprise, the engine started.

I released the hand brake, put the transmission into gear, and let out the clutch. The van crept forward. I immediately glanced into the rear-view mirror. I watched the front door. I expected Otto to come out and gaze at my van with a frown, then jump to the ground and dive into his pickup and race after me. This had occurred in approximately 23 percent of all the suspense films I had ever seen. I was banking on inductive logic to ruin my plans once again—but it was no-go. Otto did not appear on the porch.

I was deep into it now.

There was no turning back.

CHAPTER 28

I guided the van along the dirt two-track toward the fallen tree. The grade grew steep. I eyeballed the narrow passage between the sectioned tree trunk. It was wide enough for the pickup to pass through, so I was only a little worried about scraping the paint off the sides of the van. If that happened, I was prepared to give Wally a batch of inductive logic.

No problem though. When I got close to the passage I could see that the van would make it unscathed. Plenty of wagon-room. Things were running smoothly. That's when *The Children of the Damned* appeared. I had not even entered the walls of wood before the kids began filtering slowly across the roadway, blocking my path to the adobe plateau. I shifted into neutral and yanked the brake.

The kids were smiling, so they weren't really like the children of the damned. They were more like *The Stepford Wives*, especially the boys. They strolled en masse between the trunks and slowly surrounded the front of the van. A hippie boy tapped on my window. I quickly rolled it down.

"You can't drive up here," he said.

Since I was older than everybody present I said, "Why not?"

"Pollution," he said.

It was as if he had uttered a secret code word that immediately generated bleak images of exhaust pipes, clouds of smog, acid rain, leafless trees, gasping fish, and a suffocating world writhing in the throes of death.

"Oh."

I squinted past the pond and said, "I saw Otto drive his truck up here, so I thought it would be okay."

"No."

He didn't elaborate. I was deprived of the opportusnity to dismantle his system of logic point by point. I've always wanted to do that to somebody.

They obviously did not want me to follow the road to the end, but why? And how did they know to congregate and block my path? These were the thoughts I had as I backed around and drove down to the big house, where Otto and Windsong were standing on the porch watching me. I felt like I was driving toward nuns.

I parked in front of the house and climbed out.

"Where were ya headed there, Doctor Lovebeads?" Otto said amiably, standing at the top of the steps with his hands in his pockets.

"A site for Transcendental Meditation!" I chirped. "Twice a day I find a quiet place to meditate, so I thought I would head up toward timberline and pick a lonely spot to sink into the deep recesses of my mind."

"Oh wow, do you practice TM?" Windsong said.

"Ever since I was a junior in college," I said. "According to the Maharishi, it takes ten years to arrive at cosmic consciousness, so I guess I've been there twice."

"I've always wanted to learn that," Windsong said. "Could you teach it to me?"

I frowned. "I don't know if that's advisable. They told me that I had to keep my mantra a secret, although they didn't say why. But I wouldn't feel right trying to pass along a mantra without official authorization."

"I understand," she said solemnly.

I was glad someone did.

Otto sauntered down the steps. "We don't allow vehicles up on the ridge. It's bad for the environment. I do drive up there every now and then to haul wood or whatever, but we'd prefer that you walk."

"People used to take *snowmobiles* up there before we put a stop to it," Windsong said, with a certain amount of umbrage. There's no umbrage like hippie umbrage. I once knew a woman who tried to convince me to eat vegi-burgers. I don't want to talk about it.

"If you're looking for a place to meditate, why don't you just walk up to the pond?" Otto said. "I'll let the others know that you want to be left alone for a while."

"That would be groovy," I said, as my heart sank. "It only takes about twenty minutes."

"I'll let them know," Otto said. He pulled a two-way radio from his back pocket and spoke into it.

I grinned like a madman and turned away and began walking up the road. Fer the luvva Christ, now I had to act like I was meditating in full view of the entire world. Fortunately, I did know a little bit about TM, having attended an introductory lecture one evening at UCD while waiting for my buddies to get out of a Henry James seminar so we could go to a bar and get wasted.

I passed between the wooden walls with the grin still plastered to my mug, ready to say howdy to all the kids hiding behind the trunks. But after I came out the other side I found the plateau deserted. The saggy adobe watched me as I walked past. I wondered if the hippies used the adobe to sleep in at night. I wondered if the adobe had scorpions. I wondered if the scorpions were watching me. I momentarily forgot that I was in Colorado. I should do that more often.

I made my way up to the pond feeling like an idiot. I now had to pretend to follow through on something I didn't want to do. I do that about three times a year. The last time I did it I was walking toward the front door of a hardware store, but at the last second I realized the store was closed for the evening and the door was locked. I started to turn around and go back to my car but a couple of total strangers were walking along the sidewalk toward me, so I continued on up to the door and stopped at a display window and pretended to examine a wide variety of pipe fittings as if that was the real reason I had approached the store and was not bothered in the least by the fact that the door was locked. I'll admit it. I was too embarrassed to change my mind and turn around in front of people who didn't know me. After the total strangers passed by, I rushed back to my car, got in, and sped away. I don't know if I've ever mentioned this to you, but I need some kind of goddamn therapy.

I walked up to the edge of the pond then looked for a dry spot. I checked the ground for scorpions. I sat down cross-legged with my back to the big house, held my head erect, closed my eyes, and began mumbling, "It doesn't matter, it doesn't matter, it doesn't matter …" I was "faking" a mantra. I don't know why I put that in quotes. I really was faking it.

After five minutes, though, I started to feel strange. I felt like a molecule. I grew completely unaware of my surroundings. Twenty minutes later the molecule began to rise like a glob floating upward in a lava lamp. By the time it reached the light bulb, I had become conscious of my surroundings. I opened my eyes. I felt totally refreshed, alert, and full of energy. I felt as if I could run up the side of the mountain and nobody could stop me. It suddenly occurred to me that I may have stumbled across a way to make lots of money. All I had to do was scribble down the exact step-by-step process by which I had become a molecule and then submit it to the patent office. But I filed that under "L" for "Later." I had less profitable things to do at the moment.

I stood up and studied the side of the hill. The road meandered into the trees and disappeared. I wondered what would happen if I started following the road. By this I meant would my lungs or my legs give out first. If you have never lived near any mountains, let me tell you something about walking up them: don't.

I turned and made my way back down toward the fallen tree. I wanted to take a peek into the adobe and the trailer, but I kept on walking down to the big house. I knew that my every move was being watched. I had known that since the day I was born.

When I got back to the van, there was nobody around again. I couldn't figure out where everybody kept disappearing to. Then I remembered the girl who had used the word "chores" during the self-criticism moment. Suddenly I got scared. Would I be expected to pitch in and help just because I had eaten their food? What had I gotten myself into? I hadn't seen a cow yet, but if there was a cow here, it meant only one thing: hay. I've seen movies about people baling hay, and it can get ugly.

Windsong came out of the house then. So far, I hadn't been invited inside. I wanted to go inside to see if Janet and Vicky might be there, but now that the word "chores" had wormed its way into my brain like an earwig, I started thinking about dirty dishes. Suddenly I didn't want an invitation.

"Where is everybody?" I chirped, as she floated down the steps and came up next to me.

"They're busy making preparations for the solstice celebration tomorrow."

"Do you hold it right here?" I said, making a wide sweep with my arm indicating the front yard.

"Oh no, we hold the celebration up the hill."

"At the pond?" I said.

"No. Higher up in the trees. You'll see it tomorrow. They're putting up the decorations right now. Didn't you ever take part in a solstice celebration down in Taos?"

"I never seemed to be around during the solstices. I was always on the road."

"That's too bad. Well … I'm sure you'll have a wonderful time tomorrow. We'll have lots of visitors."

"I'm looking forward to it. Maybe I can make a few sales."

She raised her chin and, basically, looked down her nose at me. "Nobody works on the solstice."

I nodded. "In that case, maybe I can give away a few things. My sandals are kind of log-jammed."

A smile broke across her face. "That would be wonderful." Everything was "wonderful" with Windsong, unless it was "too bad."

"Well, since I ain't going back to Boulder today, maybe I should find an out-of-the way spot to park my van so folks won't be stumbling over it in the dark. I guess I'll just crash in it tonight."

"You can park over by the side of the house, but you're welcome to sleep in one of the hostels," she said, pointing at the crappy shacks dotting the landscape. "That's where the members of the family sleep."

I nodded. I was thinking more in terms of the comfortable-looking robot trailer, or else the adobe.

"Who sleeps in the adobe cabin up the hill?" I said.

"Nobody," she said.

"Why not?"

"Because it's haunted."

I nodded like an experienced man-of-the-world who wasn't nonplused by weird statements. I had known a few women in college who were involved in Wicca. I learned to take that stuff seriously at keggers, where the other women arrived with dates.

"Who haunts it?" I said.

"We're not sure, but we think it's the ghost of a shepherd who lived there a hundred years ago."

I stuck out my lower lip and nodded as if it all made sense. "I'm not afraid of ghosts," I lied. "Do you think the shepherd would mind if I crashed in there tonight?"

"Yes."

"Oh."

"He lets us use it in the daytime, but at night we leave him alone."

"Have you seen him?"

"No. But we hear him. The shepherd talks."

"What does he say?"

"He whispers in Spanish, so we don't really know what he's saying."

That was as far as I wanted to take this conversation. In college I had failed the Spanish 101 class that I was actually registered for.

Windsong told me she had to go in to prepare food for the evening meal. I told her I would move the van to the side of the house. We parted.

I moved the van, then looked up the hill. Would Janet and Vicky come down out of the hills to sleep in the hostels later that evening? I hoped so. I was prepared to not spend the night in Wally's rattletrap. If I saw Janet and Vicky, I was going to pull out all the stops and do my best to convince them to come back to Denver with me.

That evening a large group of hippies came marching home from the hills. I didn't recognize any of them. At dinnertime there were twice as many strangers surrounding me. Windsong introduced me to the entire group as we sat on the ground with our plates of beans and mugs of milk. I was curious to know if the milk was as fresh as milk can scientifically get. But I was afraid I might be invited to learn how to obtain fresh milk, and from what little I know about milk, it happens before dawn.

I kept waiting to be introduced to Brother Chakra, but apparently he was not present. At that point in time I was still certain that Otto was Brother Chakra. A big campfire was built for the evening meal and the entire family took part in a rousing sing-along. Do you want me to describe it to you?

I didn't think so.

After dinner I went to bed in Wally's rattletrap. I fell asleep wearing my hippie clothes. It hadn't occurred to me to bring a bedroll because I hadn't planned on staying overnight. But that came as no surprise. Things frequently don't occur to me. As a result, I created a "blanket" by covering myself with used blouses. When poor planning collides with hypothermia, only the strong survive.

CHAPTER 29

I slept badly that night. I sleep badly every night. I woke up as refreshed as I ever get and crawled out from under my blouses.

I looked at the dashboard clock: 6:00. I wake up at that time every morning, except Tuesday, Thursday, Saturday, and Sunday. The fact that this was a Saturday did not contradict the hypotheses. "Saturday" is just a word. The fact is, I always wake up at 6:00 A.M. when I have something to do. Sometimes it's cab driving, sometimes it's rescuing people, sometimes it's laundry, usually mine.

I adjusted my love beads, made sure my headband was squared away, yanked my Mexican shirt down to cover my bellybutton, and put on my sandals. The sandals sort of hurt where the straps had rubbed against the skin during the previous day. I should have worn my tennis shoes after all. But I decided to wear the sandals again. Maybe the subtle but ceaseless pain would remind me to think better.

I put on my sunglasses, shoved the doors open, and slid out of the rear of the van. I performed the final step of my wake-up ritual by adjusting my jeans. It is literally impossible to effectively adjust your jeans when you're lying prone. Maybe scientists will invent a method someday, but until then humankind will have to rely on the thumb-yank combined with the primitive technology of the "gravity-tug."

I shut the doors and walked around to the front of the van and saw hippies moving about. They were walking with a step that I would have described as "lighthearted" if I was being interrogated by the police. And why not? The solstice is to hippies what Christmas is to normal people. Ergo, Christmas comes twice a year for hippies. It kind of makes you want to become a hippie, doesn't it? Just think: you would have to buy double the number of presents, and you would get to see your relatives twice a year instead of once every twenty years.

I was scratching the general area around my wallet when Windsong stepped out to the front porch of the big house and looked at me. I quickly pulled out my comb, gave my hair a quick sweep, and put the comb back. Everything was copacetic.

"Good morning, Doctor Lovebeads," she said. "Did you sleep well?"

"Like a top!" I chirped. I placed the tip of my right index finger on my scalp and did a little dervish whirl to show her that I was a zany flower child. It worked. Windsong laughed. I assumed it was a real laugh and not a forced laugh. Believe me, I've ruined enough keggers to recognize a forced laugh as the guests walk out the door.

"One small problem though," I said.

"What's that, Doctor Lovebeads?"

"I need to use the facilities."

She smiled and pointed across the yard. I looked in the direction indicated. I saw what I recognized from the movies as an "outhouse." A half-moon was carved into the door.

Let's jump ahead ten minutes and try not to think about it.

As I was returning to my van, I saw Otto and Brent sauntering toward me. Otto was grinning. "Hey man, happy solstice," he said, raising his right hand. I could see what was coming: the hippie handshake.

"Right on!" I said, and clasped his hand in the ninety-degree angle javelin-grip. "Windsong told me that nobody works on the solstice, so I'll tell you what I'm gonna do. I'm gonna throw my doors open and let your guests take whatever they want for free. I'll be heading back to Taos by sunset anyway and the less weight I'm pulling, the less gas I'll need."

"You are one heavy dude, man," Otto said.

Brent just stood there smiling. He stank of marijuana. It made me think of coffee. That had never happened to me before.

"I don't know if I'm out of line here, man," I said, "but when I'm on the road I usually start the day off with a hot cup of coffee. By any chance do you have any here at the ranch?"

"Tea," Brent suddenly said.

"How's that?" I said.

Brent did not extrapolate.

"We drink tea here," Otto said, "but no coffee." He grinned. "I'm a coffee drinker myself." He shrugged. "The women here do make an especially strong herbal tea that might fool you."

"Hey, I appreciate it," I lied. I wondered if there was a crossroads town near the ranch that I could drive to for some take-out joe. Right at that moment I was willing to bet Otto could be bought cheap. But I didn't want to step too far out of character. Hippies were supposed to be people who gleefully went along with whatever kick was happening at the moment. Or was that looters?

Otto went into the big house. Windsong came out a little later with a clay cup filled with something hot and dark and wet. Use your imagination. I stood there drinking the liquid bark until I heard the grind of gears. I looked off in the direction of the metal gate and saw some cars trundling along the two-track. The invasion of the guests had begun.

I was surprised at how well I took it, but then this was Christmas in June. I knew everything I ever wanted to know about Christmas, since I had gone home to Wichita for the previous one. My sisters had husbands who were about as well known to me as the people who would be arriving during the next few hours, and I had discovered that by not talking to the husbands I wouldn't get to know them even better. I decided to use that strategy among the bedouins who showed up for the festival. This would be made extra easy by the fact that I was in disguise, so even if they did get to know me, it wouldn't be me, it would Doctor Lovebeads.

In a way this reminded me of a costume party I once attended. I was looking for only one girl at that time. This was the girl that I later murdered according to the wisenheimers at Rocky Cab. I never even touched the girl, except when she kissed me—but I'm getting the order of events all mixed up. Let's drop it.

I opened the driver's door and got into my van and popped Butterfly into the 8-track. I'm talking "Gadda." I kept the sound low enough to qualify as background Muzak. But I felt uneasy about bringing electronic technology into the "rain forest." By this I mean that hippies drank tea and smoked certain organic roots, but they also listened to acid rock, most of which was produced in studios, meaning the sounds were unnatural and could not be created without a complex mechanical device such as the cardboard tube that John Lennon sang through to get a "hollow" sound.

I got out and walked around to the side of the van and slid the door open for the big giveaway.

Mi casa, su casa, nature boy.

I hated to do this because it had taken me twenty years to collect a lot of the dusty books that I had never opened, not to mention the LPs I never listened to. I must've had thirty dollars worth of collector's items in there. But I felt that in order to establish trust among the flower people I had to make it look like I didn't care about making money. The fact that I actually didn't care about making money didn't seem adequate unto itself.

I may have misled you when talking about making millions of dollars off best-selling novels. All I ever really wanted was enough money to pay my rent and eat. Books I can get at the library. Clothes, hell, there's clothes scattered all over Denver. And TV? I already have one. Maybe cable cuts into my budget, but who really needs cable? I own a VCR, and tapes are cheap. People sometimes accidentally leave VHS tapes in the backseat of my taxi. Okay, I might as well come clean here. I take the tapes home and watch them before I turn them in to Rollo.

But in the final analysis, the only thing I ever really wanted out of life was to not get out of bed in the morning and go to a job. But I practically didn't do that already. Depending on whether I still had a job the following Monday, I might have to stop not doing that and not do something else. But I would worry about that then. The Birds said it best: "… To everything there is a season, and a time for every purpose under heaven …"

Wait. I think Pete Seeger said that. Or wait. Maybe it's from the Bible. Well, somebody said it best. For all I know, I said it best: "It doesn't matter." That's the Cab Driver's Prayer. A cab driver says it when things start getting so bad that he stands back and takes the long view of things and reminds himself that his shift ends at seven.

A.M. or P.M.

It just doesn't matter.

I gave my books and records one last wistful look, then shook my head. It was all for The Cause.

I picked up a plastic flute that I had bought at SA, sat down cross-legged inside the van, and started randomly tooting. I was just a hippie entrepreneur now, and my flute was my billboard.

I counted the vehicles arriving at the Smith Ranch as I tooted the flute. By ten A.M. four vans, two pickup trucks, and three automobiles had pulled into the property and parked at the outer edge of the front yard. It was old-home week, I could tell. Lots of hippie handshakes and lots of hugging. I myself am not from a hugging family. I don't know if this is true of Irish-Catholics in general, or just we Murphys, but overt physical expressions of affection within the Murphy clan consist of perpetual handshaking. If you ever show up at a Murphy party, saints preserve us, make sure you prepare your right hand. I recommend Corn Huskers® Lotion. You stand warned.

CHAPTER 30

As the newcomers piled out of their vans, I heard the muted crash of tambourines, the squeal of women greeting women, and the undercurrent of men whispering hellos to old members of the various tribes. That's what this was, I could tell—a gathering of the tribes. Maybe the last gathering ever. I mean, how much longer can adults continue to act like me?

But there were children present, too. I didn't have a lot of faith that they would follow in their parent's footsteps though. Believe me, if I had been forced as a child to live like I do now, I would have ended up president of Microsoft. Just the thought of me having access to billions of dollars ought to make your skin crawl too.

It was the kids who first drifted toward my psychedelic daisy-dotted wonderbus. Some were shy and some were brazen. Apparently their upbringing had not affected them because all kids are like that.

"What's this place?" a boy said. He was about eight years old.

"It's a free store," I said.

"Whatcha giving away?" he said, and all of a sudden I realized I had made an error in judgment.

As repulsed as I generally am by the concept of adulthood, there was one thing about grownups I did like. I knew I could count on them not to grab everything in my van and walk away. Adults were "mature" for crying out loud. But I had uttered the magic word "free" in the presence of kids.

Yikes.

I handed the boy the musical instrument.

"Flutes," I said.

He handed it back. "I don't know how to play a flute," he said.

"Me neither," I said. I blew on the flute making it screech. The kids laughed. Making kids laugh—this I knew how to do.

But for a fraction of a second I became a Little League coach. I wanted the kid to give the toy a try. Come on, boy, don't be a quitter! Choke up on that bat! Follow through on your swing! Slide, slide! Face it—the most bizarre aspect of adulthood is the belief that kids have to be taught how to play. I say give the kids a baseball and … then … just … walk … away.

But I felt bad. I didn't have much of anything in the van that qualified as toys. And why would I? I hadn't known that a solstice celebration was scheduled. I didn't come prepared. You can carve that on my tombstone.

Otto walked out of the big house and sauntered down the steps. He strolled over to the spot where I was sitting and peered beyond my shoulder. "Just between you and me," he said, "how much do you want for that Iron Butterfly cassette?"

I glanced around at the cardboard box where the tapes were tastefully scattered. "Make me an offer, man," I said.

"Two bucks."

"All yours," I said. "I'll tell ya what though. I'll sell you the eight-track version for one buck."

"No thanks," he said, slipping me two bucks. I had the feeling he didn't want Windsong to see this exchange of cash on solstice day. He handed it to me surreptitiously. I slipped him the cassette. You would have thought we were dealing in drugs if you were an optimist.

"Listen," I said. "I'll *give* you the eight-track version for free."

He pursed his lips, then shook his head no.

I handed one of the dollars back to him and said, "Please. I'll pay you to take it out of here."

"You drive a hard bargain, dude."

He reached into the box and grabbed the 8-track version of "Gadda." I was ecstatic. I felt like a novelist who had talked a vanity press into publishing his memoirs.

He examined the plastic box, then lowered it and looked at my bleached muslin. "Nice shirt," he said. "Looks like the real article. Where did you get it?"

"Tijuana," I replied.

"When were you in TJ?" he said.

"That's kind of hard to say. As far as I was able to determine from witness statements, it was during a spring break in college."

He nodded again. "Where did you go to college?"

"UC ..." I started to say, meaning UCD. But I caught myself in time and quickly transformed the letters "U" and "C" into the words "You" and "see" as in "You see, I went to a number of different colleges before I graduated, but I was a student at Kansas Agricultural University when I woke up in Tijuana next to a bottle of tequila. How that bottle got there I'll never know. The policia filled in the rest of the details. Apparently I had bought this shirt at an outdoor flea market, although there seemed to be some dispute over the word 'bought.' I failed Spanish in college."

I could tell by the look in his eyes that he understood my explanation about as well as I understood the Mexican legal system. Then his eyes dropped a notch and focused on the double loop strung around my neck.

"Nice beads," he said. "Did you buy them in TJ, too?" I glanced down at the love beads.

I shook my head no.

"I bought them at Woodstock. A flower child was selling hand-made necklaces from a tent."

"You were at Woodstock?" he said with his eyebrows raised.

"That's what my lawyer tells me."

He nodded and continued to gaze at the beads, then he looked me in the eye. "Is the necklace for sale?"

I reached down and began fingering the beads, and shook my head no. "It would be impossible to put a price on a genuine souvenir carried away from the biggest luv-in of the sixties," I said, perhaps the most irrelevant truth that ever fell from my lips.

"I can dig it, man," he said, then he turned and walked away.

I raised the remaining dollar bill with both hands, then squeezed and snapped it a couple times. I saw Otto walk past a trash barrel. He dropped the 8-track into the barrel. That really made me feel like a novelist.

I reached into my book box, pulled out a paperback, and placed the dollar bill inside it. I did this unconsciously. It was a habit. I feel compelled here to state that doing things unconsciously with money is not a good habit to get into. But I had other things on my mind.

I was hoping that Vicky or Janet would show up, at which point I might be able to talk them into going home. I knew I had to leave the safety and security of my van and start mingling with the crowd. There hadn't been any new arrivals during the past half-hour. Maybe this was the entire guest list. I wanted to know how many people might be frowning at me when I tried to take Janet and Vicky away. It might set a new record for mass frowning. I set the old one in college. It happened at KAU during Crazy Days, a spring break festival. Believe it or not, the frowning had nothing to do with my streaking incident. But given the high tolerance level of college students when it comes to bizarre behavior, it's probably best we move on.

I began drifting toward the middle of the front yard, where people were dancing the "upraised-arms" dance that you see on the "Greatest Hits of the 60s!" infomercials filmed at love-ins.

Excuse me. Luv-ins.

Some of the hippies had formed a kind of conga line and were dancing around in a large circle. Within the circle were more hippies doing the arm dance. Hippies were seated on the ground playing guitars. Tambourines were being slapped. Woodwinds were being played, though not flutes. I don't know what the instruments were. I was in band for only three weeks before I dropped out. My Maw was furious. The music store that sponsored the Blessed Virgin grade school orchestra gave ten free lessons with a private tutor if you bought a musical instrument. "Those ten free lessons are going to waste!" Maw snarled. I wanted badly to argue with her logic, but I was afraid I might lose the argument and have to go back to band practice. I played the trumpet. Badly. I still have the trumpet. It is an object of hatred. But I can't bring myself to throw it away because it cost my parents one hundred dollars, and that was in 1960 dollars. God only knows how worthless it is today.

I decided to join the conga line. I was so swept up in the freewheeling festivities that I momentarily forgot that I was forty-five on a mountain. Even in San Diego I wouldn't have found enough oxygen to last eight musical bars. I placed my hands on the shoulders of a girl in front of me. That part was okay. We hopped and kicked, hopped and kicked. Then I felt someone's hands on my shoulders. They were large. Suddenly it wasn't fun anymore. I felt trapped. I'll be frank here. I had gotten myself into another mess. A small mess, admittedly. Even an insignificant mess. But I couldn't *breathe* fer the luvva Christ.

"Improvise!" a voice inside my head pleaded. It was Joanne Woodward, and she sounded exhausted.

I thought about pretending to trip and fall down. Crude but effective. Yet I was afraid the people behind me might see right through me and get suspicious. This has stopped me from doing more things in my life than you might believe. How about a coughing fit? Maybe the dancers would think I had been toking jays. People who smoke marijuana cough frequently, so I've been told. Not to get off the point here, but the legalization of pot could feasibly result in filter-tipped reefers. As a health-related issue that's certainly a strong argument, if not totally disingenuous.

Then I saw a hippie ahead of me drop his hands and walk away from the conga line. My God—talk about up front. Where did he find the courage to do exactly what he felt like doing? Hippies were a breed apart.

I swallowed hard. I decided I was going to drop my hands from the warm shoulders of the girl in front of me and walk away. I had a problem though. What if the people behind me thought I was imitating the boy?

My shoulders drooped. Why oh *why* did I join the conga line?

The music suddenly stopped and everybody walked away.

I stood in the middle of the yard not knowing which direction to go. All of the points of the compass had been "taken" by one or another person. No matter which way I went it might look like I was trying to be like someone else rather than going my own way as would a spiritually enlightened follower of the true path.

***

The dinner bell rang.

I fell in lock-step with the crowd hiking up the hill. I realized that my lifelong contempt for the herd mentality had blinded me to the benefits of complicity. Right then and there I vowed to myself that when I got back to Denver, I would never again do my own thing.

The adobe plateau was smaller in area than the yard down by the big house. Ergo, due to the nature of solids, the human bodies were clustered closer together. That's just a roundabout way of saying it was crowded. I guess I could have just said that. I know that my English teacher in high school, Sister Mary Xavier, probably would not have approved of my admittedly frequent use of extraneous words as well as quotation marks and long dashes—such as this—when trying to make a "point." But in my defense, I already knew how to speak English when I entered first grade, and I did not talk like Ernest Hemingway. For one thing he had a lisp, which most people don't know about. He couldn't pronounce his R's clearly. When you hear him speak on Caedmon records, he sounds like Elmer Fudd. I've often wondered if the lisp had anything to do with his macho posturing, and whether a grade school speech teacher might have badgered him to pronounce his R's correctly to the point that he rebelled by becoming one of the greatest prose stylists of the twentieth century just to show up the egghead with the hickory stick. That might make a good extra-credit research paper for a college student who has nothing else to do and no reason to go on living.

It quickly became obvious to me that not all of the guests at the feast were vegetarians. I could smell hamburgers cooking. The hippies themselves did not seem to have a distinct odor. For one thing there was not, as I said, much air at that altitude, and for another thing I had driven a cab for fourteen years and my olfactory senses had gone the way of the Dodo during year five.

I noticed that when it came to distributing the food among forty or fifty people, it was indistinguishable from a picnic attended by the bourgeoisie: people were patiently lined up with paper plates, kids were screaming, mothers were admonishing them. Need I go on? Don't you have a family? Haven't you ever been dragged to a picnic?

I played it cool though. I didn't take any meat. Not even chicken. Doctor Lovebeads was a strict leaf-eater. I didn't want to give anybody even the slightest cause to suspect that I was rational.

Since I was a virtual stranger at the gathering, it didn't really matter where I sat. Plus there was the fact that everybody here was open and up front and willing to let each other groove on his own vibe. I grooved on my own vibe once in sixth grade and ended up standing on top of my desk. It's a long story that pre-dates the Beatles. Let's move on.

I held my plate of twigs close to my body as I wandered among the picnickers. I tried to make it look like I was searching for the ideal spot to sit down on the late great planet earth and commune with my food. But in truth I was looking for Janet and Vicky. I didn't see them. I didn't know what bizarre changes they might have undergone during their week at Brother Chakra's "Luv Asylum," as I had begun to think of this place. I get pretty sarcastic above five thousand feet.

I gave up and planted myself on the ground near the trickling stream where a man and a woman wearing ponchos were eating from bowls.

"Nice huaraches," I said by way of introduction.

"Hey thanks, man," the hippie replied, raising his chin and talking with his mouth full of beans.

"Are they hand-made?" I said. My intent was to bring up the subject of my traveling wonderbus and hippie emporium. In this way, I might be able to dominate the conversation and thus avoid listening to anything they had to say. My long-range goal was to keep them occupied until the end of the feast so I would not have to introduce myself to anyone else.

The hippie looked down at his sandals and shook his head. "I don't know, man, we got 'em used."

"Where did you buy them?"

"Taos," he said. "That's where we live."

CHAPTER 31

I don't normally having coughing fits when I hear things that give most people coughing fits, but his statement came out of left field. The next thing I knew fists were pounding on my back. Then someone gave me the Heimlich Maneuver.

Keir Dullea flew out of my mouth.

People started gathering around saying, "Are you all right? Are you all right?" I was still gagging but they kept saying, "Are you all right? Are you all right?" Jaysus, why do people do that?

But choking half to death may have been the smartest move I ever made. By curling into a ball on the ground, I had inadvertently ended what may have turned out to be an embarrassing conversation. As I stated earlier, it was true that I had once been to Taos but I did not know the area well enough to discuss the layout of the town with someone who lived there. Even as I was wiping tears from my eyes and checking my chin for spittle, I was making plans to get away from these kids. All I needed was Windsong to traipse by and say something like "Hey, you guys must know Doctor Lovebeads, he's from Taos *too!*"

I won't keep you in suspense. She didn't.

"What a trip!" I choked, as I stood up. I didn't know what became of my plate of beans. And I didn't care. I just wanted out of there. I had drawn attention to myself and not in a good way. I often do that at Sweeney's.

I stepped over people seated on the ground and carefully picked my way toward the adobe. I noticed that a hippie was filming me. Naturally I had to assume that he had captured me choking forever on film, although technically it was a video-tape camera. But there was no getting around it—the noun "film" had become a verb during the past hundred years, and then it had been driven further from it's original source by people who cared so little about linguistic derivation that the word now referred to activities completely unrelated to acetate. On the other hand, some people still referred to acetate as "celluloid," but that was more of a charming affectation than criminal assault on the English language.

I staggered over to the adobe, but before I was able to step inside, Windsong appeared in the doorway.

"Are you enjoying yourself, Doctor Lovebeads?" she said.

"No," I said. "Some food went down the wrong pipe and I choked. Could I get a glass of water?"

"Certainly." She took me by the hand and led me a few steps along the front of the cabin and set me down on a wooden bench. "I'll be right back," she said.

I had not yet been invited into the big house, and apparently I was not going to be allowed inside the adobe. So far the only structure on the ranch not off-limits to me was the outhouse. I counted my blessing.

Windsong brought out a clay cup and handed it to me. I drank the water. I really did need it. It felt strange not to be doing something fraudulent for the first time in years.

After I finished the water, I pointed at the Lucy/Desi trailer and asked Windsong who lived there.

She sat down on the bench next to me. "Nobody," she said.

"Why not?" I said. "It looks mighty comfortable."

"It's cursed," she said.

I raised the cup and pretended to drink more water, even though the cup was empty. But I had done this ever since I was a little kid, pretending to drink water or soda or milk when in fact I was collecting my thoughts. It felt good to be a fraud again.

I lowered the cup.

"Does it have a ghost, too?"

"No," she said. "But it has a legend."

"Groovy," I said. "What's the legend?"

She pointed at the tricking stream that gamboled down from the pond. "It is said that a man from the city bought this property many years ago, and towed this trailer here with a pickup truck and set it next to the adobe. He wanted to live on the land but he did not want to be a part of the land. He diverted the water from the stream for his sink and shower and toilet. This angered the spirit of the shepherd who lives in the cabin, and so the spirit removed the life from the tree. A week after the trailer was brought to the ranch, the tree fell over and blocked the road. The man was so frightened that he left the next morning and never returned. He was forced to leave the trailer here because there was no way to get it around the tree."

I looked at the trailer, then I looked at the tree. I enjoyed the story so much that I decided not to scoff. I felt like a member of the White House press corps.

"Did the spirit of the adobe get mad when you chopped the tree in half?" I said.

"I hadn't arrived here yet. But after Brother Chakra bought the property, he held a cleansing ceremony and apologized to the shepherd for the desecration of the land, and asked permission to carve a path through the tree so we could travel up and down his mountain."

Mister Ask-A-Million-Questions wanted to know if the ghost actually replied, but who was I to disparage someone's creative imagination. I once wrote a book called *Draculina,* although the replies I got were rejection slips.

"So nobody uses the trailer?" I said.

No," Windsong said. "If anyone were to enter the trailer, the shepherd would be displeased."

"What would happen?" Mister A asked.

"We would all have to leave the ranch, and the entire mountain would be cursed forever."

I had to admit I had never come across a better story line on *Gilligan's Island*—except the episode where Wrongway Feldman was discovered in the jungle. Imagine living alone on an island for decades, and then Bob Denver shows up.

"I would really like to meet Brother Chakra," I said. "He sounds like one cool head."

"Oh you'll meet him later tonight," Windsong said, standing up and adjusting her Mama Cass dress. "After the sun sets beyond the mountain range we are all going to walk together to the top of the ridge for the final ceremony."

"What do you mean, what's that, what's *final* about it?" I said, probably nervously.

"The celebration of the moon," she said. "The solstice marks the longest day of the year and the shortest night of the year. The sun is the yin, and the moon is the yang. Together they give birth to the day."

The next day, I hoped.

Windsong took the clay cup and floated back into the adobe. I stood up and looked at the trailer. I noticed that the windows were not merely closed but covered with what appeared to be burlap. Nice and battened down. I didn't believe for one second that the ghost of the adobe had forbidden anyone to use the trailer. I figured the trailer was where Brother Chakra stashed all the dope he sold to people like Billy who came to the ranch to score. For all I knew, the trailer was wired with dynamite so the evidence could be destroyed at the push of a button if the feds raided the ranch.

As I turned and strolled casually away, I wondered why my imagination didn't work like that when I was seated in front of my goddamn RamBlaster.

After lunch, a kind of siesta settled over the compound. There were no more conga lines. People reclined to digest and catch some Z's. Others drifted up to the pond to wade and float. They couldn't really swim very well in the pond since it was only three feet deep. Okay. I'll admit it. I sort of wandered up to the pond where a dozen naked people were. I think I'll just let that sentence end with the word "were," even though Sister Mary Xavier would not have approved. A lot of things were going on up at the pond of which she would not have approved. In spite of the fact that the people at the pond all had long hair, I was easily able to distinguish the men from the women.

I stayed only a minute though. Maybe four. But I knew I would be expected to remove my clothes if I wanted to hang out. I'm fairly intuitive when I'm around naked people. Call it a gift.

I wandered back down toward the big house and climbed into my van. I decided to catch some Z's too. If there was going to be a festival taking place at night, I wanted to make sure I had plenty of energy. I had learned this in college. Not in class but outside the classroom where the real learning takes place. Whenever a kegger was scheduled for a Saturday night, I grabbed a few Z's ahead of time so I would always be the last person to leave the party, not counting the hosts.

That was one of the reasons I had attended the introductory

seminar on Transcendental Meditation. A friend had told me that TM gives you a burst of renewed energy that can last for hours, and yet the meditation itself takes only twenty minutes, so I was curious about it. The teachers at the seminar did a pretty good job of explaining what TM was about, how it worked and so forth, but then came The Catch. Everything has to have a *catch*. But the catch wasn't the fact that you had to pay fifty bucks in order to learn the technique. Hell, I'm a firm believer in exchanging pieces of worthless paper for practically everything. But what stopped me was the fact that you had to meditate *twice a day!*

When I heard that I almost fell off my folding chair. They told us that you had to meditate once in the morning and once in the evening. Yumping Yiminy! In the first place, how was I supposed to get up in the morning and then sit down and close my eyes and meditate after sleeping for twelve hours? I was perfectly willing to meditate once a day if it meant I would eventually attain cosmic consciousness, but twice a day at twenty minutes per session? Who the hell wants an "obligation" hanging over his head the moment he wakes up? It was called "pushups" in the army.

Anyway, that's why I never became cosmic. But I did save fifty bucks.

***

The sun was setting when I woke up inside the van. I glanced at the dashboard clock. I had slept from one in the afternoon until seven in the evening, and not one hippie had paid the slightest attention to my absence. It made me feel unpopular and lonesome. Things were running smoothly.

I crawled out of the van, made quick use of the gravity-tug, adjusted my love beads, and made a quick run to the half-moon inn.

When I got back to the van, Windsong came out of the big

house and told me that I had missed the evening meal but she had saved a plate of food for me. "You must be hungry after all that vomiting."

She could read my mind.

I took a seat on the porch while she went to get the food. She brought out a plate of beans and a cup of milk. I scooped up a spoonful of beans ... but suddenly I grew wary. Otto had told Brother Chakra that I was here, and then had given me an unexpected invitation to the festival. What if this food was drugged? What if someone had laced the gravy with acid. Did you ever see *Soylent Green*? If so, then you doubtless will understand my reluctance—although I will say that there isn't any LSD in the movie. However I am forbidden by California state law to reveal the secret of Soylent Green.

I was truly starving though. I had never used LSD before so I had to go with inductive logic. I gulped it down. As far as I know the logic worked. I remember everything that happened that night, and I don't mean with the clarity of someone whose senses have been heightened artificially. Whenever I heighten my senses artificially, I'm lucky to remember my address. I always call Yellow Cab to take me home from Sweeney's. I'm afraid that if I call Rocky Cab, Big Al might show up and drive me to a halfway house.

As the ball of the solstice sun sank toward the distant peaks of the Rocky Mountains, the tribes gathered in the area fronting the adobe cabin. I walked up the hill with Windsong. We passed between the hand-hewn ends of the tree and came out onto the plateau where everyone was seated on the ground.

Windsong led me toward the adobe. We crossed the creek and sat down on the ground with our feet almost touching the trickling stream. We were at the rear of the crowd. It was like sitting in the last row of a movie theater. We waited for the show to begin. The main feature was the end of the day.

A silence fell over the mountaintop. No people talking. No babies crying. No birds singing. No crickets chirping. No breeze blowing. No weeds rustling. Shadows began to spill down from the peaks. They stretched across the plateau. They moved slowly at first, then accelerated and swept over us as the yellow ball of the sun sank behind a purple peak leaving a dazzling spray of golden light rising against a deepening blue sky. For the first time in my life I understood landscape painting. But I still don't understand Jackson Pollock.

CHAPTER 32

As if an unspoken signal had been given, people started rising from the ground and strolling toward the road that led up past the pond. I noticed that not everybody joined the slow parade. The people who had brought children stayed back. Some of the men whom I took to be fathers gave their wives and kids a hug and then joined the march. The women began building a bonfire near the stream. The few men who stayed behind began playing guitars and flutes, and the children began playing games—tag, hide-and-seek, etc. The party on the ridge appeared to be for adults only, but I joined anyway.

Windsong walked alongside me. We made our way up past the pond and into the trees where the road took hairpin turns along the slope. The laughter of children faded behind us. The darkness was almost complete beneath the canopy of pines. I could barely see the lighter shade of the road at my feet. The sensation of following a mob and listening to their feet tramping on the earth made me feel important. Like I said, I need some kind of goddamn therapy.

Then I began to hear things. At first it sounded like wind chimes, i.e., tinkling plates of glass hung on threads. Then I heard piping sounds, as if musicians were playing … flutes. I raised my chin and looked over the heads of the mob, which was easy because we were going uphill. I saw a glow beyond the trees. As I looked at the glow, it became brighter. I sensed that the source of the light was being controlled by one of those dimmer-switches that you can pick up at Radio Shack or any other store that sells electrical devices that can add a homey feeling to your refinished basement or game room. That was how my mind was working. When you get toward timberline in the Colorado high country, you start thinking about the things you left behind—some people call it "civilization."

When I was in the Boy Scouts I used to bring cans of Franco-American spaghetti on overnight camping trips. The other scouts would laugh at me. They would spend all day trying to catch fish, and attempting to cook potatoes that had been wrapped in tinfoil buried under hot coals. It took them hours to fill their bellies with fish bones and undercooked spuds. By that time I was snoring in my tent with a smile on my face. All the other scouts hated me, which made it so much easier to resign from the troop after the near-disaster of my week at summer camp. It's a long story. Let's move on.

As we drew closer to the brightening light, the sounds of flutes became mixed with the soft pounding of drums. This, too, had a dimmer-switch quality. It was as though whoever was waiting for us at the top of the ridge was aware of our proximity and was adjusting the intensity of light and sound to coincide with our arrival.

For perhaps the first time in my life, I was correct in terms of wild guesses.

The parade came around a last hairpin-turn, and suddenly a burst of music filled the air. The lights on the ridge were cranked to full intensity. I don't know how I managed not to turn back and run blindly into the darkness. Maybe it was common sense. They say mountain air gives a man a real appetite for survival.

Then I saw it: The Arch.

A rustic wooden gateway had been constructed in the middle of the road. It was the height and width of a phone booth. Colored bulbs outlined the gate from the base to the rounded top. It was like an entrance to a carnival.

"Welcome friends and family!" a deep voice hollered. By now the members of the parade had begun talking, applauding, laughing, even cheering as they filtered through the gate. I saw a hand-painted day-glo sign that said "Entrance." When I got closer I saw these words printed below it: "Welcome to the Theater of the Mind. Leave Your Body Outside."

Oh no.

I suddenly had the gut-wrenching feeling that I was in for a whole heap of cuteness.

The parade slowed to a virtual standstill as the people at the front passed beneath the arch. I'm talking your basic bottleneck. This was further proof that the laws of physics are indifferent to everything—although I'm not sure how they feel about prisms, the Disneyland of electromagnetic radiation.

When it came our turn to enter the burlesque of the brain, I allowed Windsong to go in ahead of me. I was being polite—I wasn't hiding behind her, I swear. I could just as easily have walked around the gate. I wonder why Ma Bell stopped making enclosed phone booths. In fact, I wonder why she started making them in the first place. Did Alexander Graham Bell see an opportunity to gouge people whose Model T's had broken down in the boonies?

The deep voice welcoming everybody was coming from a man wearing a large mask, which appeared to be fashioned out of papier mâché. It was obviously handmade and consisted mostly of a smile with two small eyes above it. Basically the entire thing was a two-foot wide cartoon mouth with giant white teeth.

"Welcome friends and family!" the voice boomed, as Windsong and I walked into what I will describe as a "fairground"—or "fairgrounds." I have as much trouble with plurals as I have with Algebra.

I matched the barker smile-for-smile, but I didn't say anything.

I thought it best to keep mum until I had scoped out the terrain because I sometimes have problems with my vocal chords. I often hear them saying things before my brain has completed the edit and is ready to send the copy down to the printer. As I stated earlier, it's almost as if there are two people running things from my neck up, although I suspect there might be three, one of them being Joanne Woodward. And I guess me makes four.

I raised my eyes to the tall pines as I walked into the clearing where the nighttime solstice celebration was scheduled to take place. Colored lights had been strung from tree to tree, along with glittering items analogous to Christmas-tree ornaments—strips of tin and colored balls, and what appeared to be small Japanese lanterns. The whole scene put me in mind of hard work. I tried not to think about it.

I looked ahead toward the center of the grounds and saw costumed people dancing among the guests. They were decked out in tights and pied shirts and masks, some of them pretending to blow on woodwinds, or pretending to strum string instruments. A few of the harlequins were carrying balloons, others pinwheels, others pennants. In the middle of the clearing a low fire was being tended by a man dressed in red tights and wearing a devil-head mask. He was poking at the embers with a trident that had a jerry-built look to it, just like the masks. This made sense because these were hippies, people who had turned their backs on modern industrialization, idealists who believed in manufacturing products utilizing the old-fashioned methods—some people call it "hand-crafted." I call it "nice try."

The motif had a medieval look to it, but it was not restricted to the epoch of the Black Plague. For one thing, the music wafting in the air dissolved from one form to another, from rock 'n' roll to classical to modern jazz, as if someone behind the scenes was manipulating a sound board. On top of that, there were floodlights attached to the trees and poles as well as three shacks that stood at the far edge of the clearing. The lights brightened and dimmed in conjunction with or in counterpoint to the music—again, as if someone was in control of a board of dimmer-switches. I'm talking orchestration here. A show was being put on by the host for the entertainment of the guests. Or maybe—just maybe—the guests were being put on for the entertainment of the host.

The sight of the devil toying with fire was my first indication that this was more than a mere party—it was a performance. The people in costumes were dancing and hopping around and—worst of all—miming in front of the guests who were drifting about. Most of the costumed people had masks, but not all of them. Men and women made out to look like mock butlers and maids were roaming around the crowd with trays of snacks. A hippie girl who looked like a scullery maid pranced up to me toting a tray of brownies and held it up. I plucked a brownie from the tray and started to take a bite. Then I stopped. I don't want to say exactly why I stopped. Let's just say that I once ate a brownie in college and decided I had eaten enough brownies to last a feller a lifetime.

The maid danced off into the crowd and I stood there with my brownie in my hand. I started to get paranoid. Oddly enough that's what happened to me in college. I looked down at the snack in my hand and wondered if the eggs and flour were being absorbed through my fingertips.

I looked at Windsong, who was just finishing her own brownie. "Hate to bring this up," I said, "but are there any facilities here at the fair?"

"Come with me," she said.

She took my hand and drew me through the crowd. We came

to the edge of the clearing where she pointed toward another moonhouse. It was off in the darkness, just at the edge of the circle of light cast by the tree bulbs. "The entrance is on the other side," she said.

I walked into the darkness and stepped around to the front of the outhouse.

And froze.

The outhouse didn't have a door.

Fer the luvva crimenently. This was beyond cute. But the "front" of the outhouse did face the deep woods, which were filled with underbrush so thick that it was highly unlikely anybody would take a stroll past the facilities. I assumed that the people who had built this architectural wonder had based their concept of privacy on logic. I didn't know whether it was inductive or deductive logic and I didn't want to know. Did I ever tell you how I used to place a towel over the mirror in our bathroom in Wichita when I was a kid? The odds of any hippies seeing me from the darkness of the deep woods was about the same as the odds of a television camera being hidden behind our bathroom mirror in Kansas during the late 1950s—but what's that got to do with my brain?

Fortunately none of this mattered. I was there for one reason and one reason only: to toss a brownie.

I raised the snack and squinted at the dark circular negative space in the center of the wooden seat. Then I let gravity take over. The brownie disappeared from view. After that I hung around for a bit pretending I was using the circle. Thank goodness the entrance was facing away from civilization, my favorite direction.

I finally stepped back around into the light and saw Windsong standing there. My paranoia suddenly increased. Why would anybody hang around a public toilet? One explanation was obvious, since it was not unlike a public telephone booth, but I didn't know where the other explanation that popped into my head came from and I didn't want to know. Then I started wondering if I had made any funny noises while I was "using" the outhouse. Then I wondered if I ought to have intentionally made some funny noises just to give my "pantomime" verisimilitude. I was obviously getting uptight. I told myself to mellow out. Perhaps I should have eaten that brownie after all.

We strolled into the crowd. I noted that the maids and butlers were no longer carrying trays. They were scurrying around taking people by the shoulders and guiding them here and there, making them stand still in seemingly random spots. As the minutes passed, I could see that everybody in the clearing was going to be subjected to this peculiar ritual. The statue-like guests were being spaced out on one side of the clearing, and it became apparent that they were acting as a kind of parameter for the borders of what was becoming a "grouping." The guests were going along with it. It seemed to be all in fun. If a statue moved, a butler would go after the person and bring him back and point at the earth with a kind of Harpo Marx vexation—outthrust lower-lip with an exaggerated frown—i.e., "Stay!"

I resigned myself to the fact that it would soon be my turn to be forced against my will to take part in what could only be interpreted as "audience-participation" theater. I knew all about audience participation. I once had a date with a girl in college who talked me into going to one of those gigs. I had been reluctant, but I figured it might pay off around midnight.

It didn't.

Then I got an idea.

CHAPTER 33

Three-fourths of the guests were already standing motionless on one side of the clearing. The rest of the guests were milling around on the other side, awaiting their turns to be guided toward the group. At this point I—Doctor Lovebeads—walked up to the fire and stood in front of the devil, raised my arms as well as one leg in mock-surprise … and froze.

I held this position until I got the desired response, which was attention. Grabbing the spotlight during large gatherings of people was something I had gotten relatively good at when I was a kid. Believe me, when you come from an Irish-Catholic clan the size of County Cork, getting anybody's attention is a major achievement. Back in those days I was competing with uncles who seemed to think that in their youths they had performed onstage with George M. Cohan. Before a party ended, half of them thought they actually were George M. Cohan. I never understood their mindset until I drank my first beer and discovered that I was Eddie Foy.

It was risky, though, to strike a posture in front of the masked devil. What if the butlers interpreted this as encroaching on their territorial imperative as actors, and began to resent it. On the other hand, what if they thought I was just trying to be cool and completely ignored me? I would have come off looking like a buffoon. I've had experience with that, mostly in high school … and to a certain extent in the army … as well as in college … and in Sweeney's Tavern. Anyway, I guess it wasn't really that much of a risk, all things considered. I'm so used to looking like a buffoon that sometimes I go out of my way to appear idiotic just so I can observe the responses of people who are deriding me. There's a certain viscerally satisfying sense of power in manipulating the emotions of people who … well … perhaps it's best I not speak of these things.

A maid and a butler scurried over to me and began examining my frozen body in an exaggerated fashion. I hope that my repeated use of the word "exaggerated" doesn't bother you. It's just that this whole scene was like a silent movie in which the actors were required to express themselves with distorted facial and body movements, and to me "exaggerated" says it all. Why leaf through some fancy-pants East Coast pseudo-intellectual thesaurus looking for a synonym when I've got a salt-of-the-earth working-man adjective that everyone comprendos?

Anyway, the butler and maid reminded me of the prehistoric monkey-men in *2001* examining the black obelisk. They approached me at a crouch. They raised and lowered their necks as they studied my frozen limbs. They didn't seem to be bothered by the fact that I had presumed to join their troupe without an audition. I was banking on the hope that they would appreciate a guest joining in on the fun. My success rate at joining in on fun averages 17 percent in the real world, but these were actors, people to whom reality was just something you did when you needed money.

They began signaling to the other actors who were wearing masks. The masked people ran over and squatted on the ground and began chattering gibberish. Then they did something that took me by surprise: they took me by surprise. They grabbed hold of my stiff limbs and lifted me up and carried me over to the front of the group. They positioned me so that I could see directly across the clearing, then they scuttled away.

At this point I could not help but feel that my status at the solstice celebration had risen in the eyes of all the guests. By joining in on the fun and risking his ego in front of a gathering of total strangers, that wacky Doctor Lovebeads could now be considered "in with the in-crowd." I was a citizen above suspicion.

Then my uplifted leg began to grow tired.

I realized I had made a terrible mistake.

What if I lowered my leg and one of the monkeys dashed over like an obsessive/compulsive prehistoric perfectionist and made me raise it again?

Fer the luvva Christ, I was back in the conga line.

I considered the option of lowering my leg at such a molecularly slow rate of speed that the tip of my sandal would eventually rest upon the ground without anybody noticing what I had done. But it occurred to me that people might see through that maneuver and "know" that I was trying to avoid embarrassment. Is there anything more embarrassing than getting caught trying to avoid it?

Then I thought of collapsing like a marionette with its strings cut. This would be in keeping with the playful nature of the evening—although they might think I was having a heart attack. I was forty-five, after all.

Then I thought of falling over while maintaining my frozen posture, like a statue blown over by the wind.

While I was pondering these options, my thigh muscle gave out and my foot dropped to the ground. Nobody paid any attention.

"Hear ye! Hear ye!" someone shouted.

I lowered my arms to my sides. This made me look like everyone else. I was just a face in the crowd now, but I didn't give a damn. I simply was not athletic enough to remain "special."

The door opened on a shack across the clearing. A costumed

masked man strutted out. The mask was shaped like a giant megaphone. It magnified the speaker's voice.

"The unbinder of minds hereby releases you from your bonds!"

At this point everybody but me sat down. Apparently the participants had done this before. I was the only person ignorant of the significance of the megaphone man's statement. I stood alone in the crowd feeling kind of special. But it was not a good special. I sat down.

"Brother Chakra would like to thank everybody who has come here to the ridge to celebrate the solstice and to take part in the induction ceremony!"

That caught my attention. After all, "induction" didn't necessarily mean being forced by the army to think logically for two years. Take my word for it.

"Tonight we have two new initiates who are going to be brought into the family. And the fact that the induction is taking place on the solstice adds to the special nature of this occasion."

I bristled when I heard the word "special" in reference to someone else.

I had barely gotten my hackles up when two people emerged from the door of the shack. Two women. I knew the women. I had once driven them from Denver to Red Rocks Amphitheater. When I took them there I thought I was giving them a free ride, but now I wasn't so sure.

The megaphone man raised his hand toward the girls as they strolled into the center of the clearing. They were wearing simple white dresses with hems that barely touched the ground. The girls looked like ... well ... virgins. I tried not to think about that. "May I introduce Sunshine and Moonbeam!"

The crowd applauded. I heard tambourines. I heard flutes. I glanced around but didn't see anyone playing musical instruments.

It was like hearing live canned music, if such a thing is possible—not hearing it, but being it.

"Sunshine and Moonbeam used to live in the city!" the megaphone man said.

The crowd booed. I was ambivalent about this, since I knew which city they came from.

"But they escaped!" he shouted.

Cheers.

"Sunshine and Moonbeam made their escape to Brother Chakra's sanctuary, where tonight they are going to be welcomed into the family during the disinfecting of the mind ceremony!"

I started to get edgy. I didn't know what this disinfecting ceremony was, but I did know that I had a distaste for ceremonies in general. It seemed like every time I got involved in some kind of ceremony, things went from bad to worse. High school graduation came to mind.

The megaphone man turned to the girls. "Sunshine and Moonbeam, are you ready to disavow all connection with your past, undergo your cleansing, swear fealty to Brother Chakra, and become a part of the family?"

Moonbeam (Vicky) bowed her head once and said, "Yes."

Sunshine (Janet) bowed her head and started to speak—but then she slapped her hand against her throat. "Wait!" she said. "I can't go on with the ceremony!"

"Why not?" the man said.

"My necklace has been stolen!"

"Stolen?" the megaman said. "Are you saying that there is a thief among us!"

"Yes!" Sunshine shouted. "I've been robbed! My necklace has been stolen!"

I'm not going to attempt to tell you how this made me feel. Sure, I could try to describe the knot of fear that erupted beneath my breastbone sending an electric bolt of adrenaline up my spine making my hair stand erect like wheat-straws in a tornado. But words fail me.

"Thief!" megaman shouted. "Call the pigs! Call the pigs!"

The doors of all three shacks burst open. A half-dozen men costumed in blue tights raced out wearing masks fashioned like the heads of pigs.

People started laughing as though this was just another part of the show. They squealed in mock horror when the pigs began infiltrating the group, peering into one face and then another as if looking for suspects. One of the pig men grabbed a hippie by the shoulders and raised him from the ground. The hippie waved his splayed hands in front of him, shaking his head no and saying, "I didn't do it!"

"Is this him?" the pig shouted, his voice muffled by the mask.

Sunshine shook her head no.

The pig let him go.

"Is this him?"

Everyone turned to look toward the rear of the crowd. A pig was holding a hippie by the ear. The hippie was laughing.

"No!" Sunshine barked.

I watched as the pig dropped the hippie and continued his relentless search for what I knew was me.

I faced front and bowed my head and looked at the hand-carved love beads dangling against my muslin shirt.

The laughter and squealing that had begun at the edge of the crowd came closer.

"Is this her? Is this him?"

I stared at my knees.

I looked up. Three pigs were standing over me.

Doctor Lovebeads had been run to ground.

I was ambivalent again. Should I "play along" and let them raise me bodily? Or should I volunteer to stand up, thus diminishing the audience-participation aspect of the performance by 50 percent? Or should I run like hell?

Why oh *why* was I wearing sandals?

"Is this him?"

I have lived in dread of that sentence all my life.

I sighed and stood up. I looked at Sunshine. She didn't say anything. She extended her right arm and pointed at me.

I have never been partial to that either.

"Bring him to me," the megaphone man said.

The pigs took me by the upper arms, but they didn't squeeze tightly. I knew I had a choice—go along with the joke, or shake their grasp and storm away cursing loudly. But I wasn't wearing tennis shoes. That was the first time in my life that an article of clothing played a key role in determining my fate. I don't count the time I got into a fix while streaking Wichita. I wasn't wearing any articles.

I let the pigs escort me out of the audience and up to the spot by the fire where Janet and Vicky were standing. Now that I was closer to them I could see that the girls were wearing loose belts made of golden string, the kind of schlock you can purchase by the yard in hobby shops. The dresses were simple and otherwise unadorned, which was why I had thought of them as "virgin" dresses, but also because I had seen a lot of biblical epics when I was a kid. I don't think my Maw ever had a clue as to what I was seeing when I went to the movies. There were more virgins on the screen than in the audience.

"Is this the thief?" the megaphone man said.

Sunshine took two steps toward me, reached out and slowly lifted the love beads from my neck. She raised them into the air and lowered them around her own neck. "Yes," she said.

I was of two minds about this. Actually I was of approximately twelve minds. I had done Janet a favor, had given her a free ride to Red Rocks, and this was how I was being repaid. But she did seem the sort of flighty type who would join a hippie commune, so I wasn't totally surprised. On the other hand, maybe this was all just a joke and I was expected to play along. Then there was the possibility that I actually was in serious trouble. I would rather not repeat what Joanne Woodward was saying, but if you ever watch *The Fugitive Kind* you'll get her drift.

I finally decided to assume that this was all just a joke.

"Hey!" I said, doing my wacky dance in place. "I plead not guilty!"

"Not *guilty?*" the megaphone man said.

"Yes! I'm not guilty of *anything!* Doctor Lovebeads has never done anything in his life!"

"You were wearing her beads!"

"*Her* beads?" I exclaimed, glancing at the audience with mock disbelief. "Nobody can *own* beads! Beads belong to *everybody!*"

It didn't work.

You can carve that on my tombstone.

"I made this necklace myself," Janet said. "It's the product of my labor. Brother Chakra teaches us that labor is the source of all ownership."

This cut me off at the knees because I fully agreed with that. I owned every nickel I ever earned, not that I earned every nickel I ever owned. But all wealth starts with human labor, which explains my tax bracket.

CHAPTER 34

"You stand accused!" the megaphone man said. I didn't like the sound of that.

Neither did the audience. I heard hisses and boos.

"Put him on trial!" someone shouted.

"Trial!" the group began chanting. "Put him on trial!"

As I often say, it was at this point that things began to career out of control.

Everybody got to their feet, stamping the ground and clapping in unison and shouting "Trial! Trial!" The megaphone man raised a hand and began flapping it in the air. Three pigs approached me and said, "Come with us!"

We didn't really go anywhere. They guided me around the clearing. As they did so, a dozen people lined up in a formation, which I will describe as a gauntlet, as in "running the gauntlet." They formed a double row and raised their arms the way soldiers raise swords when a buddy is getting married so the bride and groom can walk beneath the crossed blades as they come out of a church. But the hippies just touched fingertips, creating a canopy beneath which I was required to walk. The path led back to the spot where I had stood accused, but by then there was a new addition.

A tall figure wearing a black robe and a large mask topped by the thunderhead of a white judicial wig was standing in front of me. I quickly put two-and-two together and concluded that I had just been escorted through a "Hall of Justice." The symbolism of amateur theatrics has always tended toward the obvious, thank God.

The judge folded his arms.

A silence fell over the crowd.

And then softly … almost imperceptibly … the drum solo from "In-A-Gadda-Da-Vida" began drifting through the air. I assumed it was coming from the tape that I had sold to Otto. For those of you not familiar with "Gadda," try substituting the first four notes of *Dragnet.*

I braced myself.

There was no doubt in my mind that the man behind the mask was Brother Chakra, and it was obvious that he knew what he was doing. His choice of background music was worthy of William Castle. When it came to manipulating the emotions of an audience, Brother Chakra knew how to push people's buttons. But then so did Walt Disney and Elvis Presley. Jackson Pollock, on the other hand, missed the boat entirely.

The judge pointed a finger at my face and said, "Who are you, stranger?"

At that moment I would have given my right arm for an inexpensive lawyer. But since that option was closed, I was left with only one alternative: The Truth.

That was completely out of the question, so I said, "My name is Doctor Lovebeads and I'm from Taos, New Mexico."

"Who … are … you?"

"He's a fraud," a voice said.

I looked around and saw Otto walking toward me carrying a shoebox.

"A fraud?" the judge said.

"That is correct, your honor," Otto said, stopping beside me.

"What is the nature of his fraud?"

"This man is not who he claims to be."

"Do you have any proof?"

"I have evidence," Otto said.

I closed my eyes. "Evidence" is my least-favorite noun.

"Bring it forth," the judge said.

Otto lifted the lid of the box. I looked down at the contents. There was a license plate and a Polaroid snapshot.

I looked at Otto. "What's this?" I said.

He reached in, picked up the plate, and held it high for everyone to see.

"This man who calls himself Doctor Lovebeads claims to be from New Mexico. But this license plate was taken off the bumper of his van. It's a Colorado plate."

There were gasps from the audience. I couldn't tell if the gasps were theatrical or real. If they were real, I could only conclude that these people were morons.

The judge reached in and picked up the photograph. He held it up to my eyes. It was a close-up of me and my love beads sitting in front of the adobe.

"Who *are* you and *where* did you *come* from?" the judge said.

I realized that the curtain had come down on my performance. I was scared, but not as scared as I would have been if I hadn't been carrying a small plastic squeeze bottle of ammonia in my pocket. But I knew that the ammonia would act only as a brief deterrent if I found myself hobbling down the mountain leaving screaming hippies rubbing their eyes. No, the bottle wasn't going to be much help, other than to give me courage, which I normally get from glass bottles.

"I know who this man is," Otto said, pointing at me. "He's a cab driver. He came to the gate last Wednesday."

"That's right," I said. "I drove up here to get Janet and Vicky but you wouldn't let me in, so I came back to see if I could talk them into leaving this ridiculous place."

The crowd murmured its disapproval. But here's the funny thing: the more dangerous I made the situation, the less dangerous it felt. I have had a lot of experience with disapproval and I have found that few individuals are capable of expressing it without being backed up by at least one other person. I have respect for individuals who can vilify me on their own, but I had the feeling that the people at the ranch were incapable of doing anything on their own. They would be too timid to attack me without a mob to draw courage from. Now the bad news: I was surrounded by a mob.

"Why don't you take off that asinine mask and show me your face?" I said to the judge.

He raised an open palm.

"Don't hit him!" Vicky hollered.

I glanced at Vicky. She looked terrified.

"Do not worry, little Moonbeam, I am not going to hit this trespasser," Judge Chakra said, turning slowly so that his fake face faced Vicky. "As I have taught you, I do not believe in violence. I do not believe in bringing harm to any living creature. Nor do I believe that one person has the right to intrude upon the personal space of another. This mountain belongs to the family. Therefore this trespasser shall be punished in the manner of the olden times."

He raised his palm higher.

"Exile," he hissed.

I heard the sound of an internal-combustion engine starting up. At that moment I was grabbed by two pigs. They hustled me out of the clearing toward the exit gate where I saw the following words printed on the backside of the arch: "Entrance. Welcome to the Theater of Greed. Leave Your Soul Outside."

They dragged me through the gate and out into the real world. I saw the pickup truck parked farther down the road. Brent was in the driver's seat. Two men were standing on the flatbed holding torches. The headlights came on.

"Put him in the rear," Otto said.

They forced me to climb onto the flatbed. I sat on the ribbed floor. The men with the torches sat down with their backs to the cab. "Don't even try to climb out and run away," one of them said. "We'll catch you. We know these hills."

I pegged him as another member of the mob—possibly Luca Brasi.

Otto hopped in shotgun. Brent wheeled the truck around and started driving downhill. I'll admit it. I was rattled. In spite of my many years of fending off disapproval, I had never felt so disliked in terms of both quantity and quality.

We came down out of the trees and passed the pond. People were gathered around the campfire near the adobe. Kids were chasing each other, but they stopped and cheered when they saw the truck lit up with torches. I doubted that they understood what was going on, but then that was the nature of theatrics, not to mention its black-sheep brother, politics.

The truck slowed to negotiate the passage between the tree trunks, then picked up speed for the final leg of the downhill run. We came to a stop in front of the big house. The doors of the truck flew open. Brent and Otto came around to the flatbed.

"Climb off of there," Otto said.

I got down. Otto jammed the license plate into my belly and held up a screwdriver. "Here," he said. "Put your license back on and get the hell out of here. And don't even think about calling the police. We know who you work for, and it wouldn't be any trouble finding out where you live … Murph."

I didn't say anything. I took the license but ignored the screw-driver. I walked over to the van, opened the door and climbed in. I tossed the license plate onto the shotgun seat and reached into my jeans, pulled out my squeeze bottle, and set it on the seat. I pulled out my keys. I started the van. I drove onto the two-track and followed it to the main gate. The gate was open. I looked at the rear-view mirror and saw the pickup truck following me. I drove off the property and turned onto the asphalt road. I looked in the mirror again. The pickup had stopped. I could see silhouettes moving around by the gate. The peace/love generation had tuned me out.

I followed the asphalt road until I came to the picnic area on Flagstaff Mountain. I pulled the van off the road and parked in the same place where I had parked the previous day. I shut off the engine and was engulfed by silence. There must have been a reservoir of un-used adrenaline inside me because my hands started to shake the way they did after a hard night at Sweeney's—but in a bad way.

I opened the door and climbed out and walked back and forth in the darkness for a few minutes, taking deep breaths of thin air. Then I looked around to see if there were any cars parked in the area. Maybe this was a lover's lane for students at CU, which was lit up on the plains below. All of Boulder looked like a miniature version of Los Angeles viewed from Mulholland Drive. You've probably seen it in the movies. Steven Spielberg said he got the inspiration for the design of the giant flying saucer in *Close Encounters* by standing on his head on Mulholland and looking at LA upside down. To be perfectly frank, I would like to know what Steven Spielberg was doing on lover's lane when he should have been revising the script of *1941*.

The air was cold on the ridge. I pulled off my Mexican shirt. I walked back to the van and opened the sliding door and started looking for something else to wear. Suddenly I stopped.

Everything was there.

All of the blouses and sandals and books and tapes that I had sold during the day had been put back in place. Even the 8-track that Otto had trashed.

A chill crept up my spine. It was like receiving a message that served to underscore the extent of Brother Chakra's reach as the leader of an underground cult—a clear and unambiguous warning from the Theater of the Mind.

I started shivering. I dug around in the van only to realize there wasn't anything suitable to replace the shirt. I picked it up and put it back on. Full circle, like everything else in my life. I would be going back to Denver empty-handed. Once again I had failed to come through for someone who needed my help. Not that everybody I helped asked for my help, but whether they asked for it or not, they got it.

I yanked off my hippie headband and tossed it to the floor. I grabbed a bandanna out of the box and tied my hair in a half-assed ponytail to keep it out of my face while I drove. I slid the door shut, walked around to the driver's door and reached under the seat. At least my tennis shoes were still there. It was probably a good thing that I hadn't put them on before going up to the ridge. I'm the kind of person who often makes a run for it without considering the consequences. It's similar to the way I approach cooking.

I had lucked out, given the fact that I had been "chauffeured" to my van rather than chased a quarter-mile down the mountain. It was almost enough to make me never do anything on purpose again, and I had a pretty good record in that department. The few times that I did do things on purpose, it was usually to help someone out. Maybe my failure to bring Janet and Vicky home was a message from the theater of the gods that it was time to stop doing things altogether.

Janet and Vicky were living in some kind of crackpot commune, and there was nothing I could do to alleviate the guilt I felt for having given them the free ride to Red Rocks. If I had left well enough alone on that day, they might have been at home right at this moment, or at least in some place where I couldn't be blamed. That has always been bottom-line with me: avoiding blame.

CHAPTER 35

I drove down the mountain and skirted the edge of the University of Colorado. It reminded me of Kansas Agricultural University, insofar as it was a campus. As I drove out of Boulder and up the big hill that would take me back to Denver, I started thinking that I shouldn't have dropped out of KAU. I thought I should have stayed in Wichita in spite of the fact that Mary Margaret Flaherty had refused to marry me. If I had stayed in Wichita, my Maw would have let me live in my bedroom practically rent-free for the past twenty years. This would have had the effect of preventing me from getting a job in Denver as a cab driver and subsequently "helping" people, many of whom never would have needed my help if they hadn't climbed into my taxi in the first place.

I headed toward the glow of Denver. At night Denver glows, whereas in the daylight it smolders. You can always tell where Denver is. When newcomers arrive in Denver I inform them that it is impossible to get lost in the city because they can always see the mountains, assuming they understand that the mountains are to the west. If they don't understand that, then I have hit what is known as "The Wall" in the world of free advice.

I was halfway to the city limits when I noticed that my hands were still shaking. But that's how it always is for me. I remain cool and calm in the midst of disaster, and when the disaster is over I start thinking too much.

Which is to say, I could have gotten killed up there on that mountain, although it wasn't the mob of hippies that worried me, it was Chakra's henchmen. Guys like Chakra know how to keep their hands from getting dirty. Surround themselves with Ottos. Make threats. Incorporate fear. Even gentle flower children can be motivated to certain types of violence if they're threatened with the abstraction of fear—the next thing you know they're running down the streets of Chicago throwing tulips at cops.

I tried not to think about it. I had been humiliated. Stripped of my mask. Exposed as a fraud. The fact that I always knew I was a fraud helped me to deal with the situation. I mean it wasn't like I had "learned" something awful about myself that night. Fraud has always been an ace-in-the-hole. I just don't like other people to know it.

Then something occurred to me. Maybe I had been using fraud as a crutch. Maybe I had been relying too much on chicanery to get me through this poker tourney we call life. And maybe—just maybe—life had called my bluff. This is why I never bluff when I play poker. When someone calls your bluff, you are exposed not only as a fraud but an incompetent fraud. Believe me, there are plenty of strangers in Vegas who remember my name.

As I drove along the highway, I began to think I ought to try being real for once. I've always said that a taxicab is a terrible place to have an epiphany, but any motorized vehicle will do. I started to wonder what would happen if I removed fraudulence from the loop, the matrix, the paradigm of my existence. What would I be left with? I thought about that as I swung down onto Interstate 25 and headed south toward the lights of Denver. The pickings were slim but I realized that, if nothing else, I could say one thing about the real me with absolute certitude: I was an asphalt warrior.

I took the exit at Interstate 70 and headed east. A few minutes later I took an exit down an off-ramp. From there I aimed the van along a road that I had once traveled while seated shotgun in a tow-truck after a taxi I had been driving was destroyed in a holocaust of flames and exploding tires. It's a long story, and sort of funny.

Pretty soon I came to an intersection. I turned left and cruised past the main building of the Rocky Mountain Taxicab Company. I pulled into the dirt lot and guided the van down a row of parked cabs that—in the moonlight—looked new. All the vehicles looked like they had just come from the parking lot of the Denver Police Department where they had served as mobile tools in the arsenal of law enforcement. Moonlight became them, it's true, but in the stark light of day they looked like what they really were—however I won't destroy the illusion by lifting the flounce.

I drove along looking at the numbers stenciled to the fenders. I was looking for one cab in particular. If it wasn't there, that was okay, but I much preferred it over the others that were available. I was used to its saddle. It was broken in. I wished I had been able to look for RMT #127. Now *there* was a taxi with a broken saddle. But that was long ago, and in another junkyard.

Then I saw it: #123. It had not been signed out for the night. Or else it had been signed out and then brought back by a newbie who had made the mistake of trying to ride herd on the mean streets of Denver on a weekend. But you don't just walk into a rodeo with five days of driving under your seatbelt and hop into the saddle of "Ol' Thundercrack," as we cabbies refer to Saturday night.

No, you have to work your way to the top of that nightmare. You have to pull a few graveyard shifts in the middle of the week, you have to sit staring dumbly while a drunk with the legs of an Olympic athlete disappears in the panoramic landscape of your rear-view mirror. You didn't think he had it in him, did you? He could barely stagger when he came out of the Lulu Room, and there he goes with your six-dollars and forty cents.

You have to learn, baby, learn—as the hippies almost used to say.

I pulled into a parking slot and climbed out.

I walked into the on-call room, where Stew was reading a copy of *Model Railroading Magazine.* I tell ya—Stew could set up a life-size poster of himself reading that magazine and grab a few winks in the back room and the management wouldn't know the difference.

I walked up to the cage and rapped my knuckles on the countertop.

"Murph!" Stew said, setting the magazine aside. "What are you doing here at this time of night?"

"Aagh," I said, which is a code word that needs no translation among asphalt warriors. "I had a bad week, can't sleep, nothing good on TV, and my woman left me. So I thought I would come in and pull a short shift. Is one-twenty-three available?"

"Sure is," he said going into action, reaching for the key and a trip-sheet.

I had taken a chance. Up to now I had been pretending to be suspended from driving. If that was going to happen for real, it would happen on Monday, but I was afraid that if I showed up for work before Monday the man in the cage might already have been ordered by Hogan to pretend that I wasn't even there. If that happened, I was prepared to argue that the police had learned the whereabouts of the girls, which logically would have rendered my pretense moot and thus allowed me to not work for real, unless I felt like working, which was so unlikely that Hogan hopefully hadn't even thought of officially forbidding me to do what I never do anyway. That's what I was counting on. When specious reasoning collides with convoluted logic, I always come up smelling like a rose.

I paid thirty-five dollars for a short-shift, picked up my key and trip-sheet, and said, "Thanks."

There was nobody else in the on-call room, so Stew would have to wait until another cabbie arrived before he could express his wonder at the thing he had seen on this Saturday night: Murph was walking with the zombies.

I exited the room.

I crossed the lot to Wally's van, locked it up, and climbed into 123.

It took fifteen minutes to get home. I climbed the fire escape, went inside, took off my muslin shirt, and grabbed a fresh T-shirt out of my closet. The other T-shirts rustled on their hangers. I grabbed a fresh pair of jeans from a hanger. The other jeans rustled, too, as if all my clothes knew what I was doing, where I was going, and wanted badly to join me on my mission in the night. It was as if my clothes knew I was "up to something."

I removed my deep forest green Rocky jacket from its hanger, then removed my equally green Rocky cap from its hook on the closet door. I carried them into the bathroom and set them on the sink. I looked at my hair in the mirror. I reached back and yanked the bandanna away. It was like pulling the pin on a hand-grenade—the hair became a giant fuzzy ball. The same thing happened to London Lee's hair on the *Merv Griffin Show.*

I grabbed a rubber band off the bathroom doorknob where I store them—the ambient moisture keeps the rubber springy. I banded a new ponytail, adjusted my T-shirt, tugged at the waistband of my jeans, and reached for my Rocky jacket. I slipped it on and zipped up, then grabbed my cap and placed it squarely on my head.

I stood back and inspected myself in the mirror.

I was "going in."

CHAPTER 36

B oulder lay dead-ahead.
The Rocky radio was on but I wasn't paying attention to it. The soothing sounds of the night dispatcher yelling at the occasional newbie kept me company though. You don't hear that many newbie-yells at night. As I say, newbies tend to stay away from night shifts until they've made most of the mistakes of the day shift and think they know enough to work nights. I always feel sorry for the night-shift newbies. The truth is, a cabbie never learns enough to walk with the zombies. You simply do it, and pray you live to see the dawn.

My cab rolled over the big hill that led down into Boulder. The lights of Boulder were pretty in the valley, but all cities become velvet and diamonds when night falls. The beauty can be irresistible. The irresistibility reminded me of a Venus flytrap. I sent away for one of those things when I was a kid. It was advertised in the back of a comic book, and the damned thing actually worked. I woke up one morning and looked at the plant, and there was a fly—trapped. In a way it was anti-climactic. I was prepared to be disappointed. I'm still leery of sending away for Sea Monkeys. What if they're real?

I rolled down into town but kept going. I made it to the base of Flagstaff Mountain and took it slow and easy up the road. Then I was at the top.

Let me tell you something about the dark at the top of a mountain. It's as black as the dark at the top of Kansas. The only light is the light you bring with you. You can't count on the stars to guide the way, they're as worthless as the moon when it comes to avoiding ditches. You just straddle the white line and pray you live to see the dawn.

The main gate of the Smythe Ranch flickered past in my headlights. I was minutes away from my goal. I turned down the noise on my radio, but I didn't turn it all the way off. The voice of the dispatcher was my Muzak. It was my lifeline to reality. I needed some reality in my life right then because I was about to do something that had all the earmarks of unreality. I was about to walk back onto a stage where reality was just a prop in a play written by a dramatist who enjoyed manipulating his characters like marionettes. Of course this was true of all playwrights, but tonight there would be one big difference: the play was going to be revised by a novelist. And to add insult to injury, an unpublished novelist.

I was less than a mile away from the Smith Ranch but I could see the distant glow of the solstice celebration taking place on the ridge overlooking the property. The Theater of the Mind apparently was still conscious. I slowed as I approached the gate. I peered ahead as the headlights hit the metal fence. I didn't see any guards about. I liked that. It told me that the owner of the property wasn't expecting the comeback of an actor who had been given the hook.

I made a hard right and pulled up to the gate, jumped out of my taxi, and ran to the rope that kept the cows in line. I unlooped the rope and shoved the gate open, then ran back to my cab, hopped in and drove onto the property.

Was I trespassing? I had no legal authority to do what I was doing, except the authority granted by the PUC—the leniency bestowed upon a lost and confused cabbie pulling onto private property to beg directions. I love splitting legal hairs.

I could see the lit windows of the big house up ahead, could see the glow of the campfire higher up where the adobe cabin stood hidden behind the dark mass of the fallen tree, could see the brighter glow of the solstice celebration on the ridge where the colored lights created a rainbow effect against a slow-drifting haze of smoke generated by the bonfire.

I shifted into low gear as I approached the big house. Somebody came out the front door and stepped to the edge of the porch. I heard a voice yell hey as I cruised by with my recognizable rectangular Rocky Cab light blazing on my roof. I didn't stop.

The ground began to rise. I slowed as I aimed the hood toward the gap between the severed trunk. I had to make it before any bodies appeared. I eased past the wooden rings. I saw people rising around the campfire as I emerged into the light. I didn't see any kids. I was worried about the kids. But it was almost midnight and I didn't really expect the kids to be awake, not even hippie kids born unto people who had turned their backs on the bourgeois concept of Daylight Savings Time.

The hippies began drifting toward the road with what must have been uncertainty. A low-slung uninvited sedan with a strange light on top—maybe it was a cop. Maybe this was a bust. Hard to say when headlights are coming your way at night and you are only a visitor here. There was no telling how many guests were on the plateau versus how many actual members of the family, but I didn't stop to take a head-count or even ask directions like a good lost and confused cabbie. I kept going, past the adobe and on up the hill toward the pond, up into the trees until it was just me and the enveloping darkness and my headlights and the Theater of the Mind shining at the top of the ridge.

Then I was there.

The party was still going strong.

People were seated in a circle around the fire. In front of a hut a play was being performed. I knew it was a play because everybody by the fire was looking directly at the costumed kids acting out their fantasies in beams of colored spotlights aimed like crossed swords. I knew it was a play because the devil was dancing in front of the judge who reigned supreme on a jerry-built throne while pigs and girls writhed around him. I knew it was a play because the actors were exaggerating their body movements in the way of people who hide behind masks. I had never seen real people act like that, not even at Sweeney's. I didn't recognize the play but I was willing to bet it wasn't *Charley's Aunt*. I saw *Charley's Aunt* in high school. I don't want to talk about it.

I drove up to the "Entrance" arch and eased around it, but damn if I didn't wing a corner and knock it cockeyed. I kept going. My headlights cut across the circle of fire. People started looking my way. Those seated began standing up, and those already standing began backing off. The devil stopped his filthy dance and looked my way. The pigs looked my way. The girls looked my way. And finally the judge himself—Brother Chakra—looked my way as I pulled up and stopped in a swirl of dust that spun across the fire, muting its hellish glow.

Music had been playing over the loudspeakers when I drove in, but suddenly it stopped. I recognized the song—"Spoonful" by Cream. I liked that song. I liked it so much that I felt bad when my arrival put a stop to it. It was just getting to the part where Ginger Baker breaks out on the tom-toms.

A silence fell over the theater.

The roiling dust settled on the burning coals.

The crowd stared at 123.

Brother Chakra slowly arose from his throne.

While he was busy doing that, I picked up the microphone from my dashboard, turned the volume up to 9, and opened my door. I climbed out and cocked my right elbow on the roof.

"One-twenty-three," I said, loud enough for the dispatcher to hear me all the way back in Denver.

"One-twenty-three," the dispatcher said, his voice crackling across the Rockies.

"Time check," I said.

"Stroke of midnight, Murph."

"Check."

Maybe it was the sight of a semi-uniformed man holding a microphone to his lips, maybe it triggered a knee-jerk response in a few muddled brains, because a number of hippies at the edge of the crowd suddenly staggered into the darkness and disappeared.

Brother Chakra strolled toward the cab. He stopped near the right front fender. He reached up and yanked off his cardboard wig with what I interpreted as umbrage. Ergo, I reached up with my left hand and yanked off my Rocky cap—I'm talking dueling body language here.

My copycat gesture gave me the edge.

This party was mine.

"I'm back," I said. "And when I go I'm not leaving alone." I slapped my cap back onto my head.

Brother Chakra looked at me with fire in his eyes—reflected of course. He raised his right hand and pointed his index finger at me. "You are trespassing!" he boomed.

"Call the cops," I said. I matched him right-arm for right-arm, stretching my coat sleeve across the roof and holding the mike toward him.

I heard the quick shuffle of a few more hippies exiting past the outhouse.

I looked around at the faces of the crowd. Everybody was standing now. I saw fear in their eyes. It was the kind of fear you see in the eyes of people who had been taking too many drugs and didn't know what the hell was going on.

Okay. I'll admit it. I've been there. I'm no angel. I'm a Baby Boomer.

"I came to pick up two girls who need a ride home."

"Nobody here called a taxi," Brother Chakra said.

"I'm calling the taxis here," I said. "Last week I took two girls to Red Rocks Amphitheater for a concert. Somebody gave them a couple of free twenty-dollar tickets. Somebody who likes to prowl the mean streets of Denver looking for wide-eyed, eager, wholesome, innocent girls he can lure to his lair with promises of mind expansion, communal living, and all the free love you can stuff into a bong."

A murmur arose from the audience. It wasn't a good one.

Brother Chakra raised a hand to silence the crowd. "It's okay, it's okay, we have the law on our side. This man is a trespasser." He looked at me. "I don't know what you're talking about," he said, in a voice so soothing it ought to have come from the devil mask.

"I'm talking about two girls I never should have picked up in the first place. If it hadn't been for me they wouldn't be here. They would be home in their own beds where they belong."

"Oh ho!" Brother Chakra said. He grinned and raised his arms and turned to face the crowd. "See? This is what I have been talking about! Here is a man who thinks he is responsible for somebody else's life. But what have I taught all of you about personal responsibility? Donovan? What did I teach you?"

The kid who had hassled me at the pond stepped out of the crowd. He looked like a student called upon to recite in front of a classroom. He cocked his head sideways and looked up at his own forehead and said in a sonorous, robotic voice, "We are each of us responsible for our own life, our own personal choices, and our own fate."

"That is correct, Donovan," the guru said.

Donovan took a step backward into the crowd. He had repeated his lesson word-for-word like every straight-A student I had ever known. It made me sick.

Brother Chakra smiled at me. "If I may be so bold as to inquire, trespasser … who put you in charge of the world?"

"The Pubic Utilities Commission," I said. "I'm a licensed taxi driver, and when somebody climbs into my cab I'm responsible for their health, safety, and welfare until the ride is over. And this ride isn't over until I say it is. I'm talking round-trip, baby. It's the only trip worth taking."

Somebody snickered. I wrote it off as pot-induced.

I heard a door open. I looked at the center shack on the compound and saw Otto and Brent step out. They weren't dressed for a party. They were dressed for business: boots, blue jeans, denim jackets, and caps. I figured they were in charge of the music. But right at this moment I was The Music Man here.

Brother Chakra looked over at them, then made a small gesture with his right hand, a subtle bit of body language that I interpreted to mean, "Stay," the kind of gesture you might flash at two well-trained Catholic boys.

Brother Chakra glanced at the mike in my hand then looked around at the audience, which had dwindled, though not considerably. I was easily outnumbered forty to one. I was familiar with those odds. I used to bet them at the dog track. I was a sucker for long shots. Fortunately somebody cured me of that disease. His name was Big Al. But he wasn't an M.D. He was more like a witch doctor who recognized a hopeless bet when he saw one and manufactured his own cure-all: a tincture of lecture and beer. But like a man who had long ago been bitten by the dreaded Tsetse fly, I still suffered from occasional bouts of poor judgment.

Brother Chakra held an open palm toward me. "What we have here is a control freak," he said.

Another murmur from the crowd.

"This is what the city breeds," he said, playing his followers like a sitar. I'll be honest. I don't enjoy the sitar, although it has nothing to do with Brother Chakra.

"Look at this disgusting machine he drives," Brother Chakra said. "It's like an army tank. And look at the violence he has wrought in his greedy pursuit of money," pointing at the cockeyed gate. "This is what I'm talking about when I talk about …" he raised a hand and pointed toward the cities of the plains, "… *out there.*"

I looked at the faces. The fear was beginning to melt away. A few bodies drifted slowly back from the darkness. He was starting to pull them together by playing a tune they understood—the song of moral superiority.

I heard a door close. I glanced at the shack. Otto and Brent had gone back inside. A moment later music came on, only this time it was "Layla." I liked that song, too, except it had to be played full-blast to truly appreciate the thermonuclear lead guitar. But Otto had set the sound low. I could barely make out the bass.

Brother Chakra smiled at me. "The members of this family do not believe in violence. We believe in peace and love. We believe in freedom of thought. We believe in freedom of expression and free-dom of lifestyle. We revere all things bright and beautiful."

I nearly crushed the mike with my fist.

"But … in spite of the fact that you have come to this place of peace and love uninvited … twice I might add … I am more than willing to turn the other cheek and let you have your way. Passive resistance is the only form of resistance we practice in this family."

He raised his chin and looked at the crowd.

"Does anybody here need a taxi?" he said above the muffled drone of the music.

No reply.

He looked at me and shrugged. "If I am not mistaken, I believe you mobile capitalists refer to this sad set of circumstances as a 'no-show.'"

That caught me off guard. I wondered if he had ever driven a cab for a living. He looked the type, I'm sorry to say.

"And so," Brother Chakra said, "I would appreciate it if you would kindly turn this dreadful pollution factory around and go back down to the brick-and-steel slum from whence you came."

Whence.

That tore it.

I glanced over at the audience. I wanted to keep my eye on their movements, especially Otto and Brent who were still inside the orchestra hut. I looked back at Brother Chakra. "I can't tell you how glad I am to hear that you believe in non-violence," I said. "It makes my job so much easier."

I turned back toward the audience.

"Janet!" I barked. "Vicky! If you want to go home, now's your chance!"

No reply.

Everybody just stared at me.

"Time for you to go," Brother Chakra said.

"Don't try giving me orders," I said. "I'm not a member of your family. Not yet anyway. You never can tell though. Maybe someday I'll lose my sense of self-worth and come crawling back here for your approval. That's how it works, isn't it—you barter approval in exchange for the things that people give you? And I'll bet you get the better part of that deal."

I looked at the audience.

"Janet! Vicky! This man gave you two free tickets. What's he gonna charge you for those free tickets?"

"I want you off my property right now," Brother Chakra said, moving into the headlights. He stopped. The lights made his chest and face blaze. It was very theatrical. He knew what he doing. He was smooth.

"*Your* property?" I said. "I was told that hippies don't believe in property rights."

His smug smile disappeared.

But just as quickly it came back. He raised his chin and looked at his audience.

"And I have heard that money-grubbing capitalists *do* believe in property rights," he said. "I've heard that they wouldn't dream of trespassing on somebody else's property. But isn't this what I have always taught you? The people *out there* are driven by money and hypocrisy. If they can't buy something, they just steal it."

I squinted at him. "Why would that bother you, Mister Share-the-Wealth?"

Brother Chakra began walking again. He crossed over to my side of the taxi, where I stood with my right elbow on the roof and my left hand on the door. "That's close enough," I said. "I'll be leaving as soon as Janet and Vicky tell me they want to stay in this dump."

"There is nobody here by that name," Brother Chakra said. "You must have the wrong address."

"We've already had this conversation," I said. "Janet! Vicky! Sunshine! Moonbeam! I came here to offer you a free ride home. Are you coming with me?"

Silence.

I looked at the crowd. They had drawn so close together that they held a vague resemblance to a flock of sheep. The breeze on the mountaintop was at my back, so I couldn't speak for their smell.

"I want to go home," a voice said.

A young girl stepped out of the crowd. It wasn't Janet or Vicky. She looked like she was trying to keep from crying. "Will you take me with you?"

I stared at her.

"I want to go home, too," another girl said, edging her way out of the herd.

Brother Chakra raised his judicial wig and placed it back on his head. "Heather. Tammy. What do you think you're doing?"

"Whoah, brother," I said. "If these girls want to come with me, they're coming."

He smiled at the girls. "Why would you want to go back down to the killing fields when you are safe up here with the family?" I looked at the girls. I could see it in their eyes: confusion—the ace-in-the-hole of all rulers who understand the power of language.

"You don't need this clown's permission to leave the mountain," I said to the girls. "You don't even need money. I usually charge a dollar-fifty per mile but it's Christmas in June here at Murph's cabstand. Free rides for everybody who wants to go home, compliments of Catholic guilt. If it hadn't been for me I wouldn't be standing here tonight. I doubt if I'll ever forgive myself for what I did to me because this is the last place on earth I ever wanted to be, and I once lived in …"

I didn't make it to the punch line.

"I want to go home, too."

A boy stepped out of the crowd. It was Donovan.

Then I noticed something odd.

Some of the hippies were gathering up their things and drifting toward the ruins of the Entrance/Entrance gate. I had the funny feeling I had gotten through to the wrong people.

Then it happened. Janet and Vicky stepped from the crowd. They had changed out of their virgin dresses. I quickly tried not to think about that.

"I want to go with you," Janet said. "But Vicky wants to stay here."

I looked at Vicky with disbelief. "You want to stay in this place?"

She nodded.

"But why?" I said.

"She doesn't have anywhere to go," Janet said. "She's from Vermont."

"Hell, I'll drive you to Vermont," I said, starting to panic.

"He's lying," Brother Chakra said. "The people *out there* lie all the time about everything."

The fact that I agreed with Brother Chakra was no reflection on me—I hoped. I turned to him. "Listen, Brother Charade, or whatever you call yourself, I want to hear her tell me she doesn't want to go."

"I don't want to go," Vicky said. "I want to stay here."

She stepped over to Brother Chakra. He put an arm around her shoulders.

Let's jump ahead five seconds.

I quit grinding my teeth.

I opened the left rear door of my cab and told the four kids to climb in. After they were safely situated within my territorial imperative, I closed the door and looked at Vicky.

"You don't want to stay here," I said.

"Yes I do," she said, and she put her arm around Brother Chakra's waist.

"No you don't," I said. "I asked the police to give me fifteen minutes to try and talk you into coming with me before they swooped down and threw a net over this cuckoo's nest."

I would have felt guilty about making up such an alarming lie, but isn't that what improvisational theater is all about? Who says the end doesn't justify the means? Someone who's never experienced the end, that's who.

Leaving that whopper flopping on the ground like a big two-hearted trout, I got back inside my taxi and shut the door.

It took three seconds for Vicky to open the shotgun door and dive in.

Moving with a swiftness known only to men who have walked with the zombies, I reached back and locked the rear doors, the shotgun door, and my door. Then I started the engine, shifted into low, and made a circuit of the campfire, which was virtually deserted.

I guided 123 down the winding road in the direction of the pond, dodging hippies all the way. I recognized a lot of them from earlier in the day. I had a feeling the guests were checking out. By the time we got down to the pond, the message already had passed us by. But this is the nature of messages, especially rumor messages, and especially lies, my specialty. People were gathering up their things and walking down the road, passing between the trunks of the fallen tree.

I slowed as I approached the tree. People were filtering through the passage. And then something happened. They turned and blocked the road. I hit the brakes.

"Why are you stopping?" Vicky said. There was fear in her voice.

"I'm required by law to yield to pedestrians," I said, trying to sound cocksure. Cocksureness is distantly related to lying, but I didn't have much practical experience with it—it's sort of a specialty act. I'm more of your garden-variety phony.

The headlights turned the bodies white. I couldn't make out facial features. Hippies started gathering around the windows and looking into the cab. It was like a scene from every horror movie ever made where the inmates take over the asylum—except this was scary because it was real. Horror movies don't scare me, as long as I'm not alone at the drive-in.

An inmate rapped on my window.

I rolled the window down 1/32 of an inch.

"What?" I said.

"After you drop them off could you come back and pick up me and my girlfriend? We can be waiting for you down on the highway."

"What?" I said again.

"We don't even know these people here. We're just hitchhikers. Could you please tell that to your police friends?"

My shoulders drooped. I looked at Janet, then looked at the hippie.

"I'll tell you what," I said. "I'll get in touch with Yellow Cab in Boulder and have them send someone up here. But like I said, it costs a buck-fifty per mile so you better have the bread. You don't want to stiff Yellow Cab drivers. They're not like normal cabbies."

"I got the money, man, no problem."

I started to reseal the window, but then he tapped on it again. "Maybe you better send more than one cab, man. A lotta people here want to leave."

"Okay," I said.

I felt sort of bad. Hippies were probably scattering across the hills looking for a way off the mountain before The Man nabbed them. But at the same time it sort of made me laugh. Being a hippie is a tough gig. But it's like Brother Chakra teaches, probably in a minimum-security prison by now, assuming he hasn't fled to Sweden: "We are each of us responsible for our own life, our own personal choices, and our own fate."

I drove down past the big house where the ground leveled out, then made the last leg along the two-track that led to the main gate. I didn't see the green pickup truck until it was thirty feet away. It was parked parallel to the gate, blocking the road. Otto and Brent were standing in front of the truck with their arms folded. I slowed to a halt.

"Why are we *stopping*?" Donovan said. "Why is it taking so *long* to get *out* of here?"

I looked at Donovan. His eyes told me something that my own eyes didn't want to hear. He was stoned. He didn't know what the hell was going on. I wondered briefly if he would realize what he had done when he woke up the next day. But at least he would wake up in a place where he could decide whether he wanted to go back to not knowing what the hell was going on.

"Everybody stay cool," I muttered.

Otto lowered his hands and came around to my side of the cab. This time I rolled the window all the way down.

Otto leaned into the window and looked at the backseat, then looked at Vicky.

"Cops my ass," he said. "There ain't no pigs waiting outside to make a bust."

My right hand snaked toward the radio. I grabbed the mike and raised it to my lips. "I can have the state patrol here in five minutes if that will make you happy. I'll even throw in the Boulder police. I bet you have a couple of acquaintances down there."

I punched the button three times.

"All right, who's playing with his microphone?" the dispatcher said.

I held the button down. "Murph here. My mistake. Sorry."

"Come on, Murph, stay on the ball," the dispatcher said with total disgust, as usual. "What are you doing driving nights anyway?"

I gave Otto a dour look and said, "You've got your little hippie commune here, and your little dope racket, and I've got what I came for. So why don't you and I just pretend we never met, and leave it at that."

He stared at me without expression for ten seconds. I knew what he was doing. He was thinking. I've seen that look on plenty of faces. Mostly C students.

He leaned away from the window and made a hand gesture toward Brent. Brent climbed into the pickup and drove it out of the way. Otto walked over to the fence, unlooped the rope, and pulled the gate open.

Then he did something that irked me. He held out his hand and bowed to me like a butler opening a door for a guest. It was a corny thing to do, and I knew that he knew that I knew it was corny, and that it would annoy me just as it would annoy anybody with half a brain. It was a gesture that only the squarest of the square would perform, and I knew damn well that he knew that I knew that he knew …

Aaah, to hell with it.

I pulled onto the road and turned left, and started to press the accelerator with my right toe. But then I had an inspiration. I glanced at my rear-view mirror and saw Otto standing in the glow of the headlights of the pickup.

I made a fist and tapped the horn seven times—I'm talking "… shave-and-a-haircut …" which was so corny it might have been beeped by the King of Squaresville himself.

When I looked at my rear-view mirror Otto was shaking his fist at me, although it wasn't exactly a fist. It was one of those hand gestures that you never see in polite company. It has a variety of colorful names, but I call it "fist-plus."

His message was unmistakable.

Victory was mine.

CHAPTER 37

The interior of the cab was silent as we drove down the winding road of Flagstaff Mountain. I doubted that any of my five passengers was younger than eighteen, although I didn't know for certain. But they seemed like little kids to me. Fugitive kids who had been taken away from something that they obviously had wanted to get away from. Vicky might have been an exception. It had seemed to me that she really did want to stay with Brother Chakra until she thought there was going to be a police raid, i.e., until she thought there was going to be a consequence. But I didn't want to know. She could always go back if she wanted to pick up where she had left off. Brother Chakra was right: "We are each of us responsible for our own life, our own personal choices, and our own fate."

I didn't try to make conversation. I figured the kids were a bit shaken up. That made six of us. When we got down to Boulder I headed over to a steep street known as "The Hill." I didn't know who the genius was that had nicknamed that stretch of Broadway, but I suspected it was a farm boy who had matriculated in the nineteenth century. I headed to Pearl Street and saw what I was looking for: a big yellow taxi parked in front of a theater called "The Boulder Theater." This place was full of geniuses.

I parked behind it and told the kids to wait. I climbed out and walked up to the driver's window and tapped the glass. He rolled his window down. He didn't recognize me, thank God. The Word on the street said that all the Yellow drivers in Colorado once made a bet on me and lost a bundle—and believe me "bundle" is low-balling it.

I told him there were people at the Smith Ranch up on Flagstaff who were looking for taxis. I left it at that. He would either radio his dispatcher to put out the call, or just drive up there by himself. Or he might quietly let a few of his buddies in on the score. But it was out of my hands.

I got back inside 123 and drove us out of Boulder.

On the stretch between the lights of the city and the first big hill I glanced into the backseat.

"I want to make something perfectly clear to you kids," I said. "On the drive back to Denver we are not going to do a chorus of Row-Row-Row Your Boat, so you can put that out of your minds right now." I was attempting to lighten the vibes.

And then, just as we topped the hill, I heard a girl's voice softly trilling "… Row-row-row your boat …" and I realized I had made a horrendous mistake.

It took hours to get back to Denver. Less than one anyway. By the time we were on Interstate 25 headed toward midtown I had elicited addresses from the kids, all of whom were from Denver except Vicky, who was going to spend the night at Janet's house.

One by one I dropped them off in front of their homes. I found it curious that every house where I stopped had a front-porch light on. I didn't want to think about that. Janet's house was my last stop. It was in the middle of a block on a heavily tree-shaded parkway in east Denver, the only house on the block with a light on.

I waited and watched as they trundled up the sidewalk to the front door. Janet had to ring the bell. I tried not to think about that. A light came on in an upstairs window. After a minute the front door was opened by a man who stood frozen with the door halfway open. Then he yanked it all the way open. I heard their voices. Janet turned and pointed at my cab. I tapped the horn as lightly as 123's horn had ever been tapped, then I put the transmission into gear and drove away.

Logic dictated that I drive back to the motor after that and eat my lease—thirty-five dollars down the tubes. I hadn't had any intention of working that night anyway. But then, I never have any intention of working, I just do it.

I was too wired to go home, so I switched on the Rocky radio and started listening for bells. Night bells are different from day bells. Night bells tend to be few and far between, but what they lack in quantity they make up for in drama. There can be long pauses in between calls. You might wait five minutes, or even ten, before the radio clicks and the dispatcher says, "Colfax and York."

Even though a night dispatcher is never as overworked as a day dispatcher, there is something tired-sounding and wistful and lonely and distant in a night dispatcher's voice when he or she offers a bell for the taking. And sometimes nobody takes it.

A minute might pass before the radio clicks again and the dispatcher says, "Colfax and York."

The bell hangs in the air, framed by the silence of the city.

Click.

"Anybody?"

Not as many drivers work the night shift as the day shift, which partly explains why nobody jumps the bell right away. They're driving a fare some place else and it's not on their route.

Click.

"Colfax and York ... anybody?"

The silence settles back in.

But then the radio clicks and you hear the dispatcher say, "Party named Williams. She'll be waiting outside," and you know that one of your fellow asphalt warriors has jumped the bell.

In this case the fellow warrior was me. Colfax and York is an intersection on The Hill at the eastern edge where the hill begins to lose its definition. Once you get past York Street it becomes merely east Denver. But Colfax and York is still a part of The Hill. It's not that far from my crow's nest, where a part of me wanted to be and another part wouldn't let me be—the electric kool-aid tangerine-flake streamlined part.

The fare turned out to be a nurse's aid going to St. Joe's hospital, which wasn't far away. Less than three dollars, but she gave me five bucks. She told me she took a cab to work every night. This was a typical Capitol Hill run. Short trip, but decent money. A man committed to working hard could earn his nut on The Hill at night if he knew all about walking with the zombies. The only problem was, sometimes you ran into real zombies. I'm talking bar closings. I'm talking a freak show. I'm talking the laughers, the lovers, the weepers, the philosophers, the politicos, the poets, and the tough guys. I'm talking a ship of fools, a mixed crew, all of whom have one thing in common: they over-tip.

It had been a long time since I had worked the graveyard shift, which had been a desperation move, like most graveyard shifts in most lines of work. You always have special reasons to work the graveyard, and they always differ from day reasons. You work days because that's when everybody else works. But you pull graveyard for reasons of your own, reasons that you might not necessarily want to share with anybody, not even your friends. Sometimes you work the graveyard because you have no friends and there's no reason to get up with the sun.

By "reason" of course I mean "excuse." My excuse on that night was adrenaline. I knew I wouldn't be able to get to sleep if I went home where I wanted to be. I knew I would lie in bed shivering with the knowledge that the thing I had done on the mountain was both dangerous and good, like so many dangerous things. I knew I would lie there and make a vow to never again get involved in the personal lives of my fares. But I didn't want to play that broken record again. How many times during the past fourteen years had I said that to myself only to make a liar out of me? Do numbers go that high? Don't ask me. I never did like abstract concepts anyway. If I can't see it, smell it, or break it, get it out of my taxi.

"Colfax and Pearl."

"One twenty-three.

"Party named Lewis."

"Check."

By five thirty I had grossed forty-five dollars. Thirty-five for Rocky Cab, and ten for the gas that I had put into the tank. I didn't use up all the gas though. The trip to Boulder and my hours of working The Hill had used barely half a tank. I would be leaving a nice gift for the day driver, whoever he happened to be. Probably a newbie who would freak out at the sight of the gas needle standing at twelve o'clock high, and would subsequently ask the mechanics if it was broken.

Newbies.

Give me a break.

It was getting light outside when I drove 123 back to the motor and handed the key and trip-sheet to Stew, who was chugging through the last few pages of *Model Railroading Magazine*.

I walked back out to the parking lot and paused a moment to

study the psychedelic colors plastered all over Doctor Lovebeads Cosmic Wonderbus and Mobile Mercantile. I wondered what Wally would do if I left it that way.

But I knew what Wally would do. He would laugh. He was me pal. I also knew what his wife would do: flip out and make him promise never to see Brendan Murphy again. Wives always do that. I can read them like X-rays.

I got in and drove the van over to the wash-rack where the mechanics hosed down the cabs after they had finished working on them. I asked the head mechanic if I could make use of the hose—it seems some wild teenagers had sprayed graffiti all over my van last night. He shrugged. I liked that.

Five minutes later a neon rainbow was gurgling down the drain. Wally's van looked better than it had since college.

I drove out of the Rocky lot and made my way to a Safeway store on east Colfax. A Salvation Army dumpster was located at a corner of the parking lot. You've probably seen them. Painted white with an SA decal on the front above a sign saying "Please—No Trash." I returned all the clothes and gadgets that I had purchased on Thursday. I hoped the Salvation Army people didn't get mad at me for bringing back items they had already sorted through and put on display. I figured I would have to stay away from SA for at least a month. They might be looking for me.

That was almost that.

But for the presence of the van, an objective morning commuter might not suspect that I was just finishing up getting involved in someone's personal life. Washing my hands of the whole deal. Bringing closure to another near-disaster. He might think I was a normal person getting an early start on the rush hour.

That's what I was banking on.

All my life I have wanted people to think I was normal. My batting average is about .500 if you divide the world into people who know me, and people who wish they didn't.

I drove the van into the parking lot behind my building and pulled into the space where fence-meets-fence, the choice V-spot. My Chevy was at Wally's house. I had left it there after I drove over to borrow his van. I told him I would leave my car as collateral. For some reason his wife didn't laugh.

The sun was still making its way over the Kansas cornfields by the time I reached the fire escape on my apartment building. I climbed up and down a few times, hauling the remaining boxes into my crow's nest. Given the speed of light and the velocity of the earth's rotation, it was no surprise that shafts of golden sunlight began striking the nearby rooftops as I made my last climb hugging my lava lamp to my breast. Scientists tell us that if the earth drifted just one teensy mile closer to the sun out of 93 million miles, we would all burn up. The smug bastards act like they invented the planet.

I entered the kitchen and set the lamp on the table, then stepped over to the door and started to shut it. But I paused a moment to look at the sunlight plastered against the white brick wall of the apartment building next door.

I had seen the same sunlight on the same wall when going to work, but seeing it after coming home from work, and knowing that I was going to bed, gave it a different feel. It reminded me of college. It reminded me of pulling all-nighters, whether keggers or just pretending to study with my buddies during finals week. It's funny the things you do on purpose when you're young, things you try so hard to avoid doing after you grow up, or at least get older, like staying up all night. Staying up all night is like the first Everest of adulthood that you want to conquer when you're a little kid, usually at Christmas. My brother Gavin and I always tried to stay up until Santa Claus arrived. But what kid doesn't? What kid doesn't want to see The Truth with his own eyes, especially when he suspects it's a lie? I've never really understood that about myself, or any other kid. Life is filled with enough disillusionments without chasing them with butterfly nets.

On the other hand, if you encounter enough disillusionments, you might be motivated to go running back to your childhood, like Gig Young. Maybe that's why Janet and Vicky ran off to a hippie commune. I'll be honest. After I got out of the army I basically did the same thing. But I called it "college." That's what I was thinking about as I stood in the open doorway. I managed to stay in college for seven years, and I have to say that it was about as real as Brother Chakra's Theater of the Mind, and just as fun, too, if you were into strange trips—whether dancing around a campfire or studying the *Norton Anthology*. Whatever turns you on. It's just that after you graduate, you are theoretically supposed to go out into the real world and find a job based on all the skills you were supposed to have learned in school.

I just hoped Janet and Vicky learned something.

I doubt if I did.

I rarely do.

The End

DARK NIGHT
OF THE SOUL

BOOK 6 IN
THE ASPHALT WARRIOR
SERIES

COMING SOON

CHAPTER 1

My alarm clock went off at six A.M. that Monday morning. I immediately hit the snooze button. I had been up the previous evening thinking about trying to write a novel, and nothing drains a writer more than thinking about trying to write. A lot of it has to do with the energy it takes to not watch television. Not watching television is like going to a bar and not drinking. That's as far as I can take the analogy, because I've never done that.

But as I sat in my apartment the previous evening staring at the blank screen of my TV, I subconsciously got the urge to turn it on. I could feel every muscle in my body aching to get up and walk across the living room and pick up the remote-control, which I had purposely set on top of the TV to keep it out of my reach. I managed to resist the urge to get up, but it took an enormous amount of effort. It reminded me of the Charles Atlas course advertised on the backs of comics when I was a kid.

I'll admit it. At the age of ten my dream was to kick sand in the face of a bully. I had tried that once at the age of eight, however at that time I did not possess a thorough grounding in the art of modern advertising.

Later on, while reading a comic in the hospital, I realized what I had done wrong: I had not sent Charles Atlas ten cents. The ten cents was to cover the return postage on an introductory booklet for his muscle-building course—or so he claimed. After I was released from Wichita General I asked my Maw if she would give me the necessary ten cents. She said she would be glad to give me ten cents if I mowed the lawn.

I mulled this over for a few days, then came to the conclusion that it just might be worth it. If things worked out the way I planned, I might be able to extract revenge against Danny Doyle. His was the face into which, in my marketing-and-distribution naivete, I had sent a spray of sand. This was at a place called Courtney Davis, a swimming resort that apparently no longer exists in Wichita. It was like a Club Med for Jayhawkers. Why did I kick sand into Danny Doyle's face? It's a long story, but I think stupidity covers all the bases. Briefly, he had knocked an ice-cream cone out of my hand while roughhousing with his pals.

I was always amazed that bullies had pals. Where did they get pals? Did a kid have to apply for friendship with a bully? What were the requirements? Was there an annual fee?

Anyway, it took me two hours to mow the yard and by the time I was finished I no longer wanted muscles. That was the end of my business association with Charles Atlas. But when I turned thirteen I learned the secret of "dynamic-tension." This was one of those secrets that ran the grapevine of adolescent boys. Word on the street said that some kid had actually sent away for the Charles Atlas course, and had blown the lid off dynamic-tension. I suspected it was Danny Doyle. The secret consisted of flexing your muscles real hard, which was about as disappointing as learning it was impossible to literally "throw your voice" with a gadget that cost a buck. I don't want to talk about that.

Nevertheless, I immediately set out to flex my muscles—in secret of course. I didn't want any trouble with the U.S. Patent Office. I didn't have that many muscles when I was thirteen but I did manage to flex the ones I found. I was primarily determined to develop gigantic biceps and pecs, so I spent hours in the bathroom behind the locked door flexing my muscles in front of the mirror. After two days of this grueling workout I did not detect any visible signs of progress, which led to my loss of faith in comics.

But since I had given my Maw the impression that I was willing to mow the lawn, I earned forty cents a month during the summer of my thirteenth year. I ate twelve chocolate sundaes in twelve weeks, not including my usual sundaes. By the time school rolled around I had a gained a pound of muscle in my wrists from pushing the lawnmower. Also five pounds of fat on what appeared to be my stomach. On the night I weighed my wrists on the bathroom scale, me ol' Dad walked past the doorway and saw me, but didn't say anything.

Anyway, I was sitting there in my living room staring at the TV and found myself fighting the instinctive reflexes of my muscles. My body wanted to get out of the chair, but I wouldn't let it. This went on for half an hour. It was just like going to the gym where I had once paid two hundred and fifty dollars to walk through the front door twice.

At the end of the half-hour I was covered with a sheen of sweat, and I was breathing heavily. But I had spent so much time fighting my muscles that I forgot to think up the plot of a novel. It didn't matter though, because I was so exhausted that I didn't have the energy to cross the living room and turn on my RamBlaster 4000 personal computer and wait for it to warm up. It's the waiting that kills you. Instead, I staggered into my bedroom, kicked off my Keds, and collapsed into bed.

When the alarm went off the next morning I hit the snooze button. It was set for ten minutes. Unfortunately, after the radio came back on I slept through the rock songs. I truly was exhausted from my Herculean writing labors of the night before.

Suddenly "Jailhouse Rock" erupted and my eyes popped open. Whenever I hear Elvis Presley I immediately begin making calculations, trying to discern whether it's the pre-army Elvis or the post-army Elvis. I like the pre. In fact, I have a theory that the man who came home from Germany in 1962 was not the real Elvis Presley, but I don't want to get into that and neither do the gate guards at Area 51.

I stared at the ceiling for a while, then I casually rolled over and glanced at the clock, and nearly had a heart attack. It was seven twenty-five. Normally I sign out my cab at the Rocky Mountain Taxicab Company (RMTC) at seven A.M. I immediately panicked and got out of bed. I staggered into the living room and did something I had never done before in my life, which was to make a telephone call at dawn.

There is a rule at Rocky Cab that says a driver is allowed thirty minutes to pick up his assigned taxi or it will be given to someone else looking for a day lease—unless the assigned driver phones in to let them know he is coming. I had to call Rollo, the man in the cage who is in charge of handing out keys, and let him know I was coming. I had never gotten along very well with Rollo, but when he answered the phone he didn't give me any jive. He said he would hold cab #123 until I arrived.

It sort of annoyed me to have to talk to Rollo like a normal person because I like to employ subtle forms of sarcasm when speaking to him. I felt cheated. After I hung up the phone I rushed around my apartment getting dressed. It infuriated me. Not that I'm opposed to getting dressed, but I hadn't rushed around in panic in a long time.

I did do that a lot in the army where they had things like sergeants and bugles, but that was a quarter-century ago, which is a long time to not panic.

I grabbed my plastic briefcase and walked out the back door, locked up my crow's nest, and hurried down the fire escape. I hopped into my Chevy, fired it up and drove onto 13th Avenue.

I felt foolish as I negotiated the dawn streets of Denver. Everybody was heading for work, the rush hour was on, and I was a part of it. I felt like Jason Robards. It wasn't a good feeling.

I arrived at the motor at ten minutes to eight. The parking lot was dead. The seven A.M. shift-change was long over, i.e., the bustling of asphalt warriors climbing out of night-shift cabs and the day-shift drivers replacing them like soldiers at the parapets of the Alamo. Well. Something like that.

The silence was eerie as I headed for the door of the on-call room. Normally I like silence but I can do without eeriness. It reminded me of being late for school, the most gut-wrenching thing that can happen to a first-grader. I was glad to get inside where the eeriness was normal, especially with Rollo seated behind the glass window of the cage eating a donut. Rollo bears a resemblance to half the character actors who ever made B movies, my two favorites being Sidney Greenstreet and Andy Divine. Take your pick—there's plenty more where they came from. Anybody here remember Eugene Pallette?

Rollo is the man in charge of Rocky drivers in the daytime. He's like a line producer on a movie set. The man in the cage wields a lot of power in a cab company, in the way that a bottleneck wields power over anything that gets stuck anywhere. Use your imagination.

I felt foolish walking up to the cage almost an hour late. Rollo was now like a school teacher. Even before I opened my mouth, he knew he had won. I could tell he knew because he didn't lord it over me. You may find this hard to believe, but cab driving is one of the